PRAISE FOR JOE R. LANSDALE'S
RUSTY PUPPY

"Joe R. Lansdale has a wicked way with words...Hap Collins and Leonard Pine, small-town East Texas private detectives, say the filthiest things. Some of it is good-natured banter between buddies; the rest is don't-mess-with-me trash talk. And they don't just talk dirty. They fight dirty, too. One almost feels guilty enjoying their raw, rollicking adventures. But Lansdale, an Edgar Award–winning writer from Nacogdoches, has a way of winning readers over with his deceptively elegant brand of 'redneck noir.'"

—David Martindale, *Fort Worth Star-Telegram*

"The humor and humanity prevalent in the story receive star treatment...Lansdale's fans are sure to enjoy this latest installment, which rounds out an even dozen for the series, and it can also be appreciated by those who haven't experienced earlier titles."

—Jen Forbus, *AudioFile*

"A unique mix of sly humor and horrific violence. Readers will laugh at some particularly profane smart-ass repartee and then want to cover their eyes a couple sentences later as the violence explodes. Another fine entry in a great series." —Wes Lukowsky, *Booklist*

"Joe Lansdale has a knack for murder, though thankfully he limits that talent to the fictional adventures of crime-fighting duo Hap Collins and Leonard Pine." —Susie Tommaney, *Houston Press*

RUSTY
PUPPY

BOOKS BY JOE R. LANSDALE

THE HAP AND LEONARD NOVELS

Savage Season
Much Mojo
The Two-Bear Mambo
Bad Chili
Rumble Tumble
Captain Outrageous
Vanilla Ride
Devil Red
Honky Tonk Samurai
Rusty Puppy
Jackrabbit Smile

OTHER NOVELS

The Magic Wagon
The Drive In
The Nightrunners
Cold in July
The Boar
Waltz of Shadows
The Bottoms
A Fine Dark Line
Sunset and Sawdust
Lost Echoes
Leather Maiden
All the Earth, Thrown to the Sky
Edge of Dark Water
The Thicket
Paradise Sky

SELECTED SHORT STORY COLLECTIONS

By Bizarre Hands
Sanctified and Chicken Fried
Best of Joe R. Lansdale

RUSTY PUPPY

JOE R. LANSDALE

MULHOLLAND BOOKS

Little, Brown and Company

New York Boston London

Mulholland Books / Little, Brown and Company
Hachette Book Group
1290 Avenue of the Americas, New York, NY 10104
mulhollandbooks.com

Originally published in hardcover by Mulholland Books, February 2017
First paperback edition, February 2018

Mulholland Books is an imprint of Little, Brown and Company, a division of Hachette Book Group, Inc. The Mulholland Books name and logo are trademarks of Hachette Book Group, Inc.

The publisher is not responsible for websites (or their content) that are not owned by the publisher.

The Hachette Speakers Bureau provides a wide range of authors for speaking events. To find out more, go to hachettespeakersbureau.com or call (866) 376-6591.

ISBN 978-0-316-31156-4 (hc) / 978-0-316-31157-1 (pb)
Library of Congress Control Number: 2016954780

10 9 8 7 6 5 4 3 2 1

LSC-C

Printed in the United States of America

This one's for my literary agent Danny Baror and my film agent Brian Lipson, both of whom have helped make my life more comfortable, and to them I send my sincere appreciation for their consistent efforts to improve my career, which can be a full-time job unto itself, and for being good friends. Thanks, guys.

And an acknowledgment to my friend Jim Mickle for directing my works so well on screen, and for my brother Nick Damici for adapting those works so kindly and carefully.

Once you get dead, then you ain't dead any-more, and you come back because somebody pressed on your chest and you took a breath and shot a turd, you got a different view on things. That being said, if I ain't in the hospital, and I can get around, I never miss Tuesday night chili.

—Jim Bob Luke

RUSTY
PUPPY

1

I was still getting over being dead, and let me tell you, that's a comeback.

I died twice in the hospital after being stabbed, and the last thing I remember before I awoke from death was Leonard being there, shoveling vanilla cookies into his face, waiting for me to wake up. Actually, I was awake, but I couldn't fully open my eyes other than just enough to see him. I repeatedly felt as if I were drifting away on a slow boat to nowhere with a stick up my weenie. That turned out to be a catheter, but it felt like a stick. A big one.

Doctors and nurses saved me from the big, dark plunge, and I didn't thank Jesus when I came around. I thanked the medical staff, their years of schooling, their tremendous skills. I always figured if I was a doctor and I saved some person's life, and the first thing they said when they came around was "Thank Jesus," I would have wanted to stick a pair of forceps up their ass and tell them to see if Jesus could yank those out for them.

Bottom line was, I was back. It took me a few months to pull it together, but finally I was out and about regularly, and on this day

I was totally on my own. I had lost a few pounds while being on the tube-down-your-throat diet (not the same tube as the one in my pecker, I hasten to add) but as of recent, my strength was back. I felt like I could bench-press two-fifty and beat an angry gorilla's ass, but maybe not in a fair fight.

That said, I also had days when I would weep uncontrollably and had the concentration of a squirrel. Doctors told me there would be days like that, days when I not only knew I was mortal, but had come smack up against the concept. Watching cartoons helped. I came around pretty quick, and the doctors were amazed that I didn't have any real posttraumatic stress. I didn't mention it to them, but I thought, *No, I only have that when I kill people,* and I'd learned to live with that stress as if it were merely a quarrelsome comrade. I had plenty of practice there, having known Leonard much of my life. But as far as quick recovery went, I've always been like that. Recuperation skills and a hard head have served me well in life.

So there I was, doing better, back to work, feeling mostly normal, only having brief visitations from the mortality fairy and a now-and-then concern about the eventual heat death of the solar system from the inevitability of the exploding sun. I'm something of a worrier.

On this day I had office duty at Brett Sawyer Investigations, where I worked for my girlfriend, Brett, worked with my best friend, Leonard. I was sitting with my feet on the desk, noticing my socks didn't match, feeling like a classic private eye, though my detective skills were right up there with my mathematical ability, which means you shouldn't ask me to do your taxes. But I'm persistent. That's another good trait you can add to quick recuperation time and a hard head. When I was sixteen my dad got me a job with a fellow who had me help him haul brush and tear down old houses he had bought to sell for scrap lumber. My dad said to him on my first day at work, "He might fuck up a lot, but he's no quitter."

That was kind of my motto.

I was at the office alone because no one else could be there that morning. Leonard was in Houston having sex with some guy he met on the Internet, which made me nervous for both of them, and Brett was nursing a cold. She shared her cold with a young woman named Chance who had turned out to be my daughter. DNA tests proved it, and I was damn happy about it. I had only known about her a short time, but she meshed with my family of Brett and Leonard and Buffy the dog as if she had been with us since birth.

Chance was staying at our house and working part-time at the local newspaper as a proofreader, looking for full-time employment. She had a journalism degree, which is kind of like a degree in Latin. The uses are small.

Like Brett, Chance was off work, home with her cold, resting on the couch. I figured I was next to get the bug, but so far I felt tip-top. After being stabbed in the stomach and dying for a while, coughs and sniffles could kiss my ass.

Buffy, the German shepherd Leonard rescued from an asshole who was kicking her, was with me at the office, lying on the sofa. She was remarkably well mannered, and much better housebroken than I was. Ask Brett. She'll tell you.

It was a pleasant morning, sitting there in the office wearing a pair of new blue jeans that my lady Brett said for once fit me in the ass, and I had on some new tan shoes that Buffy had chewed only slightly. I had on a nice green pullover shirt without food stains. My underwear was clean. My thinning hair was combed, and I had a cup of coffee with real cream in it and one package of Sweet'N Low. I had an open bag of Leonard's vanilla cookies that he had hidden behind our office refrigerator, and they were so good. Not only because of the taste, but because Leonard thought they were well concealed. I planned to eat them all and put the empty bag back behind the fridge. I might even put a note in there that said *Cookie Fairy was here. Fuck you. You didn't share at the hospital.*

As I sat there, contemplating on my return from the dead, I think I was starting to catch on to something about that whole nature-of-the-universe thing, bordering on some incredibly brilliant revelation that might be written up into some kind of philosophical paper, when the door opened and a black lady came in.

She was well groomed, overweight, wearing red stretch pants, a loose green top, and pink house shoes. All she needed was a church-lady hat with a fishing lure and a golf ball sewn onto it. She was carrying a purse about the size of an overnight bag. She could have been forty. She could have been fifty. She was certainly tired-looking.

I took my feet off the desk.

She said, "You the only one here?"

"Yes, ma'am."

"Where's that black one?"

"Leonard or Marvin?"

Marvin was no longer there. He had sold the business to Brett, but I thought she still might be referring to him.

"They black?" she asked.

"Yes, ma'am. All the time."

"They both work here?"

"Actually, only one of them does. Like me, he's a worker bee."

"Which one of them black fellows looks like he's pissed off?"

"That would be both of them. One is stocky and sometimes carries a cane, and he's maybe five or six years older than me. He's no longer here. The other one is muscular and my age and likes vanilla cookies. Just like these."

I patted the bag.

"I guess it's the muscular one I saw."

"Now that I think about it, they're both muscular. But one is older and heavier, like a bear that was trained to wear clothes."

She was studying me hard.

"As you can see," I said, "I'm not either of the black ones."

"I was just thinking I can't tell how old you are. White people, they're hard to judge. Can I have a cookie?"

"Take two. Would you like coffee?"

"You got a clean cup?"

"You bet I do."

She told me how she liked it. I got up and fixed her a cup. No artificial sweetener for her; she took four packages of sugar, stirred it with one of our plastic spoons, tasted it, asked for one more package, and I gave it to her. While she drank her coffee, she dunked one of her cookies in it and nibbled. She knew what was up.

"I guess it don't matter which one it is. I seen him come up the stairs and go down, so I figured he worked here, and him being black, I thought I'd want to talk to him."

"Some of us white folks talk and investigate pretty good."

"I guess so."

"How'd you see him?"

"What do you mean?"

"The black guy, Leonard. I assume you weren't in the tree by the parking lot with a pair of binoculars."

"Are you being a smartass?"

"Only a little."

"I live across the street, Master Detective. That's why I'm here in my house shoes. I sort of put on what was in front of me."

"I guessed that."

"No you didn't," she said.

"All right, I didn't."

"I got some money. I don't want anything for free."

"I've offered nothing for free."

"Uh-huh," she said. She removed a change purse from her very large handbag, which had enough room for an alternate universe, and probed around in it like she was digging for King Solomon's gold. She took out a wad of bills that would have choked a dinosaur and slapped those on the desk, poured some coins on top of them.

She looked at me. I reached over and pulled the money close and counted it out. It was a big wad, but most of it was in small denominations. Forty dollars in ones, a five, a dog-eared twenty with a chewed corner, chewed by an actual dog, maybe. There was twenty-eight cents in change and a nice pile of lint and a round chunk of peppermint wrapped in plastic. She took the peppermint back and dropped it into her purse. I bet that peppermint is still falling.

"What's that buy me?" she asked.

"Honestly? A cup of coffee, some of these cookies, and maybe you and me could go to the movies."

"I don't date white men."

"I know how to show a lady a good time."

"I ain't prejudice, mind you. I just don't deal with white people any more than I have to."

"That's kind of the definition of *prejudice*."

"So that won't get me nothing?"

"Tell me what's going on, and maybe I can see what this will do for you. It might be a simple business that I can take care of quickly."

"I need you to talk to a fellow."

"I guess we'll be talking about something specific?"

"What's that mean?"

"Means you have a point to all this. You would want me, or the darker gentleman, to talk to him about something that's on your mind, right?"

"I suppose you could say that," she said. "I think my son was murdered."

"Oh," I said.

Now I was truly interested. I had feared this would be a lost-cat job, and though I've nothing against reuniting folks with their lost pets, most of the time a cat will just come home.

"I want the black man to do it 'cause he's black."

"You think that would help?"

"You might not fit into the projects in Camp Rapture."

I nodded. "That could be true. Sounds to me like you need the police. I know a good cop that can help you."

"I been to the cops. They say I need proof."

"Yep. That's the way it works."

"This *is* in Camp Rapture," she said.

"Ah," I said. "The pit."

"Shit hole is more like it," she said.

"Cop I was talking about is one of the black men you saw here, Marvin Hanson, but he's a LaBorde cop, not Camp Rapture."

"Then get the other one," she said. "I want the black man here to get proof. Dealing with cops makes my ass hurt and nothing gets done."

"When I'm not toting a bale for them ole white masters or hoeing a row of cotton, I work here as well. And I gave you the vanilla cookies. Trust me, the black one, he wouldn't have given you the crumbs in the bottom of the sack."

"You ain't never hoed no row of cotton."

"And neither have you. Only cotton around here in the last fifty years is in an aspirin bottle."

That made her grin.

I said, "I have done farmwork, though. Used to work in rose fields. I worked in an aluminum chair factory, had an unfortunate period of employment at the chicken plant—"

"You worked there?"

"I didn't fit in. It was what you might call an unsuccessful period in my work history."

"I worked there."

"When?"

She told me.

"I was there then," I said.

"Say you was?"

"I was."

"You remember that woman got attacked on the other side of the fence, and a white fellow climbed over it and saved her?"

"That was me."

"No it wasn't."

"Yes it was."

"You the one . . . you was thinner then, wasn't you?"

"Thanks for noticing."

I had just been congratulating myself on how much weight I had lost, and now she was telling me I was thinner then. Certainly I had been a bit more spry.

"I was right there in the crowd," she said. "I didn't know that was you."

"Yep. I got a free vacation from the employer out of it. It wasn't as refreshing as I would have hoped. But that's neither here nor there."

I didn't mention the black man she wanted to take her case had gotten us left by a cruise ship, and then we had been attacked by thugs on a beach, and Leonard had gone around wearing an embarrassing hat and a bad wound. We got wounded a lot. We had a way of annoying people.

"Okay," she said. "Okay. That's good. You was the one, that's good. You did good by that girl. Saving her like that. You're hired."

"Keep in mind I can only do so much for this amount of money."

"You talk to this fellow seen the murder, that's all I want. Start there."

"All right. Tell me what it is me and this fellow will be talking about. Besides murder, I mean. I'm going to need details. I'll want to visit with the cops too."

She shook her head. "I don't like that. I said I talked to them. Shit. I'm pretty sure they was the ones done it."

2

Her name was Louise Elton, and she had a hell of a story. When she finished giving me all her details, I called Leonard. He didn't pick up, so I left a message. I'd hoped he might be back in town but didn't expect him to be. He and John, his longtime lover, were still broken up, something they did about as often as cows went to pasture, and Leonard had decided to play the field. That's how he met the guy on the Internet.

Louise's son's name was Jamar. There wasn't any proof the cops killed him, except there was a guy who claimed to have seen it. But there were problems with his story, or at least that's how the cops saw it. She was convinced this guy had information I could use.

I thought I could at least talk to him and get a read. His name was Timpson Weed. The projects in Camp Rapture were where Timpson hung his hat, if he wore one. It was not a nice place and white people were still considered the enemy down there. Thing was, though, I was bored, and Leonard wasn't around, and I had a number for the apartment.

After having a lunch of some very bad soup I heated in the office microwave, I gave Buffy a pat, got my coat, and drove over to Camp Rapture. It was a fairly short drive from LaBorde, and the projects looked like a place where dreams went to commit suicide and hope got screwed in the ass.

It was a cold day, and my breath came out white when I got out of the car. I pulled my coat tighter around me, started walking along the cracked sidewalk toward a row of apartments. They looked rough. The bricks were chipped, the walls were painted with graffiti, sweet nothings like I FUCKED YO MAMA AND HER PUSSY STANK.

There were similar remarks here and there, names plastered on the wall with what the police liked to call gang signs. Sometimes, if the same signs were on an underpass, they claimed they were satanic. They liked to keep it simple. Whatever they wanted them to be, they became.

Cops in Camp Rapture had really gotten a bad rap of late, though for that matter, they had always had a bad rap, and there was some evidence it was deserved. Not six months ago, they had "discovered" a car thief in a ditch near the car he had stolen, and he'd been shot in the back of the head five times. He was written down as a suicide. That didn't hold up, of course, but I think they thought it might, which gives you some idea of their level of professionalism.

I saw a group of young black men moving in my direction. Late teens and twenties. They were walking that kind of tough-guy walk where one leg seems to drag behind the other. They had their hands in their pockets and there might have been something other than hands in those pockets. Not expecting a shoot-out, I hadn't brought my gun with me. I hated how it was for them, young men without jobs or much in the way of future plans, but mostly I hated there were five of them and there was one of me.

"How are you gentlemen?" I said as they gathered around.

"We fine," said one of them. He was a tall kid with long, lean muscles and a red shower cap on his head. I've never quite understood that fashion statement, but I will say this: If it rained or he decided on a quick shower, he was ready.

"What you want?" said the one with the shower cap.

"Money and fame, of course."

"You a smartass?" said Shower Cap. This question came up frequently.

"Yep."

"You won't be so smart with your teeth on the ground and your ass kicked up around your neck."

"I would neither be smart nor happy if that were to happen," I said. "I'm looking for a fella. You might know him. I have an apartment number."

"We know him, you can bet your white ass we won't be pointing him out," Shower Cap said.

"Well, as I prefer not to bet my white ass, thank you for your time," I said.

I walked through a gap in the near circle they had made and didn't look back. When it came to young men with nothing to do and chips on their shoulder, you handled it the way you handled junk-yard dogs. Show no fear, don't make eye contact, and walk away slowly and hope they don't bite you on the ass.

I walked toward where I thought the number of the apartment might be but wasn't. The numbers were wonky. I went around the other side of the apartment. There were a bunch of kids playing on that side, boys and girls, eleven years old or so, kicking a ball around.

They stopped as I came around the corner. White-man sightings were as rare as Bigfoot in those parts. One of the little girls said, "What you doing around here?"

She was rough-looking, had her hair in cornrows, and was wearing clothes that looked to have been handed down from someone larger. She had on pink tennis shoes with dirty white shoestrings in them. She wore an oversize T-shirt with writing that said MY ASS MATCHES YOUR FACE.

Charming.

"Looking for someone?" I said.

"You po-po?"

"I am not the po-po. Aren't you kids supposed to be in school, or maybe setting fire to something?"

"It's Saturday, fool," the girl said.

"You know," I said, "it is."

"Course it is, and tomorrow be Sunday, and the day after that be Monday."

"In school, I bet you make As."

"Naw I don't."

"But your marks in personality are high, aren't they?"

"What?"

"Nothing. I'm looking for a man named Timpson Weed. I got five dollars for the first person points me to where he lives, and if he actually lives there, I got another five when I come back from seeing him."

I was already out a large part of my initial down payment on the case.

The little girl gave me the hairy eyeball, like a banker considering your credit report. "Let me see you money."

I took a five out of my wallet and held it between my fingers.

"Right there," she said. She pointed at a door on a landing above us.

"I was told number nine-oh-five, not six-oh-five."

"You know so good, why you asking?"

"That is a very good point."

I had asked because the lady who hired me said she couldn't remember if it was a nine or a six. This way I had confirmation. Either that or I had just been worked out of five dollars.

I gave her the bill, went up the stairs and over to the door. I could smell cooking food from under it, chicken and dumplings and a lot of onions. I could also hear the TV going, a game show. I knocked on the door. I waited through a couple of ice ages before it was opened.

It was a short woman with a flower pattern on her housecoat. She was about thirty-five. She had her hair cut close. She was a little thick, with breasts that appeared to need somewhere else to live, there not being enough room in the housecoat. She wore fluffy pink house shoes, a fresher pair than those Mrs. Elton had worn; must have been a trend. They were open in the front and her toes stuck out and her toenails were painted silver. Her fingernails didn't match. They were red.

"What you want?"

"And good afternoon to you."

"What the fuck you want? I got things to do."

"I was told this was the address of the charm school."

"The what?"

I was being uppity and an asshole, but all I was trying to do was help Louise Elton get a fair shake for her son and I had gotten nothing but shit from an eleven-year-old on up. For all I knew, Louise's son Jamar was a bad guy and had died being bad, but the idea was to find out, and so far I was batting nothing. On the other hand, considering how it was in Camp Rapture, at least in some sections, I'd be suspicious too, especially if they thought I was a cop.

"Who's that at the door?" I heard a voice say.

I tried peeking around the woman in the doorway, but that wasn't possible. She had a way of moving so that she was in my eye line. A moment later a big black man without a shirt came to the door and eased her aside.

"What's all this racket?" he said.

"This peckerwood done here asking questions," the woman said.

"Go on back in there and watch the stove. And pull that goddamn housecoat together, woman."

She gave me a look that almost knocked me over the railing, then disappeared in the back to watch the stove and whatever was cooking.

"What you want?" the big man said. He was really big. Tall, wide, and though he had some belly, it wasn't all fat that was moving around under it. Somewhere in there were some abdominal muscles that wanted to show me they were still hard, just slightly marbled.

"Are you Timpson Weed?"

"What if I am?"

"Louise Elton sent me?"

"She did? She still on that business with Jamar?"

"Still is."

"That nigger's dead and most apt to stay that way. Ain't nothing else for it."

"I'm a private investigator, and she hired me to check into his death. See if maybe there was more to it than the police say."

"Course there is. Always is."

"Police aren't always out to screw you," I said. "I know some good ones."

"Ought to try being a nigger for a day."

"Black cop, I'm talking about."

"Yeah, he's just a white man painted over. I've had some experience."

I didn't see any point arguing.

"I'm just trying to help her out," I said.

"Taking her money, you mean."

"Not much money."

He studied me for a while. "I ain't got nothing much to say."

"Tell me the little you have to say?"

He had grown quiet, as if there were spies in the woodwork.

"I don't know," he said.

"It's to help a lady out. If it's not what she wants to believe, then that's better than not knowing what happened."

"Tell you what, you buy me a beer."

"Where?"

"The joint outside the city limits. Seven o'clock."

"Joint have a name?"

He laughed. "That's just it. It's called the Joint."

"Seven p.m. I'll find it."

"Might want to bring a razor and a billy club with you. The clientele is old-school."

"Meaning?"

"They don't like white guys. Hell, they ain't that fond of each other."

3

I went downstairs and started across the lot, and here came those young men again, the red shower cap in the lead, all of them doing that leg-drag act. I had a feeling they had decided to give me a bit of a bounce just to show Whitey who was in charge down here. I was glad to let them be in charge.

I glanced around to see if there was another way to my car, but there was only a clearing to the right and the projects to the left. The clearing led across a dried-out field of grass littered with broken bottles and no telling what all. On the other side of it was another housing project. I would have had to have packed a camp stove and provisions to walk that far around to avoid trouble. That's what I should have done anyway, but my pride wouldn't let me. Or, to be more exact, I was too lazy to do it.

The little girl I gave the five dollars to came out of an open door in the projects and said, "You find him?"

I stopped, kept an eye on the young men. They were still coming. "I did," I said.

"Then you owe me five dollars now, don't you?"

"Guess I do."

"Ain't no guessing about it."

I got five dollars out of my wallet, glanced toward the young men. They had stopped and started to mill, like they were waiting on me. Behind them, coming up the walkway, I saw Leonard. He had gotten my message, which meant he had been near home when I called. He was walking in that kind of swagger he has, his head held up; his eyes, even from a distance, looked like two hard nuggets of coal. He had on a shadow-black fedora, his new affectation, and he wore it like he was a black Humphrey Bogart and was swinging two sets of nuts.

"Them boys don't like you none," said the little girl, glancing in their direction.

"I don't even know them."

"That why they don't like you."

"I don't plan to agitate them."

"They always agitated. That big one, got on the blue shirt, that Laron. He lives to fuck people up."

"You got a mouth on you, kid."

"Ought to heard my mama."

"What about the one in the shower cap?"

"He bad as Laron. Laron, he don't talk much, but Tuboy, he a talker, and he sneaky. He got a razor he carry behind his back under his shirt."

"Thanks for the tip."

"Won't do you no good."

The boys were starting to come my way again.

"They gonna sort yo' shit just 'cause they can."

"It might sort out different than they expect."

"Why, you gonna turn into a bunch of white boys? That your superpower?"

"My superpower is a friend in the right place," I said, and started toward the crowd of men.

Leonard had come up behind the boys now. He had already read the situation, and since he had on his badass hat, he was talking shit.

"Get the hell out of the way," I heard him say, and they parted before him as if he were a Mack truck. Leonard isn't a little guy, but he's not supersize either. He always gives the impression of being bigger, way he talks and walks. He leads with his dick, as one old man we trained martial arts with once put it.

"Hey, man," said the big one, Laron. "What the fuck you doing? Coming up in here like that."

Leonard hooked him to the head with a right and knocked him down. Laron lay still, either unconscious or wisely aware that getting up would be a bad idea.

Red Shower Cap, also called Tuboy, turned then, brought his hand out from behind his back. I got a glimpse of the razor opening. I started running toward them.

Leonard stepped up and hit Tuboy in the mouth while he was bringing his hand around. Tuboy fell to his knees and dropped the razor. He rocked in place.

One of the young men looked as if he might try and pick the razor up.

"Fixin' to be a stack of you assholes laying up in here," Leonard said, whipping his head around, glaring at the others.

They stepped back.

I arrived.

"Good," Leonard said. "Now you show up. You stop for a bowl of chili?"

"Came as fast as I could, but I did want that chili."

Leonard reached over and grabbed the shower cap on Tuboy's

head, yanked it off. There were cornrows underneath and there was lint in the cornrows.

"What you got this on for, you stereotypical country mother-fucker," Leonard said. He looked at the others. "I ought to just slap the ever-loving pig shit out of all of you. Living up in here like a pack of roaches, wearing a fucking shower cap. What are you, animals?"

I thought, *Animals wear shower caps?*

"You ain't got no call to talk to us like that, brother," said one of the young men.

"I ain't your fucking brother. Shoo on out of here, and take these fat asses with you. I'll keep the shower cap. I'm going to shit in it."

They scattered like geese. They didn't bother to take Laron or Tuboy with them. It was every asshole for himself. Tuboy was still on his knees. His eyes were glazed. He was probably seeing little blue gnomes riding on unicorns.

"He's out, Leonard," I said.

Leonard used the palm of his hand to push him. Tuboy groaned a little, toppled, and lay on his side.

The little girl came over. "You think you're bad, don't you?" She said this to Leonard.

"Baby girl, I don't think, I know I'm bad."

"Them boys hold grudges," she said.

"Do they now? Well, that's going to worry me for days. Who the hell are you?"

"Reba. I was named after a white lady that sings."

"Yeah?" Leonard said.

"Mama liked that cracker shit. I don't. I like me some real music. I mainly go by Little Woman."

"You just made that up," Leonard said.

"Startin' now, then."

"I like Reba," Leonard said. "I mean the singer, if that's who you're talking about. You I don't like at all, you little snot-nosed pile of rat shit."

"Leonard," I said. "Kid."

"This ain't no kid. That there is a fucking four-hundred-year-old midget vampire."

"Fuck you," Reba said.

"Fuck you too," Leonard said.

"You ain't black at all?"

"What the fuck color am I? This look like shoe polish to you?"

"Uncle Tom is your color."

"Yeah, well, you want to stay in the goddamn projects and wear your own shower cap and house shoes and whine about the Man keeping you down, you go on and do it. Me, I spit in the Man's fucking face, tell him it's face wash, and he's got to like it."

"I hope you get et up by a tiger," she said, walking away.

"Not likely," Leonard said.

"Leonard, really? You're going to pick a fight with a kid?"

"She started it. Ancient midget-ass motherfucking vampire." He yelled out to her then. "I hope your fucking tricycle has a flat."

She kept walking away, and without looking back, she stuck her hand up in a fist, extended her middle finger.

4

Leonard carried the red shower cap out to his pickup like a scalp he had taken in battle. He opened the door on the driver's side, tossed it inside.

"Can you believe that? Motherfucker going around with a fucking shower cap on his head, and he didn't even have a new do drying out under it, just a nappy head. What the fuck, man?"

"You are not a nice man, Leonard."

We climbed in our respective rides and drove back to LaBorde. Leonard passed me with his window down, waving at me and showing me nearly all of his teeth. He had removed his fedora and was wearing the red shower cap.

Back in LaBorde we drove to the office, went upstairs, Leonard now wearing the fedora again. Buffy met us at the door and I took her out for a walk and to do her business. When she finished and I had a plastic bag of dog poo in the dumpster, I went upstairs and washed my hands. While I did that, Leonard hugged Buffy. He was the one who had rescued her, and I was the one who took her home. He said, "So give me the usual shit about my hat. Get it over with."

"I like it."

"What's that? My hearing going?"

"I like it."

"Be still, my fucking heart."

"No. The fedora works. Only hat you ever wore that worked, except for a cowboy hat. Though, I have to say, that shower cap was precious. Seemed closer to your true soul."

"Fuck you. What exactly were you doing in the projects, anyway? Your message was cryptic. Old as you are, you ought to know the projects ain't a good place for you to be. You might fall down and be yelling, 'I can't get up 'cause a bunch of niggers are whipping my ass.'"

"I was doing fine," I said. "Since when have a bunch of jerks like those guys scared me?"

"I give you that, but that was a double-team job. You being up in there talking to my peeps without backup, and you lily-white, that's not smart, Hap. We go into a place where it's all cracker mother fuckers, I like you with me, so you could have waited a while."

"I concede your point."

"Do you now?"

"I do. But they're not your peeps, Leonard. Except for me and Brett and your reflection in the mirror, you pretty much don't have peeps. And I don't think you would wait on me if you got a wild hair up your ass, cracker motherfuckers or not."

"True. Up in there, though, them projects, you can get your ass killed. Them ain't good people."

"They're not all bad people."

"Yeah, but there's bad enough ones there to get you killed while the good ones watch. You'd think someone would clean that place up, way it is."

"Easy to say from the outside," I said.

"Shit, man, you drove by a white-trash fucker's house and seen it falling down, a washing machine and a stack of tires on the lawn, you'd just think he was lazy-ass trash. You see black folk living like pigs, then you start handing out your liberal bullshit about how they are downtrodden."

"They are. You should know that."

"I know black folk been run over by a lot of shit, but a lot of what runs them over is their own self-pity. I was taught to work."

"They need a job so they can work," I said.

"Need to get off their ass and go look for one, same as them white-trash motherfuckers, who I bet you ain't so sentimental about. Way I see it, color ain't got nothing to do with that lame-ass shit. You go to work or you don't. Opportunities ain't always been there for black folks, but there sure ain't any when you're nested up in some shit hole living on a government check with a crack den next door."

"Wow. That is stereotypical, Leonard. You really got to stop watching Fox News and listening to white-boy talk radio and using the word *nigger* so much."

"It ain't got a damn thing to do with black and white," he said.

I knew there was no way we were even going to meet in the middle on this, so I told him what Louise Elton had told me.

"So she says cops killed her son, and this fellow you were talking to seen it, but he don't want to talk to you in the projects?"

"Pretty much it, yeah."

"He wants free beer, Hap. You take him out, buy him a beer, and he'll tell you he saw an alien eating green cheese out of a dead dog's ass on the fucking landing outside his window."

"You have very little faith in mankind," I said. "Of course, I don't have much either. But I'm going to hope on an individual. Hell, he went in and told the police for Louise. They didn't believe him, or didn't want to. Also, the backstory is a little more complex."

"Whose backstory?"

"Louise's. She gave me some background on things."

"Let me get a cookie . . . Wait, what the hell, man? Those are my cookies. Why are they on the desk?"

"Louise was company. I thought we should share."

"Fuck Louise. Them cookies were hid."

"You are a lousy hider."

"Damn near the whole bag is gone."

"She liked to dip them in coffee."

"I bet she wasn't the only one."

He snatched at the bag, pushed the fedora back on his head, and started eating what was left. That wouldn't take long.

While he ate, vengefully, I told him all Louise had told me.

5

Louise has a young teenage daughter and, according to her, a fine-looking one. And one night, driving home, she gets pulled over by the police. They tell her she's drunk, but she doesn't drink."

"That may not mean much, a mother telling you her young daughter don't drink," Leonard said. "I bet, to hear Mama tell it, she don't fuck or wear white after Labor Day neither. You know how that is."

"Agreed. But she's pulled over, and the cop, a white cop, he says, 'Tell me your birthday,' et cetera, and then 'Say your ABCs,' and she does this, doing the singsong way of saying the ABCs, and Louise said her daughter, Charm, didn't miss a lick."

"Her name is Charm?"

"Yeah."

"What the fuck happened to Alice, Mary, Karen, and such?"

"Leonard. I didn't name her. So Charm does this, and then the cop says, 'Tell me your driver's license number.' And she does. Can you do that?"

"I can't."

"Louise said Charm did, but the cop, he has her follow him to the station. He takes her in, puts her in an interrogation room, but—get this—handcuffs her. It's just him and her in there and probably no camera. That's my guess. Anyway, Charm says this officer, Officer Coldpoint, he checks her for weapons, but mostly he just rubs his hands over her tits and ass, presses his cock up against her backside."

"This is Charm's story now? Right?"

"Right. So when Coldpoint gets through, he kind of tugs her pants down a little in back, and then he takes her out and cuffs her to a radiator in the back hallway where they bring in baddies. She says she was standing there all night, handcuffed. She asked to take a Breathalyzer right away, but Coldpoint didn't do it. Said he didn't need to, had her dead to rights. She asked for a phone call, asked for a lawyer. Nothing. All night she's handcuffed there and they're bringing in druggies and all manner of assholes, and they see her as they go by, and one of them wets his finger and dips it down her pants into her ass crack, and she's got to hear all the usual smartass remarks jerks make about a good-looking woman, 'cause that kind of talk works so well for lining up dates. Dumbasses with brains a lot smaller than their balls."

"You think things like that," Leonard said. "And sometimes you say them to me, about women."

"I don't manhandle or mistreat women," I said.

"True. But you notice what you think is a good female ass. I don't know exactly what that is, liking men and all. I do know you don't have a good ass."

"Uh-huh. Next morning, this lady cop, Manuela Martinez, she sees Charm there, asks her what's going on. Charm tells her, and Martinez lets her out of the cuffs, lets her go. No questions. No explanations. She's one moment handcuffed, next moment out on the bricks."

"I'd have had me about two lawyers buried up their asses then, and one little back-up lawyer just so I'd have someone to argue with them in the hallway. I'd go hire me that fucking four-hundred-year-old vampire midget at the projects. She could just be there to give them folks shit."

"I hear you," I said. "But Charm didn't do anything at that point. Was just glad it was over. Or thought it was. Next thing she knows this cop is following her around. She drives to the store to get a quart of milk and a box of tampons, there he is. She goes to bed at night, looks out the window, he's parked there, shining a laser pointer at her, that kind of shit. She calls the police station to lodge a complaint, and no one seems able to take it. She even goes to the police station. They're not having it. This other cop, this Manuela, she's fired. Charm doesn't know why, but Manuela has been given her pink slip. So she can't even talk to her about it, least not in an official capacity.

"This harassment shit goes on for months, this cop following her, pulling her over for a broke taillight that wasn't broke before but got broke in the night."

Leonard leaned back in his chair and looked into the emptiness of his cookie bag. "That's some serious shit, man. You believe this Louise lady?"

"I believe it's what she believes. But I haven't gotten to the good part yet. So Charm's brother, Jamar—"

"What is up with these made-up names?"

"All names are made up, Leonard. So the brother, he's pissed, and he's in the car a couple times when this cop is following Charm around. He goes in to see the cops, and the next thing, he's arrested. They said for starting a fight with Officer Coldpoint. He claimed he only spoke to him, said he was mad, all right, but didn't shove, hit, or bother anyone the way they said it happened."

"This is what he told his mother?"

"That's right. He gets out of jail pretty quick, 'cause they decide to let him go. Next thing Jamar does is he starts filming the cops outside his house—"

"Wait. You said cops, but I thought it was just Coldpoint."

"And his partner. I have his name in my notes somewhere. Maybe some of the others' too. I think other cops were drafted into the cause, at least now and then."

"Hell. Wait a minute. I remember Coldpoint. You remember? He worked at the LaBorde cops for a while."

"I don't remember, but I'll take your word for it. Anyway, Jamar is videoing them with his phone, taking notes, keeping track of when they show up and what they do, and next thing Louise knows there's word Jamar got in a fight and got killed at the projects."

"That's the place for it," Leonard said.

"You're going to stay on that, aren't you?"

"I am."

"Except why was he there? Didn't have any reason to be there, Louise said."

"Louise may be more deluded than Lois Lane about Superman's identity. I mean, really, Clark is wearing a pair of glasses and has his cowlick pushed back. That's a disguise?"

"Is this going to lead to can Captain Marvel beat up Superman? Are who runs the fastest, Superman or the Flash?"

"Well, the comics always cheated on that part about who could run fastest. I think it should have been the Flash. I mean, that's his power. He's fast, and now Superman, he can do that too, he can tie him? I don't buy it. He's got all them other powers, and they have to have him fast as the Flash? That ain't right, man."

"Back to business. Jamar had never been in trouble, nothing. Straight-A student in high school, same as his first year at college."

"But still he was found dead in the projects, and probably went there in the middle of the night?"

"That's the speculation."

"You know why folks go to the projects in the middle of the night, right?"

"To score drugs, mostly. Maybe take in the beautiful sights."

"Bad things do go on there, and as you saw earlier, bad things can happen to strangers who show up there."

"The bad things I saw there were you punching people in the head. The homeys had bad things happen to them, not the strangers."

"True."

"Okay, Jamar, he could have gone there for a nice little bag of something in powder or pill form, what have you, and he didn't have the money, or the would-be seller didn't care he had it or not, could have decided to keep his wares, take Jamar's money, and mash his head. It could be that and nothing more."

"It happens," Leonard said. "Tweakers selling to tweakers, folks get crazy easy."

"Yep, but we don't really know why he was there, and that doesn't mean he needed to die. And then there's one other thing. This man I'm going to see tonight at the Joint. He says he saw cops kill Jamar."

"Yeah. That's some bad business, buddy."

"East Texas hasn't exactly been the land of opportunity for black people."

"Not that much opportunity for anyone here. Not unless you're a doctor, a lawyer, or a drug dealer. But being black and poor doesn't mean I'm going to live in the projects and be tormented by some fucking thug in a shower cap. I live where I want."

"No. You live where you can afford to live. And you're right. That is fucked up about Superman tying the Flash. I'm not buying it."

"Now you're talking."

We bumped fists.

6

We drove to Camp Rapture that night in Leonard's truck to meet up with my secretive snitch.

"You kept the red shower cap, didn't you?" I said as Leonard tooled us along, head thrown back, fedora dipped in front, one hand on the wheel.

"Did not."

"You had it on and were fucking with me."

"That was it. I was fucking with you."

"So I'll never see the shower cap again."

"I don't think so."

"Don't think so?"

"Don't pressure me, Hap."

"You do look cool in that fedora."

"Like I value your opinion."

"But you do."

"Do not."

"Do."

"So you like it?" he said.

"Stylish, brother. You found something that works for you. I know how hard that must be for you."

"You're still searching, though," Leonard said. "Your daughter doing okay?"

"Yep."

"That's working out?"

"Except she and Brett have the colds from hell. I think it might be flu. Brett actually asked that I stay at the office tonight. They are seriously infectious. And I don't want that shit they got."

"But you don't mind sharing their germs with me?"

"I don't have a single symptom," I said. "And I'm keeping it that way. I'm actually kind of enjoying being on my own at the office. Well, there's Buffy. It's nice for a change of pace. Me and Buffy can play checkers until late at night. She hasn't quite got chess down yet."

"You can stay at my place, asshole."

"I'm fine at the office. John and you might get back together, and I'd rather not hear you fucking behind the wall. I can't enjoy that. I keep thinking something is in the wrong hole."

"Long as I've known you, you are still bothered by it?"

"Not the gay, just the act. I don't want to hear it going on."

"That's the same."

"How do you feel about heterosexuality?"

"Nothing against it, but it makes me kind of go eeew."

"Now you get it."

"I'm going to tell Brett you referred to her equipment as a hole."

"I was just speaking in a general way."

"Uh-huh."

"Please don't," I said.

"I'll consider on it," he said.

We pulled up at the Joint. There was a scattering of cars in the lot, most of which looked to be on their last set of rims and hap-pily ready for the car crusher. As we walked toward the entrance we could hear hip-hop popping on a jukebox. When we got to the door, pushed it open, and stepped inside, the place was mostly dark except for neon word twists and beer signs that gleamed with col-ored light. There was the pulsing glow of an old-time jukebox to the right, and to the left mostly empty tables, except for two guys in a booth against the wall. I didn't see Timpson Weed.

The air smelled of beer and barbecue, a faint aroma of fried hamburgers and onions. There was a little kitchen at the back, to the side of the bar. There was a lit window there and a shelf where the orders could be picked up. There was a sharp-looking black woman with a kerchief over her hair. She was tucked into a pair of shorts so brief the back of them was disappearing into the crack of her ass. She had a tray with beers and food on it and was carrying it toward the rear. She turned her head and gave Leonard a look. Hell. What was I, smashed peanuts? He ain't even batting for your team, gal.

She went on by, and Leonard swaggered over to the bar and sat down on a stool in front of it. I sat beside him. A bartender glided up like a wraith. His face was dark and the blue and red neon lights along the back of the bar made his longish, wild hair shine oddly. His teeth caught the neon when he turned toward us, and the lights gave them a colorful sheen. They looked small in his enormous head.

"You gentlemen might be in the wrong place," he said.

"No, this is it," Leonard said.

"Well, I was thinking your friend here might have taken a wrong turn at Sears. Last time a white man in here probably about 1700 and he was scalped by Indians."

"You're a real historian," Leonard said.

"I've been told."

"You ain't no Indian."

"Oh, I got some Cherokee in me."

"When that Indian did the scalping was up in here, did he order a beer? I know I'm going to. Hap here, he'll have a Diet Coke or some such, and if you got Dr Pepper, I'll have that for a chaser."

"You are some tough drinker," the bartender said to me. "Diet Coke?"

"Put it in a dirty glass," I said. "Though from the looks of things, that might be standard."

The bartender smiled broadly. There were bubbles of spit on his teeth, and the teeth and bubbles shimmered with neon light. The bartender had a way of holding his mouth open when the smile was gone, like a whale cruising for plankton.

"It's just that my clientele don't enjoy me having white folks for customers," he said.

Leonard looked around. Besides the waitress, dropping off orders, in the back, two black men at a booth lingered there with all the excitement of a poetry reading. They didn't even look at the waitress, which might suggest blindness. At a couple of tables nearby, some lonely drunks sat staring into their beer bottles, hoping for genies to come out of them and offer them their youth back, along with a fresh beer.

"Looks to me your clientele doesn't know work sweat from bottle sweat," Leonard said. "You give this man a Diet Coke if you got it, and if you don't, you give him one anyway. As for that white stuff, what the fuck you think this is, 1960? You hear of integration, motherfucker?"

"You better put a wheel lock on that mouth of yours," said the bartender. "Integration worked the other way around."

"Actually it works both ways," I said.

The bartender looked at me. Leonard looked at me.

"Don't get your fingers in my jam jar, Hap. I'm kind of on a roll here."

"Only roll you gonna be on is rolling out that door with my foot up your ass," said the bartender.

"Now how can I roll with a foot up my ass?" Leonard said. "That don't make sense."

The waitress glided behind us and started through a door at the back. She paused at the door, cocked her ass, and gave Leonard a look that a straight man would remember on his deathbed.

Leonard said, "Save it, honey, I suck dicks."

She looked startled, lost her smile, went on through the door and out of sight.

"I bet you do," the bartender said.

"Oh, I do. Just not yours."

The bartender realized Leonard was serious, and his mouth made a shape like he had just bitten into a sour persimmon.

"I like my dicks clean and attractive, and I like the bodies attached to them not to look like they pull a beer wagon on its way to the barn."

"I done told you where my foot's gonna go," said the bartender, "but considering what's been up your ass, I'm reconsidering that."

"Your foot goes in there, little gel might get on it. I just had a fresh one up there this morning, and I don't mean a foot. Wasn't that good, actually. It was like fucking a bedpost with Vaseline on it. I like it warm and loving. This wasn't. That's all right, though. A dick in the ass is better than a greased cucumber any day."

The bartender was going through a list of snappy comebacks in his head, but his mouth wasn't delivering.

Leonard checked his watch.

This confused the bartender.

"How long does this fucking song last?" Leonard said. "What is that shit?"

"Music," said the bartender.

"That what you call it?"

"I like it," I said.

"You got no taste in music," Leonard said. Then to the bartender: "Jesus, you need to get you some Hank up in here, some Loretta, Kasey Lansdale, Merle Haggard, or Reba. Going too fast for you? I was wanting you to write this down. You know, make a list for your distributor."

"You some kind of hoedown nigger?" the bartender said.

"I thought you was about to put a foot up my ass," Leonard said. "I think you got a certain hesitation, is what I think."

About that time Timpson Weed came in and strolled over to us. He sat on the stool by me.

Bartender said to Timpson, "You know these motherfuckers?"

"The white one."

"That would be me," I said, raising my hand.

"I'm starting to like him better than the other one," the bartender said.

"It's all right," Timpson said, nodding at me. "I invited him in to talk. I don't know this other one."

"This is my partner, Leonard Pine," I said. "We work together."

"On what?" the bartender said.

"Freelance plumbing," I said. "Let's have that beer and Diet Coke, and whatever this man wants. Put it on my tab."

"You don't have one," said the bartender.

"Fix me one up," I said. "You got any peanuts?"

"Not for you," the bartender said.

We slid away from the bar and went over to a table and sat down.

"You have me come here so you could screw with me?" I said.

"I ain't screwed with you," Timpson said.

"Yeah, but the bartender has."

"Me and him ain't got our legs tied together," Timpson said. "He does what he wants."

"Like you don't know a honky is going to get his chain jerked in here, or worse," Leonard said.

"He looks like he can handle himself," Timpson said. "I seen them scars over his eyes, knot on his nose."

"He handles himself all right," Leonard said.

"So you were fucking with me?" I said.

"Some," Timpson said.

He looked at Leonard, said to me, "So who is this dude?"

"Same guy he was a minute ago," I said. "Leonard Pine."

The barmaid brought our drinks over, but she didn't look at Leonard this time. She put them down and moved away quickly. As expected, there were no peanuts.

I nodded at Timpson. "Tell again what you saw? Tell me what you couldn't say at the projects."

7

I could say it," he said, "but it worries my woman to hear it. She don't want no cops coming down on us. I tried to do the right thing, and that didn't work out so well. Ain't no right thing when you come from around here."

"Let me get my violin out," Leonard said.

"What?" Timpson said.

"Forget it," I said. "It's just us now. No cops. Me and Leonard work together, so we both need to hear it."

Timpson Weed gave Leonard a hard eyeball, but that didn't cut any ice. Leonard didn't blink. Timpson turned his attention to the two men in the back booth. They looked at him for a moment, then looked away.

"I went out on the landing to smoke," Timpson said. "I could see what anyone could see if they was out there. Figure there was plenty witnesses, but I'm the only one ended up talking. What I saw was this boy getting a beating out there in the lot. Last time I seen a beating like that it was on television and it was Rodney King, only he was big and this boy wasn't big at all. Teenager. They hit him so much like a piñata, I expected him to shit candy."

"Sure they were cops?" I asked.

"They had on cop uniforms. Three of them. They had nightsticks, them old-fashioned kind, and even though it's some distance, there's enough light there to see by. They looked at me, and I went in the apartment."

"How long did the beating go on?" Leonard asked.

"Before I went inside, maybe a minute or two, but a lot of smacking takes place in a minute or two, as they had them a three-man team. I wasn't all that against it, as there's these meth heads all up in there, and my woman's son by another man, he died of that stuff. She had a little problem on it herself for a while. But I tell you, in that time I seen them, they beat on that boy until he was flat as a rug, and then they looked and seen me, and like I said, when they looked and saw my ass, I went inside. I expected I'd get me a knock on the door. But I didn't. Next day I find out who that boy was. Not no drug dealer that anyone knew of. Though some said he was there to buy from some of them wandering niggers we got there, ones think they're tough. I heard a story about a man wearing a hat like you come up and knocked a couple of them fuckers so hard their nuts flew off. That was you, wasn't it? I'm putting it together now."

Leonard nodded. "I think their nuts come a little loose, not completely off. I was feeling a little poorly that day."

Timpson grinned, then almost immediately turned as serious as a rattlesnake.

"I got to thinking on that beating, and I thought, buyer or seller or whatnot, he was just a kid and he took a hard whacking, hard enough to smack his life loose. But he didn't have that drug-dealer look. You can't tell by looks all the time, but you get so you got an idea. I went down to the station and reported on those cops. No one had heard of them, way I described them. No record of a call-out to the projects. They didn't know nothing, including their own shoe size. I come back to the apartment, and then I got word to that boy's mother, what I seen, and I tried calling some people that said they could get me up in there with the police chief, but what that got me was a cop car following me for a few days. Finally I dropped it. I never mentioned it again. I didn't want to be another dead nigger in a ditch with his asshole pulled up over his head. Boy's mother tried to talk to them, brought up what I saw, and that's when the police start on my ass again. I drive to town to get a six-pack, they was there. I go in the toilet at a filling station, hell, they was damn near there to wipe my ass. I didn't say no more about it. I got the picture and the frame it was in. They quit following me again. I shouldn't be saying nothing to you. I don't want to get dragged in on it, but I can't forget how it sounded out there, them clubs laying into that boy. I could hear bones break up like peanut brittle. It was some shit, I tell you that."

"We'll keep you out of it for now," I said.

"For now?" Timpson said. "Man, I come in here and try to do you a solid, and you gonna put me out there in it again?"

"Only way you'd have to come back in it," Leonard said, "is we get enough shit on those cops that killed that boy, the law might want them to put you on the stand."

"Camp Rapture ain't got no law. It's a goon town when it comes to law."

"Case like this," Leonard said, "I bet we could get a trial moved to someplace like LaBorde. Cops there are run by a good man and a friend of ours. You'll get played fair by him."

"I don't trust any cops," Timpson said. "I could start having some memory loss."

"You could," I said. "But I think you could still hear them bones breaking like peanut brittle in your head. We find out what the hell happened and why—"

"He got beat to death is what happened," Timpson said.

"—we'll nail the killers' dicks to a wall, then maybe you'll feel freer to talk to the authorities."

Something passed over Timpson's face that was hard to identify. It could have been a heavy thought; it could have been gas.

"Don't count on it," he said. "Right now, consider me and you two done. I just come here for a beer. But I wish you good luck."

"By the way," I said. "Were these cops white, black, Hispanic..."

"White," he said. "Big mothers, except for one. Well, he was big, but not tall. He was about as wide as a beer truck without the wing mirrors."

"One more question," Leonard said. "Who all else did you see out there while you were watching? Who else might have seen what went down?"

"I didn't take note," he said. "I got my ass inside."

"Did you see a car the kid might have been driving?" I asked.

"No. I didn't. I didn't even see a cop car. I wasn't taking notes or taking pictures, just trying to smoke a goddamn cigar."

He turned his beer up and finished it, stood, and pushed his chair back.

"Good night, fellas," he said. "Try the pulled pork here, it's fucking divine."

He went out.

8

We sat and drank our drinks, watched the fellows in the booth at the back. They weren't interested in us at all. Or at least they pretended not to be. We were about to leave when Leonard turned and went back to the bar. I trailed after him. Leonard put money on the bar for our drinks.

"You know, I'm going to leave you a tip," Leonard said and leaned over the bar. "The tip is some advice."

"I can't spend that," the bartender said.

"It's worth having and possibly lifesaving. I wouldn't give you two cents more than the drinks," Leonard said, "but this advice is free and valuable. We ever come back in, don't fuck with us next time."

"Don't come back in."

Leonard pondered that idea.

"That's fair enough," Leonard said. "Where's your shit house? I need to pee."

"You can go somewhere else and pee," said the bartender.

Leonard leaned away from the bar, unzipped his pants, and got his dick out. He started peeing against the bar, splashing it on the floor.

"I have to pee now, not later," Leonard said. "All you had to do was tell me where the shitter was."

"You son of a bitch," the bartender said, and he reached down behind the bar.

"You've been warned," I said.

I eased up really close to the bar, leaned my face over it. I was maybe two feet from him. "Best be a bugle you pull out from behind there, and you better know how to play it."

The bartender stared into my face. He lifted his hand up. It was empty.

"Damn," Leonard said, shaking his dick, the nose-twitching smell of urine in the air. "That was refreshing. You're lucky I didn't need to shit."

One of the men in a booth at the back stood up, a heavy guy with a bit of a belly.

"Sit down," Leonard said.

The man stretched and sat down.

Leonard zipped up, made a show of it, slow and tedious, like he was sacking up an anaconda.

The bartender glared at him. Leonard glared back. I tried to look pleasantly amused, which wasn't that difficult.

"You know what, bartender," Leonard said. "It smells like piss in here. You ought to clean up. Maybe spray some kind of de-stinker around."

We went out, not too briskly, but quickly enough.

As we were climbing into our ride, I said, "Couldn't help yourself, could you?"

"He was rude," Leonard said.

"Thank goodness you showed him some etiquette," I said.

Leonard nodded. "You never know what will stick with and educate a man. And if he didn't learn anything, at least I got to pee."

9

I drove us away from there and said to Leonard, "What do you think about Timpson?"

"Got a good story, but maybe too good. Sounded somewhat rehearsed to me, maybe mixed with some truth. I don't know, I get weird vibes from that guy, like he's trying to put his life in the middle of the road when he's been whipping left and right for some time. Shit, I'm not sure he ain't still whipping."

"Sounded believable enough," I said.

"Uh-huh, so do them people see Bigfoot now and then, but they ain't yet convinced me there's any Bigfoot, and that Timpson fellow ain't yet convinced me that things went down like he said."

"You are very hard to please."

"Get the best out of life that way," Leonard said.

• • •

Back at the office, I took Buffy for a walk, and when she finished with her business, me and her went upstairs and I washed up. I got a jar of peanut butter and a half loaf of bread from the cabinet, pulled out a jar of strawberry jelly from the minifridge, used a plastic knife to make a sandwich.

"Want one?" I asked Leonard.

"I do," he said while washing his hands.

I made two.

I got a dog treat out of one of the drawers, a pig's ear that was actually made of peanut butter, and gave it to Buffy. She loved those things, though they did make her fart.

I got Leonard a Dr Pepper out of the fridge and a small carton of milk for myself.

We sat at the desk, me in the client's chair, Leonard in the other. We ate our meal.

"How was your date?" I asked.

"Dry. He didn't lubricate very well."

"Not what I meant. How was the date itself, without the details on your snake's journey down a dry well?"

"Feel stupid about it, going on one of those dating sites."

"Yeah. I didn't know they had those for gay folks."

"Yeah. We date too. Some of us own property."

"Not what I meant."

"It's new. They match you up. Me and this guy, Terrance, we have the same beliefs, similar background, though he's better educated—"

"An extra day in kindergarten and he's better educated."

"Fuck you very much. We fit just about everywhere, except in certain slots."

"Okay. Enough."

"I don't just mean those slots," Leonard said. "For once, I was being metaphorical. On paper, or onscreen, if you will, we are such a match it's a surprise we aren't long-lost twins separated at birth."

"That could be a messy dating situation if it's true," I said.

"He's as black as me, got the same politics, likes country music and even likes vanilla cookies of all denominations."

"Is he a fool for hats?"

"That I don't know. But we got together, and no chemistry. It was like a duck and a rat. They don't want to hang out. Nice-looking fellow, got a great ass, but dry, and me and him, we don't really have anything in common outside of what's on the dating site. I thought, damn, me and him can play country music while we fuck, have some vanilla cookies afterwards—"

"A hand wash will be in there someplace, right?"

"But I find him almost as interesting as a horseshoe tournament."

"Those can be tense," I said.

"Let's say almost as interesting as buttering toast, without the butter. Did I mention he's kind of dry?"

"I think it came up."

"He's like talking to a cardboard cutout, but with less expression. He has all the humor of a corpse after ten years in the ground."

"Maybe your humor sucks."

"He's like one of your jokes. You know the joke, but you don't know how to tell it. I told it, he thought it was hysterical. One about the big-mouth frog. You can't do the frog's small voice. That's what pulls it off. But that joke was his one laugh. I mean that, he laughed once."

"You said he thought it was hysterical."

"That was hysterical for him. You see, he knows what humans do, but he don't know what they're like. Mostly he's a mimic. He don't know how to play it so it ain't just an act. It's so obvious, he practically brings his scenery and sound track with him."

"Sociopath?"

"No. Just dull."

"I tell great jokes, by the way."

"No, you don't."

"So, you and him? No more dates?"

"Not sure. We definitely do not click. He's a juicy-looking thing, but there's no juice in him. He's like a plastic apple."

"Damn, this is interesting, but you know what? Let's talk about the case."

"I like to talk about me."

"Yeah, but let's don't. It always leads to a drilling expedition."

"You asked."

"My mistake."

"All right," Leonard said. "Here's what we got. Your lady Louise, she has a daughter, Charm, who got picked up by a shit-head cop and his shit-head partner. They treated her badly and a bad guy stuck a wet finger down her ass crack. A female cop let her go, and the cop got fired. Charm's brother decided to take care of her by harassing the cops who were harassing his sister. He aggravated the police who were following her around, and the cops killed him. We have an eye-witness who doesn't really want to talk about it, and who sounds fishy to me, and we got a dead kid. So thing is, or so it seems to me, we got to talk to those cops. Thing that bothers me, though, is how did the kid get to the projects? He had to have had a car. That hasn't come up, and Timpson said he didn't see one."

"Doesn't mean it wasn't there, and in the end, does it matter how Jamar got there?"

"It might. Was he dropped off? Was someone there with him that escaped a beating?"

"Or was he led to a beating?" I said.

"That crossed my mind. And how did he end up there with three cops beating him to death with old-style billy clubs. Who carries those these days? Timpson didn't see a police car either. Were they fucking beamed down by Scotty on the *Enterprise*?"

I took a moment to consider.

"Do you think Scotty would do such a thing?"

"No," Leonard said. "Not really. He always seemed like one of the good guys to me . . . So the cops see Jamar, and they are sick of his shit, and here they have him buying dope—"

"You don't know that," I said.

"No, I don't. I'm just fishing."

"All right," I said. "They were sick of him following them around, taking photos. They didn't like the shoe on the other foot, saw their chance to get even. Maybe he wasn't buying or selling shit, just like his mama said, but they might have wanted to pin dope-buying on him, or -selling. Make it look that way. Decided to have him resist arrest, even if he wasn't. They gave him a good ass-reshuffling for annoying them, but they got too happy in their work, did the billy-club boogaloo on his head, and he died."

Leonard nodded. "Could be. Still, something seems to be seriously missing in Timpson's tale."

"You keep coming back to that," I said. "He sounded sincere."

"And you keep coming back to *that*. Good liars sound sincere, which is why they're good liars. He sees this cop killing, goes in the house, and the cops just forget him? They were willing to kill Jamar, why are they letting Timpson go? That doesn't make any sense."

"Good point. But I get the feeling that's his story and he's sticking to it."

10

I decided I'd talk to Marvin at the cop shop. He probably knew some of the coppers in Camp Rapture, could maybe give me a lead into who was dirty there and who wasn't, who might be a contact worth having, but when I phoned him, he was out. I left a message, and then me and Leonard left for the day. I'm sure there was plenty we could do to find out who did what, but to tell you the truth, I wasn't sure what it was or how to go about it. I wished right then I had Sam Spade's private number. Of course, he'd be really old by now, might be missing a step or two. McGruff the crime-fighting dog could be available, though. We damn sure needed someone's help on this.

Me and Leonard aren't so much detectives as we are persistent bumblers, though some detective skills were wearing off on us in spite of ourselves. Thing was, though, Leonard wasn't exactly on his best game. He was acting tough, as always, and frankly, it wasn't much of an act. He was the toughest son of a bitch I knew. But he was acting tough, not only in skin and bones, but in emotions as well. He was tough enough, all right, but no one is that tough. I knew he was hurting over John.

For a while John and his niece had moved in with Leonard, then John left again, and Leonard helped the niece, Felicity, set up her own apartment. She had a job at a Starbucks and it was a good start. Like her uncle John, she was gay, and catching hell from her father because he thought gay was like choosing a haircut and all you had to do was let it grow out or get another haircut. Unlike her uncle John, Felicity knew who she was and was proud of it, and Leonard was her hero. I could understand that. He was kind of mine sometimes.

Anyway, John left again, for the umpteenth time, and Felicity stayed in LaBorde. Her having only a part-time job gave her time off, which made her think she might could get some college in come next semester. She wanted to be a pharmacist.

Leonard had plans that night to take her to dinner and a movie, give her a pep talk or some such, so his head wasn't really into the business at hand. Honestly, we could take a bit of time. Jamar wasn't going to get any deader.

I put Buffy in the car and we went home, daring ourselves to catch what the ladies had, though I guess Buffy was immune. In spite of my telling Leonard how I was enjoying a bit of time away from home, I was starting to get lonely. I missed not only Brett, but Chance as well. Each day, I found myself bonding more closely with my daughter.

Daughter.

That was really hard for me to wrap my head around, but I liked the idea a lot.

It was quiet in the house, and Chance lay on the couch as if dead. Brett was in the kitchen heating water. Buffy went over and sniffed Chance, then lay down in front of the couch.

Brett spoke softly when she saw me.

"Cold medicine. It knocked her on her ass," she said. "I'm just now recovering from the same stuff."

Brett's face was pale and her nose was red and her eyes looked watery. She had her hair pulled up and tied at the back of her head. I thought she was beautiful.

"Feel better?"

"For the moment," she said. "I think it's actually more than a cold, some kind of flu. I do okay, and then I'm not okay. It's like constantly being run over by a train, revived, and run over again. You really should stay at the office. Let me assure you, you don't want this stuff."

"As a nurse, don't you know what this stuff is?"

"Former nurse."

"So you forget everything when you quit being a nurse?"

"I was never very good at diagnosing myself, because I so rarely get sick."

I moved closer to her. She stuck her palm against my chest.

"I'm not kidding. No kissing or hugging. This virus is a bitch with a hammer."

"Maybe a kiss would make it worthwhile," I said.

"Hey, I kiss like an ace, but even my wonderful wine-sweet kisses wouldn't be worth it."

"Actually, your lips do look dry."

"They are. I'm making hot tea. Want some?"

"Sure."

"Get the honey."

I prowled through the cabinets for the honey. It was in one of those plastic bears. I put it on the table, told Brett to sit, and finished making the tea. I found some animal crackers, something I liked and Chance loved, and put the box on the table.

"My stomach won't take it," Brett said.

"More for me," I said.

"You better save Chance some of those," she said.

"Do I have to?"

"She's your daughter. Do you want to become like Leonard, way he is about vanilla cookies?"

"I do not."

"You and her are a lot alike. Genetics isn't for nothing, you know."

"Love of animal crackers is no doubt a deeply embedded genetic trait. As for environment, I'm not sure we're offering her the best there is. That being my fault, of course, not yours."

"We are doing fine. You are doing fine."

Brett sipped her tea.

"All I can taste is hot," she said.

I tasted my tea. It was fine and sweet with honey, but then again, I wasn't sick. My taste buds were working. I had an animal cracker.

"Tell me what you have going?" Brett said.

I told her about Louise and our interview with Timpson Weed.

"Sounds like you've earned your sixty-five dollars, and then some."

"I suppose so," I said.

"But you want to keep digging?"

"You know I do."

"All right," Brett said. "Let's talk about it. So the kid was following the cops around, and the next thing you know, he's dead, and Weed says he saw him beat to death in a field by the project houses by some cops?"

"Yep."

"Know what bothers me about that?" Brett said.

"The fact that three cops in plain sight beat a kid to death? Leonard also brought up the part about them just letting Timpson Weed sail loose, and that no cars were seen by Timpson, or so he said. People live there, they notice things like that. They knew I was on-site before I actually got out of my car."

"What I'm thinking is, why were the cops that stupid? Why didn't they arrest him, take him in, or, if they really had a grudge, why didn't they take him somewhere else and kill him? That would have been smarter."

"Perhaps they didn't intend to kill Jamar," I said. "They were mad and it got out of hand. And maybe, simply put, it was a situation of opportunity, and they're not that smart."

"Could be," Brett said, and sipped at the tea and made a face.

"Stupid people get jobs too," I said. "Thing is, folks that get the badge a lot of time couldn't get a merit badge from the Cub Scouts, but they want the job and are persistent, qualified or not. Next thing you know, they're carrying a gun and an attitude and have a badge pinned on their chest."

"There are good cops."

"Of course. Marvin is the best. I know a few others. But there are still plenty that when they were kids they got a participation trophy for coming in dead last, and they're still mad about it. What is a fact is the kid, Jamar, was following them around, pissing them off, filming them. They didn't expect it, didn't like it, and the kid ends up dead."

"Uh. I'm feeling worse."

Brett stood up with her cup of tea and poured it in the sink.

"Should I take you to the doctor?"

"Nope. I'm a nurse. Remember?"

"Were."

"Hasn't been that long."

"Now suddenly you're falling back on your nursing credentials."

"I like to work it the way it works best for me."

"You make a good nurse but a lousy patient."

"That's probably right," she said. "Look, I got to go back to bed. Will you check on Chance, see that her fever is going down? Mine sort of comes and goes, so I guess she's in the same boat."

"You look pretty weak. Need help upstairs?"

"No. I got it."

Brett headed up and I went over to the couch and gently touched Chance's head. It was warm, but not on fire.

I went back to the table and finished my tea. I sat there and thought about what Brett had said, and the more I thought about it, the more I wondered. Maybe she and Leonard had the right kind of suspicions. Would the cops just beat the kid to death there in plain sight? They wanted to kill him, why not get him in the car and take him some place isolated and fix him so he's fertilizing grass. Thing was, why were they following Charm in the first place, which was the business that led to them following the brother? Those thoughts ran around and around in my head like a mouse on a hot stove.

I finished up with the tea, put the cookies away, cups in the dishwasher, started for the hall bathroom. I stopped when I passed the couch. I looked at the young woman sleeping there, my daughter. She was covered in an old quilt Brett had inherited from some relative, and all that was visible was her head on a couch pillow, her black hair tumbling over it. She looked like her mother, or at least the way I remembered her. I could see parts of me there too. Not in a Frankenstein-monster stitch-up kind of way, but in a blend of two people.

Being a father had as much to do with being present as it did with genetics. More, actually. A lot of what we say is genetics is proximity, by my reckoning, and the way we learn to be human is by example. I wasn't sure how good my example was. I had killed people, and I had hurt people. All for good reasons, I told myself, but at three in the morning, and sometimes in moments like now, I wasn't so sure I was anything more than a thug who justified his actions. Leonard, at least, believed in himself and the choices he made. I was more shaky about those things.

Chance stirred a little. I went over and sat in a chair across from the couch. She opened her eyes and saw me.

"Hey," she said.

"Hey. You still have a fever. Brett said it was really high before. Not as much now. I felt your forehead."

"I dreamed a bird lit on my head. That was you."

"Most likely. Any better?"

"Just feel unbelievably tired. Hard to pick up my arms sometimes. Brett, she's been really sick."

"I know. She was up a bit, but now she's back in bed."

"It's more than a cold."

"Brett thinks the same. Flu is my guess."

"You're going to end up with it," she said.

"I hope not. You get better, you and me, maybe we could do something."

"Arm wrestle?"

"We could."

"Badminton? Perhaps a little polo, take part in a tractor pull?"

"You're kind of a smartass."

"From what I can tell, you and Leonard and Brett are all smartasses."

"It's not as positive a trait as you might think."

"But you stay a smartass."

"Some of us have looks and some of us have brains, and some of us are just smartasses. We embrace what we have."

She sat up on the couch, pulled the blanket around her. She reached down and gave Buffy a pat on the head.

"Can I get you something?" I asked.

"Orange juice."

I went into the kitchen, washed my hands, poured her a glass of orange juice, and gave it to her. "Can you eat anything?"

"I don't think so. I don't get quite as ill as I did thinking about food now, but my stomach is still not crazy about the idea."

"Okay, then."

"You know, you look all right."

"Well, I'm not sick," I said.

"Not what I mean. You said some got the looks and others got the brains. Mama thought you looked good. I think a lot of women might."

"So you're saying I didn't get the brains?"

She laughed a little. "Brett likes you for some reason."

"There are still desperate ones in the world," I said, "and I think in Brett's case, her eyesight might be failing, and she likes having someone less intelligent than her around."

"You undercut yourself a lot, but I'm not even sure you believe it."

"Oh, that's where you would be wrong."

"And you three, you, Leonard, Brett, you're all bright. I like being here. I like talking about something besides what Mama's boyfriends talked about. Guns. Jesus, which was funny, considering they were gun fanatics and drunks, and when they weren't talking about Jesus, they were cursing black people, gays, and so on. A few of them had been in prison. None of them had read a page of the Bible, but to hear them tell it they were God's right-hand men." She paused a moment. "Leonard seems to really like guns, but he's okay."

"Leonard likes what they can accomplish, but he's not someone who dresses them up and talks to them. He doesn't talk about ammo and gun grips like he's talking about beloved family members. Well, actually, he doesn't have any family members."

"There's you and Brett. Me, I hope."

"Yeah," I said. "You're right. He's my brother. And, Chance, I want you to know, I'm not a perfect kind of guy. I have some skeletons in my closet. I need to be clear about that."

"Brett's told me some of it. I figure there's a lot more to it than she's told me, but I know this: you're a good man."

I actually blushed. "I'm not so sure," I said.

"I am," she said. "I know you are."

"Who you want me to be."

"I truly believe you are a good man."

"We'll give that some time to sort out," I said.

Right then, one thing was for sure—I wanted to be a better man than I was. For Chance.

11

After sitting by myself in the kitchen, reading an old and not-too-good Western novel now and again, I answered a brief call from Marvin and took a moment to make myself another cup of tea, which I drank quickly.

Chance was asleep again on the couch, Brett was still asleep upstairs, both of them loaded to the gills with fresh flu medicine. I was bored. I called Leonard and he came by and picked me up. I brought Buffy out to the truck with me and let her hop in the backseat. It was one of those four-door truck jobs with a shortened truck bed so as to allow a backseat.

"Wasn't sure you'd want to leave your house," I said.

"Why not. Me and Felicity went to eat, then to the movie, and, well, I could tell she wanted to go home and look at Facebook or some such shit, so I took her. Only so much time a young person wants to spend with a middle-aged person."

"Middle-aged, huh? Double your age and tell me that you are truly middle-aged."

"I'd rather not," Leonard said. "I went home, sat around, and there's no one there but me. I played with my dick awhile, but the dick wasn't interested. Ever have that happen?"

"My pecker is always curious and up for adventure."

"I don't doubt that. I remember one time when we were on a fishing trip. We were up, let me see, Caddo Lake, I think, and we were coming back, and we stopped in that little town—"

"Dangerfield."

"Maybe."

"Pretty sure that was it. Pretty sure I see this coming."

"We found this café, stopped to get a bite, and you start chatting up the waitress."

"Hair black as a raven's wing. Lips like rose petals falling apart, to quote a Bob Wills song."

"Yep," Leonard said, nodding. "So you start chatting, and the next thing I know the place is closing and we're going to take her home, and she has you get in the backseat with her, and damn if you two aren't going at it like a couple of goddamn jackrabbits back there, and there I was in the front seat, a few inches from all that business. Didn't know where I was going, just driving around like an idiot because she never gave me her address, and if that wasn't bad enough, you didn't just screw her until her lights dimmed, you kept going, trying to put them out. She kept saying, 'Oh, baby, I've come, can't you come?' And you're just pounding her so loud that old wreck of mine is vibrating like an egg timer, and you say, 'I'll get there when I get there,' and then she's screaming and yelling, 'I'm doing it again,' and then you still didn't quit."

"I am virile," I said.

"You are an animal. It went on and on. I had to stop for gas, and you two, you're back there still pumping away while I get gas, and might I say the sight of your raw white ass riding up and down was not a pleasure."

"Then why were you looking?"

"I wanted to see how it worked. Shit, what do I know about being heterosexual? Curiosity set in, you see."

"I think you wanted to see my butt."

"That was an accident, and frankly, it's left me a little scarred. So I put in the gas, drove to a hill overlooking a park bench, and you two went at it for hours."

"It wasn't hours."

"Well, it was a long time. The car was rocking so much I was getting seasick. I got out and sat on the bench and watched the car rock. When you finished back there, I thought, *Thank goodness*. But then the two of you were at it again. Had no shame."

"We were young and passion made us stupid and immodest, and I think you are exaggerating a mite."

"I kept sitting there, and the car kept rocking, and I know for a fact that was how you actually met Chance's mother."

"I know you know."

"What I been thinking is how could a beautiful girl like Chance be made from you, and, if you'll pardon me, I think her mother would have screwed anything with pants on and maybe a few others wearing short-shorts or a kilt?"

"Our urges have nothing to do with Chance."

"Actually, they have everything to do with her," Leonard said.

"Well, okay. But not that night. I don't think."

"What messes me around is Chance looks like you, but somehow on her it's good. Hear what I'm saying? Her mother looked good too, the way I think heterosexual women are supposed to look if they look good, but Chance looks like you."

"Is there a point to all this?"

"Yeah. Don't ever tell Chance how you met her mother, outside of saying you met in a café. I know you have a way with the women sometimes, and I don't get it, but then I wouldn't. Still, that was cheap. The two of you making a sausage sandwich, and now I know what came of it."

"She forgot to take the pill, or the pill didn't work. I asked her if I should use protection, and she said she was on the pill. I'm no idiot."

"You are an idiot, Hap. You took the word of some woman you had just met. But, considering the result was Chance, then or later, I guess that makes it kind of all right and makes me an uncle, but wow, you buy a hamburger, and the next thing I know you two are in the backseat doing the nasty."

"We just clicked, man. I liked her."

"You liked something. And I think she did a lot of clicking."

"We dated awhile, and you need not be so judgmental. You're dating off the Internet, and dry holes at that. That's no better, you know?"

"You have a point. I think because I couldn't get it up today, and you always can, or so you say, I was a little jealous. And the other thing, well, I didn't like what you did that night. There wasn't any courting going on. Just wham-bam-thank-you-ma'am."

"I got her number. We spent time together after that."

"Time is one thing to call it."

"This coming from you. Once again, let me remind you: Internet. No courting. Quick fuck. Dry hole."

"Yes, but I've come to expect more of you."

I laughed. "You are a piece of work, Leonard. That was many years ago. I hadn't been broken up with Trudy that long, and it was the one time in my life I was prone to drink. The only time I ever drank, to be exact. And I didn't do anything she didn't want to do. Why are we talking about this?"

"I'll say it again. A bit of jealousy at your ability to perform at the drop of a hat, and for a lengthy period of time. And also, I thought about it today, and thought it might be an embarrassing memory, and that would be fun. But you don't look embarrassed."

"No reason to. So, having trouble with your pecker, huh?"

"I think it's psychological. It's all this stuff with John. Used to, I got up in the morning, had a cup of coffee, I'd start climbing the walls like a goddamn monkey, masturbating all over the place. Had John there, well, I'd bend him over and fuck him hard enough to drive him to town and send him through the car wash."

"You are such a romantic," I said.

"Now, my dick droops, looks like one of those things they used to sharpen knives on. A strop."

"But smaller. Listen, Leonard. Don't let it get to you. Jealousy of my sexual prowess has ruined many a man. And I'm sorry you got a look at my ass, because once my godlike body is revealed, no man or woman will ever suit you again."

"You are so full of shit. I have seen your charm fail you more than once. Even a blind squirrel finds an acorn now and then."

"First I was a hot sex machine, now I'm a blind squirrel."

He chuckled. It was all absolutely juvenile, but we had done it for years, and I think ribbing each other over everything from sex to hair loss was our way of connecting; verbal comfort food.

"Part of the problem is fucking and loving aren't always the same, Leonard. Romantic you're not, but I think the way you talk about John is bullshit. You love him."

"Yeah. Damn me . . . Hey, why are we riding around with Buffy? We dropping her off at the mall?"

"Because my family has the flu."

"And you're bringing flu germs into my ride, along with dog odor?"

"I'm not sick. Brett and Chance are asleep, so there's no one for me and Buffy to play with, so I called my bestest friend forever."

"And when he couldn't make it, you called me. Again. But why is Buffy in the backseat?"

"She likes your ribald stories," I said.

"We're going to get ice cream cones at Dairy Queen, aren't we?"

"Buffy likes a good cone."

"You really wanted me to take you to get your dog an ice cream, and that's why you called me, isn't it? You wanted to save gas and give Buffy a cone and not have Brett know about it. You heard her say the dog is getting fat."

"I left a note and said we were going riding with you. No secret. Brett will figure out where and why I went."

"Unless you get home before she wakes up."

"Then I would have to remove the note, and me and Buffy would be silent conspirators together. And you will also be involved."

"I'm your patsy."

"That is correct."

"You, Hap Collins, are a liar."

"It's a white lie. And look at it this way. You got to tell me about your dick problems, and you got to tell a true-as-shit story about my manly prowess."

I looked back at Buffy. She was leaning over the seat with her nose pressed against my cheek.

"She knows we're going for a cone," Leonard said.

"Brett thinks I spoil her."

"You do," Leonard said.

"A princess deserves special things. Also, I thought we might do something else. Talk to the cop that got fired for letting Charm go."

"Manuela. You know where she lives?"

"Right before I called you, Marvin called me. He says the cops in Camp Rapture are known as shit stains on the underwear of law enforcement. And that's a quote. He did say he knew the deputy that got fired, though, and called her a 'good egg.'"

"A good egg? He's been watching old cop shows again, hasn't he?"

"I think so. He gave me her address."

"I underestimated you. I thought you were merely using Buffy to get yourself an ice cream cone, but you are after evidence."

"We are detectives."

"This fired cop's place close to our Dairy Queen?"

"Not that close," I said. "And besides, Buffy needs to go to the office."

"She have paperwork?"

"No, but she does like to tidy up."

"All right, then, after we have our cones and drop the Buffster off, we'll drive a little faster on our way over."

12

We went through the drive-through at Dairy Queen. I got a chocolate cone, and Buffy and Leonard had vanilla. Dogs aren't supposed to eat chocolate, and Leonard always prefers vanilla.

We didn't actually speed up, as Leonard had suggested, but drove around town slowly, eating, listening to Lightnin' Hopkins on the disc player, me holding Buffy's cone so she could lick it until she was down to the cone itself. Then I gave it to her. Her tongue turned blue from the ice cream, and when she was done she stretched out on the backseat and closed her eyes. I think her brain was frozen.

Finished up, we drove Buffy to the office. I took her for a short walk out in the grass beside the office, cleaned up her poo, put her inside, then we drove to the address I had for the deputy, Manuela Martinez.

It was solid dark when we got to Ms. Martinez's place. The CD in the player was now finishing up a Kasey Lansdale tune, "Can't Blame You for Trying." The house was a small house in a less expensive part of town, and it was on a street with similar houses on both sides. Nice houses, but nothing dramatic, middle class with a view to moving upwards. A little better house than mine and Brett's place, brick, with a yard lit by a porch light strong enough to make the moonlight wish for greater wattage. The flowers near the porch were wilting.

There were lights behind the windows, and there were lights on in most of the houses along the street. There was a black pickup truck and a white Ford under the open carport at the Martinez house. Leonard parked at the curb and we walked up the sidewalk that led to the porch and I pushed the doorbell.

We could hear it ding-dong inside, and then a small dog started yapping, and after a few moments we heard a female voice say, "Shut up, Trixie."

Trixie shut up briefly, but by the time Manuela came to the door and cracked it, the dog was barking again.

"Hush, Trixie," Manuela said. I could see the dog through the cracked door. It was a small, mixed mutt, and this time it went quiet and sat, looking at us with what I deduced was an angry-dog expression.

"Yes," the lady said. She was petite with thick black hair and a fine face that was almost model material, but she had a long scar from her left ear to the tip of her chin. I liked it. It wasn't deep, it was just a strong white line on a fine dark face. She wore a loose black T-shirt and yoga pants. She was barefoot.

"Sorry to bother you," I said.

"Are you?" she said.

"Yes, ma'am."

"My hand that's behind the door," she said. "It's holding a Smith and Wesson."

"Is that some kind of old-fashioned typewriter?" Leonard said, and grinned.

"No. But it does make a rat-a-tat sound if I pull the trigger just right."

"We're not here to bother you," I said.

"Well, recently I have been bothered."

"We are not whoever it was that bothered you."

"Selling Jesus or sewing machines, you are still on my shit list."

"Neither," I said. "I don't think they sell sewing machines door to door, so you can mark that off your list. Jesus has mostly moved to the Internet, I think."

"It might be cool, though," Leonard said, "if Jesus was selling sewing machines door to door."

"You are Manuela Martinez?" I asked.

"I am."

"We're here to talk with you about a young lady named Charm. Her mother, Louise, asked us to. She claims her son was murdered by the law and that her daughter was harassed by them. She has us looking into it."

"Private detectives?"

"Very private," Leonard said.

"You carrying?"

"Just our handsome selves," Leonard said.

She smiled a little. "All right, come in, but I'll hold on to my gun for a while, if you don't mind, and I'll have to pat you down."

"Really?" Leonard said.

"Really."

"Would it matter if we minded about your gun?" Leonard said.

"It would not."

"That'll be just fine, then," Leonard said.

13

The house was simple but nice inside. Through an alcove I could see into the living room. The couch in there was fat with colorful cushions. A painting on the wall of a great fish jumping appeared to have been stolen from a motel. On the left side of the room, mounted on the wall above the couch, was a very large game fish with a long snout, like the one in the painting. It was coated with dust.

Manuela patted us down, finding no weapons except our razor wit, which was much more self-contained than usual due to her holding that pistol.

She eventually invited us to sit on the couch. Manuela sat in a fat cushioned chair that matched the couch. Trixie jumped up and lay down across her knees. Manuela put one hand on the dog's head, and in the other she held her weapon.

"We have a few questions, just to verify what we were told," I said.

"Who actually sent you? I'm thinking you ought to talk to my lawyer. I have a lawyer on this business, the firing, so if you're sent from the department in any manner, shape, or form, you can fuck off."

"We're not trying to trick you," Leonard said.

"We work for Louise, really," I said. "She said her daughter, Charm, was picked up for drunk driving, but when she asked the cops for the Breathalyzer, they refused, chained her standing up with her pants slightly pulled down in back, left her that way until morning. You came along and let her loose. Is that accurate?"

"What are your names?"

We told her. We told her about the agency and mentioned Marvin Hanson.

"Marvin," she said. "Sure. I should have gone to work in LaBorde, but he wasn't chief there then. Still, would have been better off than Coldpoint and Camp Rapture."

"It's starting to sound as if going over Niagara Falls on a log would be better," Leonard said.

"That's the truth," she said. "All right. You know Marvin, and you used to work for him, so I'll talk. A little. I don't know about the Breathalyzer part, but she was cuffed, and her pants had been pulled down slightly in back, showing her butt crack, and no one would let her pull them up. Her hands were chained in front of her. The officers in charge were mad when I pulled them up for her, and they were madder yet when I uncuffed her and let her go."

"What made you decide to let her go?" I asked.

"It's a boys' club there, and I had a bad feeling about it, and then I looked at the arrest report, and it seemed dodgy. I mean, here's a girl not in a cell, but bound to a radiator, right where perps are brought in, and they're ogling her booty. I knew enough laws had been violated there wouldn't be a real case anyway. I figured Coldpoint was the main one who had violated them. He doesn't like it when people don't do exactly what he says, legal situation or not.

He can talk calm and sound intelligent, because he is, but he is a narcissist of the first degree. You know he was in trouble for a shooting some years back, black teenager who got a warning shot in the back of the head, as we say."

"And you were fired over letting Charm go?" I said.

"They said I wasn't holding up my end, but that's not the real reason. Like I said, it's a boys' club of the worst kind, so I wasn't all that upset to leave. I was married for a while, and that job ruined my marriage. Wish they'd let me go a couple years ago. At least then I'd have my marriage and not just some trophy fish he caught mounted on my living-room wall. That really has to go, by the way."

"Yard sale," Leonard said. "Some bozo will buy it and claim he caught it."

"You know, maybe it is best my husband is gone. I never did understand all that trophy fishing and hunting. Had a lion's head somewhere. Maybe he took that with him. Might be in the garage attic. But damn, I did like my job, and I did take it home with me, so I can't blame Brian for becoming annoyed with that."

I waited a moment while she studied the fish on the wall, then turned her head to study us again.

"Did Charm say anything to you?" Leonard said.

"She was crying and she had a camera around her neck, and she said it was starting to wear on her, that it was heavy, and could I at least take that off of her, but I let her go. My guess is Coldpoint wanted to con her into sex, saying if she did that he'd let her go. I don't know that, but rumor is that's his brand and that it works more often than you might think."

"Lot of rumors," Leonard said.

"That's true, but that place stank like week-old fish, and there's things I know that aren't rumors. I've shared those with my lawyers. Charm wasn't playing the game the right way for him, so he decided to punish her. Like I said, he can't stand to lose. He was mad at me already because I wouldn't have sex with him. He said he could help me move up the ladder. I told him there was nothing at the top of any ladder he provided I wanted, and I didn't think my vagina was a ladder, or for that matter a basement."

"A camera?" Leonard said.

I was focused on the vagina part, but Leonard had been more practical.

"Yeah. It wasn't a big camera," Manuela said, "but with it hanging around her neck all night, and with her standing, it probably felt like a truck tire."

"Anything else you can tell us, Miss Martinez?" I asked.

"Not really. And everyone calls me Manny. I let Charm go. Because of that, I went to court, and Coldpoint lost the first round, though I still have more court dates ahead of me. That shit never ends. Main reason they lost on me letting that girl go was they didn't have any Breathalyzer results and the usual judge they have on their payroll wasn't presiding. He was on a fishing trip, so it didn't work out so well for them, and it not working out so well for them isn't something they're used to. Anyway, after the trial, that's when Coldpoint started harassing the brother for harassing them."

"You knew about that?" I asked.

"Yeah. It took them a while to drum me out, so I was around, and I picked up on what they were doing, heard them talk when they didn't know I was listening. As for me, they wanted to make my firing about something else so it wouldn't look suspicious, so it took about a month to get me fired. I kept having to go up for evaluation, this not being right, this being wrong. All bullshit. But I knew Coldpoint was following Charm around, and then when the brother started filming them in return, that damn sure put Jamar on their shit list. Heard the guys gripe about it. They are a sorry bunch, just about all of them. Couple okay fellows, but even they go along to get along. Thing was, Coldpoint wanted me out because I wasn't a team player. And another thing was, early on, he wanted me to lay down in the back of his cruiser and be initiated, same as some female prisoners, and I wouldn't do it. And there's more going on than that. I don't exactly know what, but there's something else, maybe a lot of elses. I think for one they resell the drugs they get from the druggies, make sweet deals with dealers. They use a bit of the product themselves from time to time. You been around that stuff for a while, brought in enough users, you recognize the signs."

"But that's speculation?" I said.

"In court it would be, but I'm more than certain that the sexual favors, drug use, and drug sells are going on. But I couldn't prove it in a court of law. Thing about Charm, though, seemed to be something else going on there. She wasn't your usual druggie, or prostitute, or even someone with a reputation as being the local poke. It seemed when they didn't get their way, they were out to humiliate her, couldn't stand that she and I wouldn't play their game. As for Jamar, can't say they did anything to him. I don't know. But if you had me guessing, I'd guess they had something to do with it. Quite a coincidence that she is harassed, and then her brother harasses them and is found dead."

"Anything more you can tell us?" I said.

"I may have talked too much, more than my lawyer would want, but I do dislike those guys. I'll just say this: You dig deep at the Camp Rapture department, you're going to find a well of rotten shit. And another thing: Be careful while digging. The whole damn town's high rollers are attached to them. They're all playing grab-ass with one another, and if you try and get in the middle of that, you might end up a Rusty Puppy."

"Rusty Puppy?" Leonard said.

"You know where the old sawmill used to be?"

"There are a lot of sawmills," Leonard said.

"I mean the really old one, one goes back to the thirties. On the hill at the edge of Camp Rapture. Closed down now."

"I know," I said.

"Yeah," Leonard said. "Had an older cousin worked there, right before it was shut down in the eighties. Dangerous place to work. Cousin had one finger missing on one hand, two on the other, and the tip of his thumb got sawed off too. Folks called him Lobster. We called him clumsy."

"There's a big pool of brackish water out there now," Manny said. "It used to be a pit where the sawdust gathered, but over the years it sunk in and got rained on enough to make a deep pond. They have dogfights out there, and dogs that die in the process, or if they fight badly, they shoot them in the head and dump them in the pond. All that old sawmill dust has mucked up in there, and when the dogs floated up, because sometimes they did, they looked like they were covered in rust. Humane society rightfully got up in arms. They told the police, and they went out and looked at the dead dogs, dubbed them Rusty Puppies. Probably half the dogs in there were owned by people on the force. They love dogfighting. Still fight them out there. Cops didn't do a thing about it because they were the ones doing it."

"Now I really do hate them," Leonard said.

"Wasn't just dogs showed up there; there were a few human bodies, which were also called Rusty Puppies. They lie in that sawdust long enough, it composts them. No telling how many were turned into compost. Sawdust, it eats a body up like acid, and it does it pretty quick. The others were found before that happened, but again, how many weren't? I'm going to bet there were plenty."

"Anyone know who the bodies in the sawdust were?"

"Oh, yeah. Local ne'er-do-wells. Beat to death and dumped there. A few prostitutes and drug dealers who maybe knew too much about how the folks on the force were operating. Sometimes folks fresh out of jail. Mixed bag, really. Now and again another body pops up out there. None of those murders are ever solved, nor will they be. I figure it's the cops who put them there."

"That's a strong accusation."

"I worked in that department, not you. Let me tell you, those boys answer to no one."

"Up until now," Leonard said.

14

As we drove away, I said, "Nice-looking woman."

"I was waiting for that," Leonard said.

"Just noting," I said.

"You can't fail to notice, can you?"

"Do you fail to notice attractive men?"

"I note them, but you are at heart a goddamn hound dog. A loyal hound dog, but a hound dog nonetheless."

"As long as I don't go into someone else's yard and hump their dog or get the water hose turned on me, I think Brett is happy."

Leonard grunted. "Know what I was thinking?"

"Another ice cream cone would be special?"

"No. We are not having another ice cream cone," Leonard said. "I was thinking, why was Charm in Camp Rapture in the first place, and what was she doing with a camera, and what was on the camera, and where is that camera?"

"Whoa," I said. "You are fucking Charlie Chan."

"Yeah," Leonard said. "I think I may have tripped over a clue."

"Oh my God," I said. "Sounds to me like you are doing some actual detective-type thinking."

"What I thought," Leonard said. He looked pleased enough with himself to be a parade-float captain.

"This means we got to talk to Charm."

"What I was thinking," Leonard said.

As we drove over to the house across from our office, Louise's place, a car drifted along behind us for a while. It was a dark sedan, not a cop car, but I noticed it. Leonard turned the pickup where we didn't need to turn, and it sailed on by, made a curve around Shawnee Street, and kept going.

"You saw it too," Leonard said.

I nodded.

We may not be the world's greatest detectives, but cars following us we generally noticed. Tonight it appeared to be merely paranoia. Leonard turned around in a driveway and headed back to our destination. No dark sedans were seen.

Not long ago we had dealt with another woman who spied out her window and ended up sending us down a dark rabbit hole with strange killers and stranger circumstances. It also nearly got me killed. Not long before that event, Leonard was almost killed. We liked to argue over who was the most dead for a few moments, but the thing was, I had this uncomfortable feeling that the current rabbit hole we were diving into was deeper and darker than it appeared.

We parked in our lot, near the bicycle shop, walked across to Louise's house. There was a dim light in the window. The house was older, and most of the street had upgraded to more modern styles, but her place was still small and made of wood and the roof needed a bit of work. You could tell that when you looked out the second floor of our office. I had stared at that roof a lot but never knew who lived there until she came to the office that day.

We knocked on the door.

After a long while, Louise answered. She was wearing a long nightgown. "Oh, you're the detective."

She said this directly to Leonard.

Then to me: "You're the white guy I hired, right?"

"Right."

"Wasn't sure. You people look so much alike."

"So you've said. Sorry about it being late. But we need to talk."

She invited us inside. I said, "We're really here to ask Charm a few questions. Is she home?"

"She is. I'll wake her."

We stood just inside the front door. The house was nice and tidy and there were shelves that had more knickknacks than a flea market. Leonard had his hands in his pockets. He said, "I'm actually, very carefully, fondling my balls."

"Oh, shut up."

"He studies the shot. Thinks he can make it. If he only had a smaller cue stick. The one he has is really too enormous for the job."

"Ha-ha."

"Here goes, one black-as-night ball in the side pocket."

"Stop it."

About that time, Louise came out from a room across from us and Charm came out behind her, dragging her feet, looking sleepy.

"Missed the shot," Leonard said so only I could hear.

"I hate you," I said.

Charm was short and petite and so pretty she'd make a monk's back teeth ache.

"Hello, Charm," I said.

"Hi," she said.

Leonard nodded at her and smiled.

"I guess your mother has explained to you who we are and what we're doing?"

She dipped her chin. "Yes."

"Good. Louise, would it be okay if we speak to Charm in private?"

"I don't know." Louise was still holding Charm's elbow.

I saw something move across Charm's face, a shadow of teenage lies, perhaps.

"It's all right, Mama. I don't mind."

"I mind a little," Louise said.

"It's up to you two," I said.

"It's really all right," Charm said.

"Okay," Louise said. "But I'm going to be down the hall there, and if you need me, call me."

"I will," Charm said.

"Sometimes it just works better if we talk in private, so no one feels the need to answer in a certain way," I said.

"We tell each other everything," Louise said, and she gave me a look that said she was certain of that statement, and if I didn't like it, she was up for three rounds and no referee.

"I'm sure of that," I said.

"Damn straight," Louise said. She started down a short hall, threw back at us, "I'm just right here."

"It's okay, Mama," Charm said.

Louise disappeared into a room and closed the door.

Me and Leonard ended up sitting on the couch, and Charm took a stuffed armchair. It was a kind of replay of our roles in Manny's house.

"I want you to know we are very sorry about your brother," I said.

"Thank you," she said, and her chin quivered slightly.

"We want to get to the bottom of why what happened to him happened," I said. "That's why we're asking you questions. Not to harass you or make you feel uncomfortable."

"I understand," she said.

"You going to be a journalist, huh?" Leonard said, and showed her his nice teeth.

"That's the plan, though right now there's not a lot of jobs in the field, newspapers disappearing and all. I thought maybe magazine work."

"Hap's daughter, she's got a job in journalism."

"Where does she work?"

"Right now, local newspaper," I said. "But only proofreading for the moment. Part-time."

I realized I was speaking very proudly of Chance, even though right then she was living in Leonard's old room in mine and Brett's house.

"Here's a question," I said. "Why were you in Camp Rapture in the first place? Before you say anything, we'll keep your answers as private as possible, and remember, this is about your brother. We are trying our best to find out what happened to him. So as straight an answer as you can give us would be appreciated."

"Mama said she didn't have any real money to pay you. Will that make a difference in how much you do?"

"No," Leonard said. "Hap here is privately rich and supports me. When this is over we're opening a coffee bar in Tibet."

Charm gave a wan, sleepy smile, one that said, You know, that's not really that funny, but I'm going to go with it.

"I was there to take photos before sunset," she said. "I was told when the sun went down it made the trees and the old mill and the water pit look interesting. It was a photojournalism piece I was doing on the lumber industry in the 1930s. It's like a high school final."

"Were you leaving the mill when you were pulled over?" Leonard asked.

"I was. I went there after the party."

"And you took the photos, I assume?" I said.

"Correct."

Leonard said, "So you were leaving the mill and were back out on the road, and were pulled over, and then what?"

"A big cop, him and his partner, got out and one of them——"

"Coldpoint?" I asked.

"Yes, sir. I didn't know that was who he was then, but that's him. He got out and claimed I was weaving, that I was drunk. I proved I wasn't, but it didn't make any difference. When he wouldn't give me a Breathalyzer test, I knew it wouldn't matter what I said, what test I performed. He said, 'You want to blow, we can work it out so you blow, but not into a Breathalyzer.' I didn't take the bait. I think he was certain I would."

"Unfortunately for that asshole," Leonard said, "he was working from experience. Probably his idea of a date."

"What happened to the photographs you took?" I said.

"They took the memory card out of my camera at the station," she said.

"Any idea why?"

"I just know when I came down the hill from the sawmill they were waiting. They followed me to the edge of town and turned on their lights and pulled me over."

"This other cop," Leonard said. "Know his name?"

"At the station, I think they called him Seerfault."

"Could it have been Sheerfault?" Leonard said.

"It could."

I glanced at Leonard. He looked as if he had just sucked on a shit-stained lemon.

"You sure he was a cop?" Leonard said. "He wearing a uniform?"

"I'm sure," she said. "And he was."

"Any idea why they were following you in the first place?" I said.

"No, sir. Really, I have no idea. They took the card out of my camera and hung it back over my neck and chained me to a radiator. I think you know the rest."

I said, "May we have a peek in Jamar's room?"

"I suppose that's okay," she said.

She led us to his room, which was down an opposite hall. We went inside, and Charm left us alone. There were photographs and posters of boxers, and there was a shelf near the bed with boxing trophies.

Leonard picked one up. "First place. A university boxing event."

We looked around a bit more, then went out. Charm was waiting on the couch. We sat down across from her.

"Saw your brother was a boxer," Leonard said.

"He was pretty good. One time there was talk of him going to the Olympics, but he didn't want to. He had other interests. Boxing was more like a hobby, but he was very good."

"You think of anything else, our office is across the street," I said.

"I know," she said.

"You were at the sawmill just for photos?" I said. "Nothing else? I wouldn't ask, but it could be important."

"I was supposed to meet a boy. Kevin Conners. He didn't show."

"But you didn't want your mother to know that?" Leonard said.

"I didn't. Does she have to know?"

"I don't think so," I said. "You didn't see him anyway, so no need."

"I won't ever see him now, at least not on purpose," she said.

"Thank you, and tell your mother we thank her for letting us into her home," I said.

As we stood up: "This Sheerfault," Leonard said. "Can you describe him?"

"Yes, sir. Rough white guy, looked like a professional fighter," she said. "You know, scars around the eyes. I know something about that because Jamar watched fights, was interested in boxers. One of Sheerfault's eyes sagged slightly. The right one. His nose had been broken. It had a knot on it, and it was a little out of line. He looked like he worked out. Not in a bodybuilder way. But he was in shape."

"You will make a fine observant journalist," Leonard said. "Sheerfault was a professional fighter. I know him."

We thanked Charm again and left.

15

W e walked across the street to the office, and I took Buffy out for another walk. Afterward, I made sure she had fresh water, then I got me and Leonard bottled water out of the fridge.

"You know Sheerfault, do you? Never heard you mention him."

"He's a sore spot. Back when I was kickboxing he beat me in the ring. On points, I might add."

"Counts in sport."

"It does."

"But you're bitter about it?"

"I was beat on points a few times," Leonard said. "I always fought like it was real. Up to a certain level, anyway. It's the referee's job not to let it get too real."

"If I remember right, I out-pointed you once, back when we were first starting to know one another. I don't mean touch points, I mean real points. I got a whole seventy-five dollars, a trophy that I threw away, and a really sore face for about two weeks."

"Shit," Leonard said. "We fought to fight, wasn't no money in it then. We were testing our skills."

"Now they get paid big-time, and some of them get paid more than big-time."

"Those were the days," he said. "Fighting for pretty much nothing in the way of payment and enjoying it. Sheerfault pointed me, quite a bit. He was quick. He hit pretty hard, but he didn't land much that was solid."

"You're quick," I said.

"Not like he was. He was quick like you're quick. I hit harder than you, but he was bunny-fuck fast."

"Why the grudge?"

"Something about the guy rubbed me the wrong way. We both had a tough background. I actually knew him a little from around LaBorde, and he was a bully. He liked to rough people up and take what little money they had. A street thug. He acted like that point win against me made him the toughest motherfucker in the badass basket."

"You feel like you beat him? Don't you?"

"I thought I hit him harder than he hit me, and I made him run a little. Losing on points to that asshole chapped my ass. Something about him. But he's tough as a nickel steak, no doubt. I gave him some shots that would have made an elephant shit a stack of lawn chairs, and he kept dancing. He has a head like a block of stone. But had we been on the street, which is where I'd like to get that motherfucker, I would have beat his ass like a tom-tom. Hit hard, hit fast, go to the house, like they say in Shen Chuan. Sport is a sport. I get beat that way, normally it's no harm, no foul, but Sheerfault, he's got a way about him that sets my teeth on edge."

"You're both older now," I said.

"I can still whip ass," Leonard said.

"No doubt," I said. "I meant maybe he's matured, even if you haven't."

"Ha, ha."

Buffy came over and laid her head on my leg and I scratched her behind the ears.

"Back to what's important," I said. "I think we need to find out what it was about Charm's camera, about where she was taking pictures, that got the Camp Rapture cops nervous. How about tomorrow we go out to the old sawmill?"

"Yeah, and let's bring our own camera," Leonard said.

16

Leonard dropped me off at home. I tore up the note I had written Brett, since it was obvious neither she nor Chance had stirred. Buffy checked on Chance on the couch, sniffed her, then came over and lay at my feet. I sat at the table and wrote a new note about how I was sleeping at the agency, still avoiding flu, and then loaded Buffy in my car and drove back to the office.

Now that I was involved in this business with Charm and her mother, I damn sure didn't want the flu to slow me down. I wanted to be at my best. I figured we had a tiger by the dick, but I wasn't exactly sure if we could yank on it enough to cage him.

I drank a bit of cranberry juice I had in the refrigerator straight from the container. I was the only one who drank it, so I figured it didn't matter. I folded the couch out and got the rolled-up foam mattress from the closet and put it on the couch frame and made it up with sheets and blankets, a pillow. I turned out the light and climbed into bed, Buffy at my feet. I lay there trying to figure how

Charm and her camera went together and how that fit with her brother being murdered. As I drifted off, I thought too about those poor dogs and people in that sawmill pool, crusted over with ancient sawdust, congealed into sticky flakes that made the dead look rusty.

17

Early the next day I drove me and Leonard out to the sawmill on the edge of Camp Rapture. The morning was fresh with cold air, and the sun was creeping over a horizon lined with trees and houses, turning the sky red as a ripe, polished apple.

Both of us had lived in this area once, between LaBorde and Camp Rapture. Terrible things had gone down with me and Leonard at his old house, back when he owned dogs and we both worked in the rose fields, back when my former wife, Trudy, came calling and messed us up. Or, to be more precise, I messed us up because she had me under her spell and I wanted it that way. That had been a turning point in our lives. It had changed us. Set us on a different and more brutal course. I always thought of Leonard as the naturally brutal one, but the truth was, my choices had led us into all this, and here we were, at the zenith of those choices and mistakes, two middle-aged men, tough of flesh, but tired. At least on my end. Leonard wasn't one to complain about it much. I didn't know if he had noticed he'd aged. I had noticed I had aged. I felt it in my bones on cold days like this one, and I thought about the avenues missed when I put my head on my pillow at night. But it wasn't all bad. There was Brett, and now Chance, and I had my brother Leonard with me. That's the kind of thing a lot of folks want and never get. But as Leonard has said, I'm hard to make happy.

As we drove, I remembered Leonard's old place, where Trudy had died. He no longer owned it. In fact, his old house was no longer there. It had caught fire and burned down after he moved, and a double-wide mobile home had been hauled in and blocked up in its place. There was a real lawn now and it was always mowed. The trees that had been along the edges of his property had been cut down and a series of shrubs had been planted. The shrubs were green for about a year after they first got ripe, as I liked to say, and then they became brown clutters that ran along either side of the property.

The worst part was that at one time, well behind Leonard's house, deep in the woods, there had been a massive oak. It was the last of the great oaks and came from an older time when trees grew for a long time without fear of the saw, grew fat and tall. The oak had thick limbs you could climb up on and stretch out on and sleep without fear of rolling off. I know. Both of us had done it, just because we loved it out there. We would lie in the tree in the spring with the canopy of leaves above us, shiny and green, and in the fall we were sometimes there too, when it was cool, before the nights turned truly cold. We would lie there on separate limbs and talk. We had some great discussions.

We called the tree the Robin Hood Tree, like the humongous tree where Robin and his merry band gathered to talk and feast. I also called it the Tarzan Tree, imagined how you could build a tree house on its wide limbs and have plenty of room to live with a lithe, blond Jane and do more than call elephants and swing on vines. I guess Leonard might have dreamed of having

Tarzan as his mate, though no doubt, he would have made Tarzan his bitch.

Leonard and I would meet at the oak, me having to hike through the woods from my place, which wasn't all that far away if you came by wooded path and then broke off the path and took a deer trail and finally a winding trace through a series of tall, blackjack oaks until you arrived at Fisherman's Creek. Across the creek the trees thinned in number but not in magnificence. There were sweet gums and hickories and, of course, pines.

The Robin Hood Tree was the granddaddy of them all. The oak rose higher and spread its limbs wider than all the others. Its bark was healthy and dark, and in the spring the leaves were green as Ireland. To stand beneath it when it rained was amazing, because the limbs were so thick and the leaves so plush that during the spring and much of the summer, if not the fall, when the leaves were crisp and brown and yellow and dropping, you would hardly get wet. When it stormed, the limbs shook like angry Spartans rattling their weapons, but the limbs didn't break. The soil beneath the oak was thick and dark with many years of dropped and composted leaves. There were fat acorns on the ground, and sometimes when you came to the tree, squirrels were under it, rare black squirrels that made that part of the woods their home. They would be in the tree as well, chattering and fussing as you arrived.

Leonard and I met there many mornings, usually having a breakfast of boiled eggs that we brought in brown paper bags. We drank coffee from thermoses. We brought our fishing gear with us. We would sit beneath the tree and eat and talk and take our time drinking coffee. Finally we would go away from there, carrying our gear and cooler, one of us with a bucket of dirt loaded with worms. We walked through the trees and along the narrow creek bed to where the pond was. It was a big pond, and at one time there had been a house near it. Now the house was a pile of gray lumber and rusty nails and a few bricks that showed where the fireplace had been. Beyond that was a clapboard barn that still stood, the wide doors gone, probably removed for lumber for someone's project. Trees crowded the barn, and one sweet gum had grown up and under the roof and was pushing it loose on one side.

The pond had been dug maybe fifty years before and filled with fish, and we were fishing their descendants. There was a small boat down there, one we had tediously carried along the creek bank, and we left it there for when we wanted to fish. No one bothered it, because no one besides us came there anymore. The land was owned by someone up north who had mostly forgotten about it. The pond was always muddy, but the fish were thick. We caught them and generally threw them back, unless they were good-size enough and fat. Then they went home with us and became our supper.

We fished with cane poles, not rods and reels. It wasn't a place for rods and reels. It was a place for fishing in an old and simple way. We put lines on the poles, sinkers, corks, hooks, and bait, usually worms. Out in the boat we would dangle lines and drift and watch the fish jump, the dragonflies dip down on the water, see the shadows of birds flying over. Now and again there was the sight of a leaping frog or a wiggling water moccasin. Turtle heads rose like periscopes, then fell beneath the water with a delicate splash and a ripple.

In the spring it was cool for a long time, and in the summer it grew hot, but with wide-brimmed hats on, we still fished, and we lazed, and sometimes we talked softly, fearing we might frighten the fish. We talked about all manner of things we believed in, same as when we were in the tree. We talked about how we differed from one another. I told Leonard about my women, and he told me about his men. We talked about brotherhood without speaking of it directly. I told bad jokes and Leonard grumbled. We were tight before those times, but that was when we bonded like glue.

When Leonard moved from the house next to the woods, and I later moved from where I lived, we lost that spot.

Some years later the people up north remembered the land. They brought in pulp crews and cut the woods down, even the great and ancient oak, which must have fought the saws valiantly with its old, hard wood. But the saws won. It tumbled down and was coated in gasoline and set on fire. They didn't even bother to make it into lumber. They wanted the pines. The land where the great oak stood was a black spot for a long time.

Eventually they filled in the pond. A company that raised chickens for a supermarket chain bought the land, and a series of long, commercial chicken houses took the place of the original pond and the woods that had surrounded it. Now there is a wide gravel road that leads out of where the trees once grew and on to the highway. It's odd, but looking out here now, it seems like such a short distance to where the pond once was. It seemed a long ways away when the trees were there.

As we drove by, Leonard refused to look in the direction where the chicken houses now stood. I looked, but I didn't like what I saw. The rain still falls and the wind still blows, but the oak and the pond and the rare black squirrels are gone.

18

We arrived at our destination. My memories had placed me in a melancholy mood, and somehow that ancient abandoned mill made it more so. It stood precariously outside of Camp Rapture, on a high hill, behind a thick swath of trees that covered most of the rise. The trees grew all around it as if to spite the developers who'd mauled many of their leafy clan into lumber on that very spot. One pine, very brave and defiant, was pushing up through a gap in the roof. The evergreen needles glistened as if with sweat.

There was a good-size pond to one side of the mill, and the morning sun gave it a bronze sheen, and the heat on the cold water made it mist over. It was an ugly pond, not like the one Leonard and I had loved, back where the chicken houses now stood. That one had been muddy, but it had been fine.

We parked as near as we could to the mill, where the road ran out, walked over, and looked at the pool of water. The mist was slowly evaporating as the sun rose, and we could see the pond was dark with caked sawdust. It looked like quicksand, and it was the reason for the water's bronze appearance.

Once upon a time a chute had projected from the sawmill and sawdust had been sent down it as the whirling blades inside milled the trees into lumber and progress ate up the East Texas forests. Rainwater had gathered in the pit beneath the chute and had made the stagnant pond. The pond gave off an acidic odor.

"So," Leonard said, "Charm took a few photos of an old sawmill. So what? Everyone knows bodies have been found here, so no news there. What could have been so important Charm got pushed around by angry cops and had her sim card taken and her brother killed? Seems to me, they were better off just letting her be."

"Could be it's not what she photographed but what they thought she photographed."

"And then she got set loose and they just gave up on her?" Leonard said. "Why?"

"They had a chance to look at the sim card. Nothing there bothered them. But what could Jamar have known that would be of any concern to them?"

"Again, he was annoying them."

"Still, seems like a big jump from him being annoying to a bunch of cops punching and kicking him to death. Even these yo-yos in Camp Rapture couldn't be that stupid."

"As we have done noted many times, people who do stupid things are usually stupid. You and me come to mind."

"You have a very good point," I said. "Let's look in the mill."

We walked along a weed-coated drive. The weeds were bent down and brown, and you could see where cars had been driving over them, and recently. The gravel crunched beneath our feet like broken glass.

There was a large piece of plywood leaning against the side of the mill. I could see a strip of light between the edge of it and the building. I pushed the board aside. There was an opening into the mill where the wall had gone to rot. Inside, the morning sun dropped into the room through holes in the roof and lit up the floor and made the pine growing through the rip seem much greener. There was a large saw with a great rusty, dust-covered blade and dusty old belts attached to massive pulleys attached to a bulky engine.

When we walked, the floor beneath us felt like carpet where the sawdust had congealed. Mice darted across it and disappeared under split boards and into holes in the wall. There was a thick, wire fencing around the pine, probably about twenty feet out from the trunk. The fence made a complete circle around it. On our side there was a little open gate made of chicken wire and slats of wood and rusty hinges.

"Dogfighting," Leonard said.

"Looks that way," I said.

We went inside the circle of wire. The ground was covered in sawdust there as well, but it was kicked up, and you could see the dirt floor was scratched over by the struggling paws of unfortunate dogs, or so I presumed.

Maybe they thought Charm was secretly photographing the dogs fighting, and perhaps it was like Manny said, the cops were sponsoring it, a thing they called a sport, as if the dogs had volunteered. They might have thought she got photographs or video of a fight that could have been going on that night, feared that if she got images of the people who were there, and if the cops and prominent town officials were some of those people, it would blow back on them.

Leonard had brought a camera, and he took photographs of the place, and I used my phone to take more, and I mailed them to my computer at home.

We strolled outside, put the plywood back, and walked to the car. As we were about to get in, a blue sedan rolled up the drive behind our ride, blocking our exit. Two men got out and came around to stand in front of the car. One was dressed in jeans and a loose Hawaiian-style shirt. He was big and his head was shaved and the top of it was sunburned in contrast to how white his face was. His face looked as if it had been paddled by a two-by-four. The other man was shorter and stockier and ruddy-skinned, with a thick head of black hair and a bent nose and a walk like his balls were too heavy on one side. He stood with his mouth open, sucking air. I kept hoping a fly would land on his tongue.

"Well, well," Leonard said to the man in the Hawaiian shirt. "If it isn't Your Fault his own goddamn self."

I got it then. This was Sheerfault, the guy Leonard had fought and lost to and didn't like. He was a physically capable-looking guy.

"Leonard Pine, why, I haven't seen you in a coon's age," Sheerfault said. "No offense. I want you to know that wasn't a nigger joke . . . I think last time I saw you . . . Let me see. Didn't I whip your black ass?"

"Points," Leonard said.

"What losers say, but I had you dead to rights. I could have knocked you out if I had another round."

"I doubt you could have knocked me out with a hammer," Leonard said.

Sheerfault grinned. It was the kind of grin that made you want to feed him his teeth.

"I wanted a rematch," he said, "but as I recall, that's about when you retired."

"I didn't want to lose again on being tagged, not hit."

"Oh, you were hit, all right." Sheerfault's grin spread even wider, which seemed impossible, but he managed it.

"Who's your little friend?" Leonard asked. "He looks like he might need to be paper-trained."

"Bobo Townsend. He isn't what you'd call a thinker, are you, Bobo?"

"Ain't no thinker," Bobo said.

"He got hit by a train about five years ago, and he wasn't exactly a mental giant before," Sheerfault said. "Train hit his truck crossing the track, smashed the truck into a wad, and knocked some wires loose in Bobo's head. Bobo has a simple approach to life, don't you, Bobo?"

"I like to hit people," Bobo said.

"That sums it up," Sheerfault said. "He likes to hit people. Also, he hears a train whistle up close, he shits his pants."

"Can't help it," Bobo said.

"You should carry toilet paper with you," I said. "Change of underwear."

"I could hit you," Bobo said.

"No need for unpleasantness," I said.

"Go ahead," Leonard said. "Hit him. See how that works out for you, Banjo."

"Bobo," Bobo said.

"No need to prove anything," I said and tried to look calm and in my happy place.

"Go ahead, Banjo," Leonard said. "Hit him. We'll be sure you get a nice burial, and then when you're down deep, I'll pack what's left of your partner in the hole with you, take a big shit on top of both of you."

Damn you, Leonard. I thought Bobo looked pretty sturdy, and I would rather not start my morning with my nose broke and a tooth missing.

"I ain't gonna let you hurt my friend," Bobo said.

"That's sweet," Leonard said. "But Hap will sort your shit for you, and I'll sort your friend's."

Bobo stepped forward, dropped his chin. Sheerfault reached out and took him by the shoulder. "Not today, Bobo. The boy is just blowing."

"Not as much as you might think," Leonard said.

Bobo stopped, relaxed. He looked at me with his blank eyes. His face hung like an empty sack. Inside his head, a brain cell used a stepladder to find a high-shelved thought.

"Yeah," Bobo said. "That's all right. Another time."

"You cracker motherfuckers just out for a little sun?" Leonard said.

"All we come up here for is two things. First, Pine, I wanted to remind you how bad I beat your ass, and second, we wanted to tell you that you ought to stay away from Manny. She's kind of a liar. She's claiming cops wanted her body, and the thing was, no one did. It disappointed her to not be desired."

"So, a beautiful and smart woman like that wanted to hump you ugly bastards, but no, you turned her down because you are so fine and noble and stalwart," Leonard said.

"We ain't queers like you, Pine," Sheerfault said, "but sometimes, some nooky, well, it stinks, and you just don't want it. Manny, she stinks."

"Metaphorically, I assume."

"Maybe both ways," he said. "Never got the chance to get down there and sniff."

"She turned you down is what you're saying?" Leonard said. "Sounds like a woman with taste."

"Stay away from her," Sheerfault said. "It would be best for her and you."

"Or what?" Leonard said.

"I don't know," Sheerfault said. "Something might happen. I mean, I wouldn't want you breaking the law in Camp Rapture, on account of you could get arrested, and even in a sterling jail system like we have, sometimes folks get hurt. You know, by other prisoners. We got fellows there, they don't like being thrown in with a person of color. Isn't that what you people say? Persons of color? See how I'm avoiding the word nigger. I am, if nothing else, progressive."

"What about you, Sheerfault?" Leonard said. "You want to hurt me your own self, not leave it to some prisoners?"

"Already have."

"You only made me a little tired."

"I won. I got the money."

"Hope you invested that seventy-five dollars in some extra health insurance," Leonard said. "'Cause you want to kick my ass, which you have yet to do, you'll need it."

Sheerfault smiled. "Still a sore loser."

"Oh, I lost the match, but I didn't lose a fight," Leonard said. "I lost some bullshit dance contest."

"You keep thinking that, Shiny," Sheerfault said, went around to the side of the car, opened his car door, smiled, and slid in behind the steering wheel.

As Bobo started to climb in on the passenger side, I said, "You a cop too, Bobo?"

He paused at the open car door and put his arms on top of it, collected a couple of thoughts, said, "I ain't no cop."

"Good. I was afraid you carried a gun, you might shoot yourself in the foot."

Bobo thought that over, said, "Thank you."

He climbed into the car without closing the door, and then he climbed out. He had found another brain cell with that stepladder.

"Was that some kind of crack?" he said.

"Sleep on it," I said.

He studied me, slipped back into the car, and closed the door.

When they drove away, Leonard said, "I really hate that guy."

"I can see that."

"Don't think I care for Bobo either, fucking animated fireplug."

"Bet Bobo's mother wishes she had smothered him with his teddy bear when he was a child," I said.

"Maybe I'll do it for her."

"Oh, and thanks for trying to have him start a fight with me, brother. I owe you for that one."

"You'd have fucked him over. Way you move."

"You're a troublemaker."

"A little," Leonard said.

"Thing is, guys that want us not to think anything is going on are certainly doing stuff that makes me think some bad shit is in fact going on."

"Perhaps they really are stupid," Leonard said.

"Or nervous."

"We're good at making people nervous."

"Ain't we?" I said. "Hell, I make myself nervous."

19

On the way back to LaBorde, Leonard said, "That story Timpson Weed told. It still bothers me."

"You keep coming back to that."

"Because it still bothers me."

"Shall we pay him a visit?"

"I think we should," Leonard said.

We drove over to the projects, and, with Leonard wearing his fedora, we made our way across the wilted grass toward where Weed lived. The group of guys that were there before were there again. The one who had worn the red shower cap was now wearing a blue one. The big one, Laron, had on sagging pants with his underwear hanging out.

"Goddamn," Leonard said as we walked along, "what's this shit with the fucking shower cap?"

"Protecting the do, I guess."

"Last time he had that red cap and no do. I bet he ain't got one under there now. What the fuck he need to have a do for anyway?"

"Some folks are cosmopolitan, Leonard. Some are not. You are not."

"Yeah, and a punk in a shower cap is?"

"Depends on how you define cosmopolitan."

"Yeah, sure. And the guy with the sagging pants, don't he know that little fashion statement comes from prison, showing you're ready to take some thug's dick, that you're a jailhouse bitch?"

"I'm betting he doesn't know. And frankly, Leonard, who gives a shit?"

"It's just stupid," Leonard said.

The guys stared at us, trying to look tough. Leonard shot them the finger. They didn't shoot it back. No razors or pistols were produced, just sour faces. So good so far.

"Pull up your fucking pants," Leonard yelled at Laron.

Laron didn't pull up his pants, just continued to glare.

Since we weren't there to give out freelance fashion tips, we went up the stairs and onto the landing and stood in front of Timpson Weed's door and knocked.

The sweet lady from before answered, bringing with the opening of the door a smell of fried fish and onions. She was wearing a large muumuu and shoes with her heels breaking them down in the backs. "What the fuck you want?"

"You talking to me?" Leonard said.

"I was talking to this peckerwood, but you can take a little of that if you want it."

"Can I now?" Leonard said.

"We just want to see Timpson for a minute," I said.

She came out then and closed the door.

"You want to see Timpson?"

"That's what he said," Leonard said.

"Yeah. 'Cause you such close friends?" she said.

"Because we have a bit of business with him," I said.

"Yeah, well, you want to see that nigger, you gonna have to go down to the fucking funeral home and see him."

"He works at a funeral home?" I said.

"Fuck no, he don't work at no funeral home, unless he gonna get up dead tonight and sweep out the goddamn place."

She was starting to cry a little now, tears running down her face. I had a little pack of tissues in my coat pocket. I took it out and pulled a tissue from it and handed it to her. She snatched it like a hawk grabbing a mouse, patted her eyes, then blew her nose on it, handed it back to me.

"You keep it," I said.

"Come up in here and me grieving and Timpson dead as a bag of nails, act like you all kinds of friends with him."

"We said we have business with him," Leonard said.

"That business gonna have to wait until you get to the Pearly Gates, I can tell that to you. He over at J. Greely's funeral parlor cooling out."

"What happened to him?" I said.

"What happened?" she said. "What didn't happen? They beat him, then run over him with something a whole lot bigger than a bicycle, and then he got his black ass thrown in a fucking ditch beside the road, or some such."

An East Texas classic. Killed and thrown in a ditch.

"Who did it?" I asked.

"How the fuck do I know? You care? Bullshit. You just the same as the cops, just another dead nigger."

"I happen to be of the black persuasion myself," Leonard said. "So it concerns me. It concerns my friend here. Shit, this motherfucker, Hap, he wears a shower cap around the house, and he once wrote a letter in Ebonics."

"I do not wear a shower cap in the house," I said. "And the letter was well meant."

The woman looked at Leonard and smiled a little.

"You got a woman?"

"I got a man," Leonard said. "Sort of."

"What?"

"I'm queer as a three-dollar bill."

"Naw you ain't."

"Am."

"Naw."

"Am."

"Damn, man. That's a fucking waste. Come over here some night and let me make dinner for you, and I can turn you."

"That's a sweet proposition, but you sure have moved on fast," Leonard said. "Snot in a tissue, and you're ready to bring in fresh meat."

"Timpson just stayed here when he wanted. He had him other women on the side. I think it was one of them he got the clap from. I come down with that shit, and let me tell you, that is some whole 'nother kind of experience. Had to get shots. He come home with crabs one time. Have to near set fire to yourself to get rid of them."

"That is a delicate situation, for sure," Leonard said.

"Telling you," she said.

"Any idea who killed Timpson, and why?" I asked.

"I ain't got no idea," she said. "He might have got hit crossing the road, for all I know. Somedays I'd have run over him. Hit me once, but I caught his ass a good one upside the head with a stool. One of them little wooden ones got four legs. They solid, I'm telling you, and it's like they was made for swinging. I knocked him plumb out. Nigger was sprawled on the floor like a throw rug. He woke up and got his shit and got out, but he come back around after a time. He done had a sniff and a taste of the good stuff I got, so he come back. He made me keep the stool in the closet from then on, though."

"I see," I said. "When was Timpson killed?"

"Other night. Said he was going to see someone at the Joint, which usually meant he was gonna get stagger-ass drunk and come home and puke in the sink. The fucking sink. Got a toilet, and he pukes in the sink. That shit don't wash down so easy in the sink, and he wasn't gonna clean it up. No, sir. He left that mess for me. He had it good here. Good cooking, cleaning up after him, and then he had this fine ass."

She slapped herself on the ass.

"Pleasant companionship," Leonard said.

"Damn right."

We thanked her and she went back inside with the fish and onions. We went downstairs.

I said, "Damn."

"Probably run over himself so he wouldn't have to fuck that bitch," Leonard said.

Walking across the lot, we saw the project boys were leaning on Leonard's truck. The four-hundred-year-old vampire girl, Reba, was with them.

Leonard picked up his pace.

We came to his ride, and he said, "Your nasty asses scratch my truck, I'm gonna rub out the scratches with your faces."

They moved off the truck immediately. Except the four-hundred-year-old vampire.

"You done come back asking about that boy, ain't you?" Reba said.

"That's right," I said.

"That's just a rumor run up through here. That boy wasn't killed here. We all know that."

"Ain't no rumor," Tuboy said. "It's a goddamn lie."

"Back that truck up," I said. I sort of liked that phrase and was just waiting to use it again.

"How come that's the story gets told, then?" Leonard said.

"That Weed telling that," Tuboy said. "Now his ass stretched out at the funeral home. Or in a box or some such. Put in a sack. Whatever they do."

"Why would Weed tell a lie like that?" I said. "Who asked him?"

"Ain't got no idea who asked him," Tuboy said, "but we know it's a lie. There was people all over the place that night. And he's the only one seen it. Bullshit."

"He said others saw it," I said.

"Figure he say that, you don't think to ask around, see if it's true," Tuboy said. "You ask around?"

"No," I said. "I didn't find the relationships here all that fascinating."

"That Egg Breaker Timpson was a motherfucker."

"Egg Breaker?" I said.

"Uh-huh," said Tuboy. "You know he go to jail once for fucking chickens?"

"I hope the chickens got compensation," I said.

"Naw. They was dead. He fucked them to death. Got drunk as a rat in a beer barrel, went out and found someone had some chickens, and fucked them."

"He fucked the chickens or the owners or both?" I said.

"I done told you who fucked what," Tuboy said. "Oh, you being funny, huh?"

"He tries," Leonard said.

"They brought him in on it," Tuboy said, "and he told the cops it was good for the eggs or some such. Tell you one thing, didn't do them chickens' asses no good."

"Guess not," Leonard said.

"Everyone round here call him Egg Breaker, not Weed."

"When did this chicken event take place?" I said.

"When he a teenager, before we was born. But it done followed him around like a dog."

"Shit," Leonard said. "Fuck a few chickens, and no one gets over it, but lie about a dead man, and everyone moves on. Why the fuck didn't someone around here say something?"

"We ain't got no reason to say," Reba the four-hundred-year-old vampire said. "We talk to the po-po, it never work out. Next thing we know we pulling time. Besides, he wasn't one of our niggers. That Egg Breaker, he been up in jail a lot for this and that. Last time he was up in there he come out with a head looked like a fucking pumpkin."

"They beat him, you mean?" I said.

"Yeah, they beat him. He didn't want no more pulling time, 'cause he thought he might not come out next time. I can feel his worries on that."

"You're a child, what the hell do you know about pulling time?" Leonard said.

"My daddy done up in that Huntsville," she said. "He got another twenty years to go, then they start another thirty on him. Consecutive bullshit, they call it. He ain't gonna finish that last one out. Which is good. He ought to be up in there. He killed a whole mess of people while he was fucked up on some shit."

"Who do you live with?" I asked.

"My uncle Chuck," Reba said. "Sometimes my grandma."

"I bet that is a treat for them," Leonard said. "I figure your daddy's doing time just for making you."

"Leonard," I said. "Shit, man. Cut it out."

"All right, all right."

"You are one shitty motherfucker," the little girl said.

"I just don't like you," Leonard said.

"Like you some kind of peach," she said.

"Let me pull this back to where we were," I said. "So there was no body found here? How did it get around there was?"

"Egg Breaker," Tuboy said. "We done told you. What the fuck, white man. You deaf?"

"I just like to be certain," I said. "Cops said he was found here, wasn't just Weed . . . Egg Breaker, Chicken Fucker, whatever."

"Uh-huh, and we ain't got nothing for that," Tuboy said. "Them cops probably took him out and killed him and said he was found here, on account of everyone knows we ain't nothing but a bunch of losers."

"I second that," Leonard said.

That comment didn't bring a smart remark from the project kids, just a momentary silence.

"Yeah, you right," Laron said. "Kill someone here, ain't like you losing a future Nobel Prize winner."

"Damn, boy," Leonard said. "I didn't know you could speak."

"When I got something to say."

I was more confused than ever. Why would Weed, aka Egg Breaker, tell that lie? Who would ask him? And worse yet, would it be smart to pin it on the cops if he didn't see them do it? Egg Breaker said the cops were the ones told him to shut up. What seemed like a simple truth had turned into a complex lie.

"So, no idea who killed Jamar?" Leonard said. "Jamar's the boy Weed said was killed here, by the way."

They shook their heads.

"He got a cool name, though," Tuboy said.

"Any idea who gave Weed his trip to the funeral home?"

"Coulda been anybody. Wasn't nobody but Tamara like him."

"Tamara?"

"Lady he lived with," said Reba. "One you just talking to. Tell you one thing, don't never eat nothing she cooks. It all tastes like onions. That woman can't boil a cup of coffee without putting an onion in it. She ain't no smart one neither. Can't sort socks right, even if they all the same color, but she know how to survive."

"Look here," I said. "I'm going to give you one of our cards. You hear anything, want to tell us anything, call us. Might be some money in it."

"How much money?" Reba asked.

"I don't know," I said. "You won't be buying a car with it. Besides, you don't even have a driver's license."

"I could sell that car," she said.

"There is no car," I said. "A bit of money."

"I don't get out of bed for five dollars," she said.

"Since you made ten from me last time," I said, "I know your price."

"To point to a door, yeah. Not for everything else."

"So you got something?" Leonard asked.

"No," she said. "Just asking. I can pay attention a lot better for enough money."

"We'll make it worth your while," I said.

"What I'd like to do is give you to some kind of clinic for experimentation," Leonard said. "Something to do with cutting off heads and packing them in ice."

"You can go fuck yourself," she said.

"Get back from my truck," Leonard said. "All of you. All the way away from it."

Everyone moved away, but Reba the four-hundred-year-old vampire took her time, strolling lazily away from it. She said to Leonard as he was getting in the truck, "They experiment on me, it's 'cause they want my essence."

"Essence?" Leonard said. "You ain't got no essence, girl, unless it's from lack of taking a bath."

Reba shot him the finger. "I'm up in that shower ever' morning, you wiseass motherfucker."

He shot her the finger back.

We left out of there.

As we tooled along, I said, "You have such a way with children."

"I got deep love for them little stinky-ass motherfuckers."

20

At the funeral home we spoke to a pleasant young black man in a black suit and white shirt with a black tie and black shoes with a shine so bright it hurt my eyes. He asked us to wait and went away.

Leonard stuffed his hand in his pants pocket, said, "And he shoots."

"Shut up," I said.

About five minutes later a very fine-looking black woman in a black dress that, though conservative, looked more than adequate on her and showed just enough of her sleek legs that no one could cry foul came out and shook hands with us.

"I'm Karen Wilson," she said.

We introduced ourselves, then followed her into an office positioned off the chapel. When she was seated behind her desk, and we were sitting in comfortable chairs in front of it, the young man brought us all coffee on a silver tray, along with spoons and packs of sugar and sugar substitutes. The coffee was in nice china cups with flower designs. They were about the size of a thimble with a cup handle that I could barely get my little finger through. We prepared our coffee and sipped it and I tried not to spend too much time checking out the mortician, because she was certainly nice to look at, and my first impression had actually not done her justice. Forties, very dark-skinned, with thick shoulder-length hair and a smile that showed some very well-taken-care-of teeth.

The young man stood near the door while we sipped, his hands folded in front of him and over his crotch as if they were a fig leaf.

"This is my son Kevin," Ms. Wilson said. "I don't know what I'd do without him."

We nodded at him, and she smiled at him, and that must have been his cue, because he went out.

"No one has even asked about Mr. Weed," she said. "Well, there was one lady, but she was mostly interested in finding out if he had died with money in his pockets."

"Why, that would be the lovely Tamara," Leonard said. "That was quick."

"There's no one to pay for his funeral, but we're going to do as nice a job as we can."

"You're absorbing the price?" I said.

"Well, unless you're friends or family."

"No," I said. "I only talked to him a couple times. The cops have the body examined?"

Her lovely features soured. "They weren't even curious. Whoever did what they did to him rolled him out here. I think it was some sort of joke to them. We called the cops, they came by, said, 'Yeah, he's dead. Hit by a car.' I pointed out that he had taken a beating, had several bullet wounds, and that there weren't any cars I was aware of that fired bullets, and he had been run over several times, so, yes, a car was involved, but the bullets had been part of the equation. He had mud ground into his body along with the tire treads over his face. There won't be an open-casket service, and besides, who's coming? I know that sounds harsh, but that's the truth. I'm going to give him a simple coffin and a burial at what we call Potter's Field, which is the back end of the old black cemetery. I don't know his preference of religion, if any, but I am a minister as well as a mortician, so a few words will be said over him. Anyone deserves that much."

"What did the police say after you told them about the condition of the body?" Leonard asked. "Explained he wasn't just hit by a car?"

"They acted like they were writing things down, then left. I followed up this morning and they said the case was closed. I asked did they catch who did it, and they said they couldn't discuss it, and the next thing I know I'm listening to a dial tone."

"Interesting," I said.

"I thought so too," she said, and then paused. "You know, I really don't know who you two are."

I explained what we had been hired for but didn't give out any major information, because, frankly, we didn't really have any. I gave her a stripped-down version of events, leaving Charm and the sawmill out of it.

"I know about Jamar's death," Ms. Wilson said. "We prepared him for services. Most business of that sort for the black community ends up here."

"You mean you embalmed him?" Leonard said.

"Of course."

"Beat to death," Leonard said. "Maybe not as bad as Mr. Weed, but bad enough they both ended up in the same condition. Dead."

"Correct," she said.

"Let me get back to Mr. Weed," I said. "We were thinking his death and our case might be connected."

"They both had a lot of bruises and cuts, like they had been hit a lot," she said, "but Mr. Weed had bullet wounds and was crushed by a car. Jamar was beat to death. Still, similar enough to make me curious. But then again, I'm not a detective."

"So cops didn't ask you about the condition of the bodies, didn't have an autopsy done on them, didn't see a connection?" Leonard said.

"The police seldom seem interested if someone is killed in this part of town," Ms. Wilson said.

"Or dumped in this part of town," Leonard said.

"Good point," Ms. Wilson said. "And now that you mention it, I think Mr. Weed was killed up near the old abandoned sawmill. I hadn't really thought that much about it, but it makes sense."

"Why would you say that?" I asked.

"His shoes, knees of his pants, had sawdust mashed into them."

"There's a lot of sawmills in these parts," Leonard said.

Karen Wilson nodded. "True enough. But that's the nearest one, and if he was killed there, and whoever did it wanted to get rid of him, this is a close and ironic place to dump him."

"So you think the murderers are into irony?" I asked.

"Actually, I have no idea," she said, "I'm just winging it. I've read too many murder mysteries."

"Maybe we should read more of them," Leonard said.

"Another curious thing," she said, "Jamar had sawdust on his body as well. I think that's interesting, don't you?"

"We do," I said.

"I've probably said too much," she said. "I don't want any trouble. I'm a mortician, not a detective."

"You said that," I said, "but you are proving to me you're pretty astute in the detecting area. That stuff about the sawdust, for one."

"Well, I really don't know much about anything," she said.

I could see she immediately regretted what she had said earlier and was trying to patch it up a bit. I understood that. This was the community she had to work in, and the police in Camp Rapture seemed to pretty much do as they pleased, so it was best not to get on their bad side.

"Anything we've talked about here," I said, "it won't get back to the Camp Rapture police. A lot of it we already know, and what we didn't know about Mr. Weed's body, what you told us, that's something the cops already know. They saw the body. They know what it looked like and they know how he died."

"And maybe who killed him," Leonard said.

"I'm sure they are doing the best they can," she said.

That sounded about as sincere as a nine-year-old boy's fart apology.

"No worries," I said, and stood up. I reached across the desk and shook her hand. Leonard did the same, and we left.

21

While Buffy licked the last of the food out of her bowl, I used a ladle to dip chicken soup out of a pot into deep blue bowls, then placed one in front of Brett and one in front Chance. They sat at the table with their heads in their hands, staring into their soup. They looked miserable. Red noses. Swollen eyes. Listless.

Finally Brett lifted her head and looked at me. "Crackers."

I got a box of crackers and opened them and placed them on the table. I poured them each a glass of ice tea.

Brett sniffed and raised her head, showing me her Rudolph the Red-Nosed Reindeer nose. "So, how's the investigation going?"

"It sucks," I said, and poured myself a bowl of soup. I gave them large spoons, took one for myself, then sat on the far side of the table away from their diseased bodies. There was hot sauce on the table and I poured a bit of it into my soup. It goes with all kinds of soup, not to mention just about everything but ice cream, and Leonard says it's pretty good with that, you mix it right.

"Appreciate the soup, Dad," Chance said. "I think I'm worse. I was doing better, but now I'm worse. It's bad, and then it clears up a little, or seems to, but it's just going out for reinforcements. What really peeves me is I had a flu shot."

"This brand of flu wasn't one they expected to be a real threat this year," Brett said. "It wasn't in the vaccine. They were wrong. I had a flu shot too, and I hate needles. I got needled for nothing."

"You're a nurse and you hate needles?" Chance said.

Brett nodded slightly. "I didn't mind sticking someone else with one, and I don't get sweaty when I need to have one stuck in me, but I don't like it. I mean, who does?"

"I hear you," Chance said. "Wow. This soup is hot. Face-of-the-sun hot."

"Yep," I said, "just burned all the hair off my tongue. Let it cool."

"It's like lava," Brett said.

"You can cook for yourself next time," I said.

"But it's good lava," Brett said. "Nice chicken lava."

"That's better," I said. "I suppose you don't want any hot sauce. it's a different kind of hot, and it really spices the soup up."

"No spices," Chance said. "My belly won't take it."

"Do you have any guesses about the murders?" Brett said.

"They're connected," I said. "That's my best guess, and not exactly a Holmes and Watson moment. But I don't think I'm going too far out on a limb to say that. They were both beaten, though in Timpson Weed's case, he was also shot and run over by a truck. The confusion is why did Timpson say he saw the cops beat Jamar to death, but no one else in the projects saw a thing?"

"Perhaps they're all lying," Brett said.

"I don't think so. I think the four-hundred-year-old vampire can be trusted."

"Who?" Chance said.

I explained about Reba.

"I'm not even sure Jamar's body was found at the projects any-more," I said.

Brett slurped her soup.

"Sorry," she said. "It's cooled enough to eat, and it's good, and I sound like Oliver Twist sucking up his last drop."

"You can have more," I said.

"More please?" Brett said, and held the bowl toward me.

I took it and put more in the bowl, placed it in front of her, and sat back down.

Chance was staring off into space. She said, "What if Weed was telling the truth about what he saw, or telling the truth mostly, but wasn't telling the truth about where it happened? Maybe he's more involved than he wanted to let on, so he's assuaging his conscience with a half-truth."

I felt like a lightbulb turned on. It was low wattage, but the bulb was burning.

"Sorry," Chance said. "I took a criminology course."

"Let me think on it," I said.

22

At the office, Leonard said, "So what we have here—besides this excellent bag of vanilla cookies that I have brought for myself, and none for you—is an idea Chance threw out that you grabbed onto? She is one smart young lady, but if it looks like a duck, walks like a duck, quacks like a duck, and tastes like duck once you cook it right, it's a duck. And I think this case looks like a duck."

"I got lost somewhere," I said.

"Yeah, I think I extended that metaphor too far."

"I think Chance may be onto something," I said. "I think what we were getting from Timpson Weed was guilt, but not the sort I thought it was. Originally, I thought he felt guilty because he had seen a murder and couldn't get the cops to do anything about it. Could be more to it than that, because I was also thinking about what Reba said."

"Oh, that little fountain of wisdom."

"She said Timpson had done a lot of jail time."

"Chicken fucking."

"That was when he was a teenager, but remember she said last time he came out of the jail, he was beat up."

"He is black and lives in Camp Rapture. That's kind of the way it goes. Get arrested. Get beat up. Nice lunch on the county, shit on a shingle. Pay your fine, and after another ass-kicking, go home."

"Guess I'm thinking we may be looking at the wrong duck," I said.

"So you admit there is a duck?"

"I do. What if Timpson, the old chicken fucker, knew what happened to Jamar and lied about how, not what?"

"Because he had a conscience? I don't know, Hap. He didn't lose sleep over those chickens, I bet. Here's a hole in your theory, and you've heard it before, and I keep coming back to it because it makes sense and you don't. Why would he go to the cops if he saw the cops kill Jamar? That would be like climbing into a hot frying pan and asking for lard to be poured over you."

"Perhaps we should find out who Timpson spoke to at the station. I say we go back to Manny."

I reached for a cookie. Leonard pulled the bag away.

"Nope. You did me dirt with that old lady, giving her my sweets."

"It was a joke."

"My joke is you put your hand in my cookie bag, you draw back a bloody stump."

"Man, you do not forgive, do you?"

"No, sir, I do not."

23

We arranged to meet Manny at a dog park in LaBorde. She said she wouldn't meet in Camp Rapture.

It was a nice cool day. The dog park was a large fenced-in area down by a creek with a number of hardwood trees growing around it. Leonard had once punched a smartass college kid on the jogging trail there. A sweet memory.

Inside the dog park there was a concrete bench beneath a large pecan tree, and we all three sat there while Trixie ran about barking at larger dogs who seemed to be sizing her up for a sandwich.

"Those assholes drive by my house frequently," she said. "Not Coldpoint. He's the superior, so he sends Sheerfault. Sheerfault rides around with this guy that isn't even a cop. It's against regulations, but if we start talking about the regulations they break, you'll have to go buy a couple pens and half a dozen notebooks to list them."

"This guy with him," I said. "Bobo?"

"Ah," she said. "You've met."

"We have indeed," I said. "He wanted to dance, but I declined."

"He looks like a guy that might step on your feet a lot," Manny said.

"Yep, that's what I'm thinking," I said.

"We got a question you might can answer," Leonard said. "Timpson Weed."

"Chicken Fucker, or Egg Breaker, some people called him," she said.

"You know our man," Leonard said. "Question is this. According to what we heard, and keep in mind we got this from a four-hundred-year-old vampire midget—"

"Say what?" Manny said.

"Ignore him," I said.

"This midget said Weed was arrested quite a few times, and he came back and looked like he'd been beat on," Leonard said.

"There are rumors," she said. "Sorry I have to come back to rumors, but that's what I've got. That and suspicions. There are people they arrest on a regular basis, people on the margin, with little money and little recourse to real law, and they often end up beat up. There's always some excuse. The inmates were in a fight. One of them gave a jailer or an officer some trouble and they had to get rough with them. Mostly it's men, sometimes women."

"You see any of that happen?" I said.

"No. I knew it went on, though. A multitude of rumors of that nature is why I quit and am now living on savings. My bit of pension seems to be held up in a pit of legal quicksand. I'll get it, but they're making it difficult. They're claiming I sexually harassed them. Them being Coldpoint and Sheerfault. They're doing that because I have a suit against them for harassing me, and for other transgressions, as my lawyer puts it."

"Was Jamar ever arrested?" Leonard asked.

"I don't know. As for this Weed character, definitely he was arrested. Drunk driving. Drugs on him. About once a week for a year he got arrested, but he was always loose in short time, and then he kind of fell off the radar until the kid was killed."

"He reported Jamar's death to the police, right?"

"Now that I think about it, I believe he had a lawyer do it."

"That's new," Leonard said.

"He could afford a lawyer?" I said.

"It was Tom Barker. Ambulance chaser. Cruises hospitals and such, does a lot of work where if he wins, he takes a bite out of the settlement. I'm sure he saw some kind of money in it, eventually. Guy like Barker, he lives a lot on eventually. My guess is he thought the department might want to settle the case without accepting fault, and the settlement would give him a nice payday."

"Okay," Leonard said. "Lawyer thinks he might drum up some kind of suit and make some dough, that makes sense. But the thing still bothers me is why would Weed want to go to the police if the police were the ones responsible? Why would he think that would work out? It would put a target on his back with the Camp Rapture department."

"You got me there," Manny said. "But I can talk to the one or two people I'm still friendly with at the department. They aren't actually in cahoots with the rest of them. I can make a few phone calls. But no promises."

"Good enough," I said.

"Yeah," Leonard said, "but watch your ass. I don't think these dudes are playing around."

"I assure you," Manny said, "they are not. But neither am I."

24

On Monday we looked up Tom Barker and drove over to his office in Camp Rapture. It was off an alley and you had to go through a paint-peeling door to reach the hallway that led to his office. The hallway was dark enough to grow mushrooms.

Barker's pebbled-glass door was decorated with time-worn black stenciling that read TOM BARKER, ATTORNEY-AT-LAW. Underneath that was a list: SEMI-TRUCK INJURY, PHYSICIAN MALPRACTICE SUITS, DUIS, PERSONAL INJURY. I GOT YOU COVERED.

"He's got us covered," Leonard said.

"Seems like it."

"Might be a good idea. We have a lot of personal injury."

I opened the door and went in. The outer office was small and tight with a desk taking up much of it. A young girl behind the desk who looked like she still had two years to go before she was a high-school student glanced up at us.

"Excuse me," I said, "Is Mr. Barker in?"

"He's out," she said.

She was a little thing with shoulder-length brown hair, a bit of baby fat, and a cute face sprinkled with acne that had been covered over with makeup that appeared to have been designed for another skin tone.

"Do you know when he'll be back?" Leonard asked.

"Uh-uh. I don't work here, really. I'm his daughter, Connie. He doesn't have a receptionist right now. Last one quit a year ago. Hasn't hired anyone else. Sometimes, after school, I help out."

"Okay," I said. "Maybe I could give my name and a phone number—"

That's when the door opened and a man with a very similar face to the girl's, minus the acne and the makeup, came in. He was short and a little portly, but it wasn't baby fat. This was hard-earned marbling. He had thinning brown hair and wore a brown suit that fit him about as comfortably as a three-piece suit fits a groundhog. He gave us a practiced grin, letting us know he could get that settlement for us, though we might have to go around with neck braces for a couple weeks. There were a few bottom teeth missing on the left side of his mouth. Like the suit, he had seen better days.

"Gentlemen, what can I do you for?"

"Can I go now?" the girl said.

"Sure, honey, go on ahead. You go on."

Connie started toward the door, was stopped by Barker. He got out his wallet and gave her a twenty and she went out and shut the door. When he'd opened his wallet I noticed there weren't many other bills in it and they looked like ones.

"Kids," he said. "They go to lunch, they got to have soup to nuts and a cookie to go. Kids."

We smiled. We couldn't think of anything else to do.

"Come in the office. Come on."

He opened another pebbled-glass door, this one minus the stenciling, and in we went. There was a saggy leather couch in there, and there was a blanket on the couch, and a pillow. Barker picked up the blanket and folded it and took the pillow and carried all of it to an open closet and stuffed it inside and closed the door.

"Me and the wife," he said. "We're kind of taking a break. I been sleeping here."

"Sure," I said.

Barker sat behind his desk and we sat in hard wooden chairs in front of his desk. Thirty seconds later, my ass felt like it was broken.

"Oh." He stood up suddenly. "I forgot to introduce myself." He leaned over his desk. Leonard and I stood up and shook his hand in turn. "Tom Barker."

"Yes," Leonard said. "We know."

"Of course you do. Of course."

We all settled into our seats.

"I'd offer a beverage, some coffee, but you know, I'm plumb out. Need to make a store run. Been real busy. Plumb out of everything."

He looked like the last time he'd been to the store you had to harvest your own coffee beans.

"Sure," I said.

"We work for a private investigator, and we're looking into the death of Jamar Elton," Leonard said. "And while we're at it, we might as well throw in Timpson Weed."

"Oh . . . Oh . . . I see. Yeah. Well, I don't know that I can help you with that. Just don't know I can."

"But you know about it," I said.

"A little. Very little. Just a tiny bit."

"You were the spokesperson for Timpson Weed, as I understand," I said. "You told the cops what he had seen."

"I did. I did. That I did."

He looked nervous, like his dick was in a sausage grinder and someone angry had a hand on the crank. The man's repetition of words and phrases was starting to crawl along my backbone.

"We just wanted to know what was said, and why Timpson had you speak to them about Jamar, and how that worked out."

"There's really nothing. Nothing. I was just doing a kind of favor."

"There were no money possibilities in it for you?" I said.

"Not really. Not really . . . Well, maybe. But it didn't come to anything. I like to make myself available, you know."

"Could you maybe tell us a little about what Mr. Weed had you do, and why?" I said. "Jamar's mother is our client and obviously it's all tied together. Here, let me show you who we work for."

I took out one of the cards Brett had made up for us and put it on his desk, then leaned back in my chair. The card lay on the desk in front of him. He leaned over and looked at it.

He read the card out loud, like we might not know what was on it. " 'Brett Sawyer Investigations. Hap Collins, Leonard Pine.' That's you two?"

"Still is," Leonard said. I was hoping my man didn't get too testy and start pissing off Barker. Leonard is not patient with bullshit. Start laying that on him, Leonard goes negative and mean, and sometimes pretty damn funny pretty damn quick.

"Jamar's mother hired us," I said. "We're just trying to find out how he died."

"I see. I see."

Barker wasn't actually acting like he did see.

"I sort of hit a wall with that. Hit a wall."

"What kind of wall?" Leonard said. "A blue wall?"

"It's not really anything I can talk about," Barker said.

"Or won't talk about?" Leonard said.

"Now, there's no need to be smart, be smart, you see, no need."

"Would you rather us be dumb?" Leonard said. "You're treating us like we're dumb. We know you went to the station for Timpson Weed, and you told the cops he saw Jamar beat to death."

"I don't like your tone. I don't."

"We aren't trying to be tuneful," I said. "We are trying to find out what happened to a young man for his mother, and I guess, while we're at it, we'd like to know what happened to Mr. Weed, and what this has to do with the Camp Rapture police force, and what was said by them when you told them what you told them. And just for icing, why does this all make you so nervous?"

"I have to leave, leave now," he said. "You need to go first."

"I guess so," Leonard said. "You leave, we'd feel pretty silly sitting in your office by ourselves."

"We could play checkers," I said.

"Like you remembered to bring a game board and checkers," Leonard said.

"We wouldn't be drinking a cup of coffee, that's for sure," I said.

"I'm quite ready for you to go now, go on out," Barker said.

"Who the hell is going to know what you tell us besides us?" Leonard said.

"All right. All right. It's time for you two to go. Go on now. Go."

We sat for a moment. Barker stood up, pushed his chair under his desk, put his hands on the back of it, and looked at us.

Taking our time, we got up and started out. When we got to his inner office door, I turned around and looked at him.

"What if it was your daughter, Barker? What if something happened to her and you thought someone might know something. Maybe just a piece of something, and they wouldn't tell you? How would you feel?"

"That's a low blow, bringing my daughter into it. A low blow."

"Jamar's mother suffered an even worse low blow," I said. "Her child isn't coming back."

"Get out now, or I'll . . ."

"Were you going to say 'call the police'?" Leonard said. "I don't think you're going to call the police. I think maybe you're afraid of them."

"Go. Go now."

We went through the outer office, down the dark hall, out to the alley, and back to our car. There was a flyer for a gun show under the windshield wiper.

25

As we sat in the car at the curb, Leonard said, "Okay, there is definitely a big turd in the soup somewhere."

"Agreed, and on that note, how about lunch?"

"Just as long as we don't have soup," Leonard said.

We drove back to LaBorde and to a café downtown on the square. A diner. It was our first time there. We had been meaning to try it.

An older woman with silver hair so severely bound back it damn near pulled her cheeks over her ears showed us to a table. I asked her if they had crayons for Leonard, but she just stared at me.

"He likes to color," I said.

"Oh," she said and, without a hint of humor, said, "We do have crayons."

"He's messing with you," Leonard said.

"Oh, I see. Long morning. I should have got that."

"Bad joke," I said.

She took our drink orders and went away.

"I can't draw a direct line to what's going on with all this Jamar business and the Timpson Weed aka Chicken Fucker business," Leonard said.

"Maybe not a direct line, but you can draw a wavy line right through Charm, Jamar, Weed, and Barker. That's enough for me, the connections. And I bet if we look real close, we'll see that line runs right through Coldpoint, Sheerfault, and the train-fucked Bobo."

"And there's Manny too," Leonard said.

"She's just to one side of the line, at least as far as I can tell, but yeah, she's in the vicinity."

"She has too many rumors and not enough solid information," Leonard said. "And I'm wondering about Timpson turning in information to that lawyer, and then the lawyer telling it to the cops, and suddenly the lawyer is frightened out of his skin."

"He did look scared," I said.

"Yeah. You'd have thought we were the Ebola virus."

" 'Hey, how are you? We're the Ebola virus, and we've come to kill you.' "

"Yep. That's how he acted."

"Barker looks like he scrapes by. He doesn't seem like a mastermind, and doesn't seem like someone cops would have on their payroll normally, but what if they paid him to keep his mouth shut?"

Leonard shook his head. "But he didn't keep his mouth shut. He told them about Jamar being beat to death, told them what Weed told him to tell them. Since then he's gotten nervous. Well, he was most likely always nervous, but now he's like a pig that just saw the butcher pull up."

"I think the money may have come after he said what he said to them. They told him, 'That's a nice story, but if we hear it again, we're going to pull your asshole over your ears and drop you down an old well somewhere.' "

The waitress came back with our drinks and menus. We glanced at the menus, and before she could go away, I ordered a chicken salad and Leonard ordered a hamburger with fries. A hamburger and fries was what I wanted, but I forced myself to have a salad.

"So what we know is what we know," I said, "but now we know what we know is more shadowy than we thought."

My cell buzzed. I took it out and looked at the number. I didn't recognize it. "Get me some more tea, will you?" I said to Leonard, having already sucked down the glass I had while we were talking. I'm a serious ice tea drinker.

I got up and went outside and answered the cell.

"Hey, this you? White man with the loudmouthed nigger?"

I recognized that voice. It was Reba, the four-hundred-year-old vampire.

"You got him," I said. "But cut the nigger stuff, okay?"

"You paying good money?"

"For what?"

"Information, asshole. You was the one said it."

"Depends on the information. But please, I had asshole legally dropped from my name."

"That was a mistake."

I walked along in front of the restaurant, glanced through the plate-glass window, and saw Leonard watching me. I walked on farther down the sidewalk and stopped in front of a shop that sold Texas souvenirs.

"That Timpson not only screw the ass out of chickens, he kill that boy himself."

"That boy?"

"Jamar. The dead fucker. You and me talked before, right? I ain't dialed the wrong number and got the wrong honky."

I let that sink in.

"I'm the right honky. How do you know?"

"I want to see some money first before I tell you squat."

"How much money?"

"I figure it's worth ten thousand dollars."

"Oh, really. I haven't got ten thousand dollars. What the hell, girl? Ten thousand dollars. You out of your mind. I look like Rockefeller?"

"Who?"

"Never mind."

"Okay, a hundred."

"A hundred thousand?" I said, just to mess with her.

"Yeah, I guess."

"Nope."

"All right, then," she said. "Hundred dollars."

"That sounds more like it, if you have something that's worth a hundred."

"I want to see that hundred dollars. Take a photo and text it to me."

"I haven't got a hundred dollars on me. I use my debit card mostly. I got a few bills, that's it."

"Well, then, you ain't gonna get no new information, is you?"

Leonard was right. This wasn't a little girl. This was indeed a four-hundred-year-old vampire.

"How about this? I get a hundred dollars out of the bank, text a photo of it to you, then you call me back with the information."

"Naw. You send that photo to me, then I'll call where we can meet, and then you feed me something good at McDonald's."

"They have something good at McDonald's?"

"Don't get snooty on me," she said. "I like me some McDonald's. And to me, you look like you'd get down on some supersize French fries in a New York minute."

"Like you'd know a New York minute."

"Yeah," Reba said. "I ain't got no idea what that means, but it sounds fast."

"When does this need to happen, this trip to McDonald's?"

"I got business now," she said, as if I would really think she had business. And as I thought about it, she just might've. She could have business terrorizing squirrels, shooting birds the finger, knocking streetlights out with a rock.

"When, then?"

"This afternoon, say five thirty. Meet me on Choctaw Street. It's below the projects."

"I know where it is," I said.

"But we don't got no business till you text me a picture of that hundred."

"I could just show up with it," I said. "Either way, you got to trust I'm going to give it to you."

"You give it to me, and then I give you the information."

"What if your information sucks?"

"It don't."

"Yeah, but what if it does?"

"Then you out a hundred, ain't you, Mr. White Man."

"I hate you," I said.

"Hate me on up to five thirty, then show up with a hundred dollars in your hand."

26

When I went back inside, Leonard was eating my salad.

"What the hell, man?"

"It came out first. I was hungry."

"So you're eating my salad?"

"Looks that way, don't it? And you know what I did? You're going to thank me for this, Hap. I ordered you a hamburger and fries, 'cause I know that's what you want."

"I'm trying to be healthier."

"Not today. This salad is damn good, though. Who was the call?"

"My broker."

"Yeah. I hope you fire him. I know your finances."

I told him all that Reba had said.

"You can't count on her doing nothing but working a deal," Leonard said.

"Crossed my mind," I said.

"Instead of a hundred dollars, you ought to bring a stake and a mallet, and drive it through her heart."

"I'm starting to think you might be right."

"Damn tootin', I'm right."

We ate and I paid the bill. Leonard seemed to have forgotten his wallet.

As we were getting in the car, my cell rang again.

It was Barker.

"Maybe we ought to talk," he said.

"All right."

"You got to understand I'm putting my neck on the chopping block, right on it."

"Not if they don't see you put it there," I said.

"That's the problem, they just might, they just might."

"When?" I said.

"How about you come by the office, say five thirty?"

"Can't. I have another meeting with someone about this case."

"Who?"

"Client confidentiality."

"You know there's nothing legal about a private investigator and their client having confidentiality."

"Nothing legal, but I gave my word."

"You might give all you know up if the wrong people get hold of you," he said.

"I don't doubt that," I said. "I think I would cave right away if they brought out a pair of pliers and a ball-peen hammer. But right now I'm sitting pretty in my car with my best friend and I have a bellyful of hamburger and nobody is threatening me."

"Six thirty, then?"

I considered. I looked at Leonard as I muted the phone.

"Barker. He wants to meet at six thirty."

"We can make it work," Leonard said.

"Seven," I said.

Leonard shrugged.

I pushed the mute button off, said, "Seven p.m. Your office."

"Oh, hell no. How about we meet at the old Camp Rapture High School, out by the tennis courts. No one goes there anymore, not since they built the new school."

"Seven p.m. Old Camp Rapture High School tennis courts."

I hung up and Leonard said, "Now, if someone would call and say you've won a million dollars, this could be a real good day."

"When it rains it pours."

"Someone did call with some money like that, you'd split it with your dear friend and brother, wouldn't you?"

"Not likely," I said. "Remember the cookies?"

27

The four-hundred-year-old vampire had quite an appetite.

"Be careful there," Leonard said, "you nearly ate the paper napkin."

"Go fuck yourself," Reba said.

"You've just about had the left side of the menu," I said, "so is there a point where you actually give me some information about how it was Timpson Weed killed Jamar? Or did you just con us into a free meal?"

"I'm going to need a couple fried apple pies."

"Are you?"

"Don't know I got a thing to say I don't get a couple pies."

"Would you like a cup of coffee with that?" Leonard said. "Maybe a silver sugar bowl and a matching spoon, and when you finish I can wipe your mouth for you?"

"Naw, but I'll take a glass of milk."

"Eat any more, you're going to blow up," Leonard said.

"I can eat a lot," she said.

"We've seen that," Leonard said.

"I ain't eat nothing all day, so thought might as well get my fill, but I ain't there yet. Still got an appetite."

I went to get the fried pies and the milk.

When I came back, Reba was licking her fingers.

"I hope you washed good or that ain't your wiping hand," Leonard said.

"You a funny nigger," Reba said, but she didn't actually look amused.

I gave her the pies and the milk.

"That milk ain't as cold as I like," she said.

"Well, shit, Hap," Leonard said. "You go back there and tell them to ice that milk. The princess likes it real cold."

"Enough of this," I said. "I texted the photo of the hundred. We've bought you a week's worth of groceries, and so far we only know you like milk with your fried pies."

She sipped the milk and it gave her a frothy mustache.

I pulled the hundred-dollar bill from my wallet and put it on the table. I carefully put my wallet back in my pocket and pressed the bill out with both hands.

"It's a crisp, fresh one hundred right out of the bank. Probably flown in from the mint this morning."

"How pretty it is don't impress me none," she said. "It's how it spends."

"For Christ sakes," Leonard said. "It spends like a hundred-dollar bill. That's how it spends."

"Can't buy as much with a hundred as you used to," Reba said.

"Used to," Leonard said. "You hardly been alive long enough to know when the price of gas last went up."

"Our deal was a hundred," I said.

"I'm thinking now you could maybe add a twenty to that to sweeten it on up to serious sugar," she said.

"They're fixing to find you in a ditch tomorrow with a goddamn McDonald's sack over your head," Leonard said. "Get on and tell us what you brought us here for."

She didn't say anything.

I sighed. I got my wallet out and removed a twenty, which was all I had left, and put it on top of the hundred.

"That's it," I said. "You either got information or you don't. Tell it, or we walk, and with the cash."

She reached over for the money.

Leonard slapped his hand down on the bills.

"That ole dog ain't going to hunt," he said. "You got to at least give us a taste of this big information you got. We don't get a taste, you don't get a taste."

Reba leaned back in her chair. She took her carton of milk and sipped it like it was fine bourbon.

"Timpson was the cause Jamar got killed, and he was upset about it."

"And you know this how?" I asked.

"I heard him and this fat white fella talking about it, out in the parking lot. I was in a tree."

"There's one fucking tree in the projects, except for those down on the creek, and you were in it?" Leonard said. "Lying on a limb like a constrictor snake at just the right time to overhear a conversation between Timpson and a fat guy? That's some rich shit, girl."

"I climb up there all the time. There's a hollow up there I keep stuff in. Here come this fat white fellow and he pulls up right under where I am. Sits in his car. Could see him through the window glass. Calls on his phone, and here comes Weed out of the projects, coming down to the parking lot. Fat man gets out of the car and he and Weed lean on the car door and they talk."

"And you heard all this from a tree?" Leonard said.

"They right under me, so, yeah, I did."

"Could've told us this before," I said.

"Wasn't nothing in it for me until you made that offer, and I wasn't gonna talk in front of them niggers out there, or they'd come down on me when I got the money."

"All right, then," I said. "What did they say?"

"When they start talking, I got quiet and still, 'cause I figured this wasn't something I was supposed to know, way they was meeting and all. My mama may have been a drug addict, but she didn't raise no fool for a daughter."

"Go on," I said.

"So Weed, he tells this fat man he wants him to do something for him, 'cause on the back end there might be some money. He says he wants him to tell the cops he gonna go to another bunch of law and tell them that they made him fight Jamar, and that he near beat him to death, and then they finished him off. Told him to say the body was in the projects. But it wasn't."

"You're sure you heard right?" I said.

"I ain't old enough to be deaf yet," she said. "Said if the law didn't pay him some real money, he was gonna say they did it, and he was gonna say they did it up in the projects, 'cause there was gonna be a whole lot of politicians could say it was police brutality, up there where all the black folks were."

"He was going to blackmail the police force?" I said.

"If that means he was gonna tell what really happened and say he didn't have no choice but to do what he did, yeah, then he was gonna do that, and he was gonna be quiet, they give him some money."

"Not exactly feeling his conscience," Leonard said.

"Maybe a bit of column A, a bit of column B," I said. "So, you're certain Jamar was killed somewhere else?"

"I never seen nothing, and them niggers run the lot from daylight to dark didn't see nothing either."

"How would you know if anyone else in the projects saw something or didn't?" I said.

"Please. Them fuckers can't keep they mouths shut if you glued they lips together with superglue."

"Really doesn't matter where he was killed," Leonard said. "He was killed, and that's what matters."

I nodded at Leonard, then turned my attention to Reba. "Any idea how Weed knew the fat man?"

"I ain't never seen him before," she said. "I don't even know what he do."

I looked at Leonard.

We had a real good idea what it was he do, and who he was.

28

We dropped Reba off on Choctaw Street with a to-go order in a bag. Four hamburgers and four fries and four apple pies. She didn't say *Thank you, Kiss my ass,* or *Hope you get hit by a car.*

She got out, slammed the back door, and started walking toward the projects.

"I miss that little bitch already," Leonard said.

We sat parked at the top of Choctaw and waited until we thought Reba had gone into the projects, added time for her to get to her place, then I coasted us down and past the projects. There was one great oak at the edge of the lot. It was big and the limbs were wide. A little girl like Reba, she could have been up there, and if no one looked up, they might not have seen her. Past the oak and the projects were more trees, and then there was a creek. I drove over a short concrete bridge, found a place to turn around, and drove past the projects again, on up Choctaw Street.

We still had time before seven p.m., so we went to a coffee shop Cason Statler had taken us to once, sat there with strong cups of coffee, and watched the clock.

"What do you think about Reba's information?" I said.

"I got to think she got a nice crisp hundred-dollar bill, and about a century's worth of greasy food she'll be shitting out about the time we take our old-age pension."

"You don't believe her?"

"I guess I do, but I keep thinking, okay, she just happens to be in a tree in the parking lot. The only tree, and Barker, 'cause that's who it sounds like it is, pulls up and Weed comes out and she hears their conversation?"

"I believe her," I said. "Not that I don't think the sweet Reba might tell a little lie, she took a notion. But I think she's telling the truth. That description fits Barker to a T. It's such an odd story it strikes me as true. Even she couldn't pull a story like that out of thin air."

"I have more faith in her lying, conniving self than you do," Leonard said.

We waited until six forty and drove over to the old high school. I don't know exactly when it was abandoned and the new one was built, but the old one was a lot better constructed than the new one that was off the edge of the main highway. The new one looked like a prison.

The old one had been built by the WPA during the thirties. There were some additions in the fifties. There was a football stadium within walking distance. Out back were tennis courts. Somehow it was decided a new location was better for the students, and the new school was built. One day, I presumed, they would knock this one down, along with the stone memories of all those men Roosevelt put to work.

The side road at the back of the school was dark. The few street-lights had been rocked out or shot out some time back. I parked by the old gym. I got a flashlight out of the glove box. Leonard put his fedora on the seat between us, and we got out and started walking along a narrow street behind the school, near the tennis courts. I turned on the light and flashed it along the gym. It was covered in graffiti, most of it instructional of a sort and anatomically impossible.

"What the hell is Barker?" Leonard said. "A bat?"

I turned off the flashlight.

"I'm not liking this," I said.

That's when we saw headlights and a car turning off the main street and into the little avenue that split the gym and the tennis courts. The stadium loomed in the distance, reminiscent of a small Roman Colosseum.

After a moment the car stopped and the driver's door opened and we could see someone get out. It was Barker. We could tell by his shape.

I flicked on the flashlight and we walked over there.

When we were past the tennis court, almost to the little, dark avenue, lights came on at one end of it, and then another car came the way Barker had come and pulled up near Barker's car. The car on the other end pulled up close and kept the lights on. The lights were harshly bright and we were pinned between them.

I looked at Barker. He was standing by his car, his hands having no place to rest comfortably; they fluttered against the sides of his legs.

"You fucked us over, didn't you?" I said.

"I had to," he said. "My daughter."

"We live through this, she may still be fatherless," Leonard said.

Doors slammed at both ends of the street, and we could see shapes coming toward us. In front of the bright headlights they looked like dark cutouts.

"Hey, if isn't my colored friend," a voice said.

"Sheerfault," Leonard said. "Of course. I only dreamed you were dead."

A shape moved closer to us, and now we could make out Sheerfault. Behind him trailed his pet gargoyle, Bobo.

"Bobo," I said, "how's the ole cucumber hanging?"

"Shut up," Bobo said.

Now from the other end another man came toward us. He was well tailored in a nice blue suit and had perfectly combed blond hair. He had a face that looked as if it belonged on the front of a men's fashion magazine, not somewhere in the shadows behind an abandoned school. When he was close I could smell his cologne.

I said, "I'm going to guess you're Coldpoint."

"That's a good guess," he said. I noted now another part of his wardrobe that I had overlooked at first. He had a handgun held down close to his leg.

"It's nice you invited us out here," I said to Barker, "but I think maybe we'll head out now. "

"No," said Coldpoint. "You won't be leaving until I say you're leaving."

He and Bobo and Sheerfault were all close to us now, and no one looked particularly friendly. Coldpoint continued to let the gun hang by his side.

"I guess we could stay awhile," I said.

Coldpoint smiled. "Of course you can. What we got here is just a friendly chat."

"Gun makes it less friendly," Leonard said.

"This is merely a room monitor of sorts," Coldpoint said. "We're not in a room, but you get the idea. Barker here told us you were meddling in police business."

"Monkey business," Leonard said.

"Hell," Sheerfault said. "You should know, them monkeys being your kin and all."

"No need for racial invective," Coldpoint said.

"Sorry," Sheerfault said. "Just don't like niggers, and this one in particular."

"'Cause you know you didn't really whip my ass, and can't," Leonard said.

"I got the trophy," Sheerfault said, and gave us his shit-eating grin. "I got the money."

"I'm going to ask everyone to shut up, and I want you boys to get in the car," Coldpoint said.

"I take it you don't mean our car," I said.

"You take it right."

He pointed to the car he, Sheerfault, and Bobo had climbed out of.

We didn't move.

He lifted his gun but didn't point it at us, merely held it in such a way as to be a persistent reminder. "Afraid I got to insist."

Barker, still standing where he had been, lifted his head, said, "It isn't personal. Really. It isn't personal."

"Go fuck yourself," Leonard said.

"Go away," Coldpoint said to Barker.

Barker got in his car and started it up, backed down the little avenue and onto the street, turned it into place, and drove away.

At gunpoint, me and Leonard got in the car. Sheerfault and Bobo rode in the backseat with us. Like magicians, they had produced handguns. They poked them against our ribs. I had Bobo on my side, and I figured I got the worst of that deal. He had breath that stank like a dead skunk's ass.

"I bet you get a lot of grooming products for Christmas," I said.

"What?" he said.

Coldpoint climbed in behind the wheel, turned on the engine and the lights.

"Can we go through a drive-through?" Bobo said. "I'm hungry."

"Later, Bobo," Coldpoint said.

"I could use a sandwich too," Leonard said.

No response. Coldpoint eased the car between the stadium and the gym, and gunned it along the dark and silent street.

"I guess yelling for the police isn't going to help much, is it?" I said.

They didn't bother to respond to that.

Coldpoint drove on.

"You two, you think you're helping out people that are downtrodden, don't you."

"Our client paid us."

"I researched you two, and what I get out of it is, you are do-gooders."

"That how you see it?" Leonard said.

Coldpoint nodded. "You got to understand, this is a dog-eat-dog world. My mother, she was a party animal, never saw her. Dad liked to drink with friends. Drop us off outside a bar, and he'd go inside and drink. Us being me and my sister. We got food out of the dumpster out back of the bar. A piece of this, a piece of that. Sometimes something nasty was on it, but you know what, we ate it."

"I don't give a shit," Leonard said.

"I figured right then and there you had to get yours, and you had to get it the way you wanted to get it. My sister, she didn't think that way. She became a public defender."

"Still don't give a shit," Leonard said.

"And she was good at it. One of her clients, he ended up knifing her. Guy she was trying to get off. People, they're shit, fellows. Me, I do some good things for the community, but I do it in a way that gets things done, not in a way where I beg for control or power to do something that protects citizens."

"Damn," Leonard said. "I am getting teary-eyed."

"Shut the fuck up, nigger," Sheerfault said.

"Ease off of that," Coldpoint said. "So, I made myself what I am today."

"I don't doubt that," Leonard said.

Sheerfault poked him in the side with his gun.

"My sister, Jewel, she was trying to live her life right, help people, but the people she was helping, they didn't deserve it. Criminals all of them, and one of them killed her. You think life is about doing the right thing, but I say the right thing as the law sees it isn't always the right thing. The end truly does justify the means."

"We agree on that, to some extent," Leonard said.

"And you, Mr. Collins. What do you think?"

"I'm sorry. Did you say something?"

"Doesn't matter," Coldpoint said. "I just thought you should know my philosophy a little better. Maybe you can understand my choices."

"Nope," Leonard said. "Not getting it."

29

We took a little ride in the country. The moon had been sacked by some ambitious black clouds and it had started to rain. I thought, Oh hell, I've seen this movie, and it doesn't have a happy ending. The shadowy trees on either side of the road looked like mountain ranges in the night. The headlights were foggy with mist.

Coldpoint tooled us out to where the old sawmill road was, drove up it. All I could think about was that sawmill sludge in the pit out front and how flesh and bones dissolved in it like snowflakes on a hot skillet.

There were other cars parked up there, and I could see a light seeping out from where the plywood covering was, and there was more light leaking out of the hole in the roof where the brave pine grew.

"Get out," Sheerfault said.

They walked us to the plywood barrier. We could hear hooting and hollering inside, the sounds of something smacking something else.

Bobo slid the board back, and we all went inside.

A generator was humming, and a crowd was gathered around the fence with the pine in the middle. The generator was near where the great saw was. The generator was one of those boxy things you roll in on wheels. It was the source of the lights and had a long cable coming out of it that fit into another box with a lot of long, thick extension cords running out of it. The extension cords led to where lights were arranged on high racks that looked like old-fashioned TV antennas. They were placed primarily around the fencing.

"Get up closer," Coldpoint said.

We did.

"Give some room," Coldpoint said to the crowd, and they moved aside. I noticed the handguns had gone back under their coats.

When we could see what was going on, we saw two young men, teenagers, in the middle of the circle. They were wearing gloves, boxing shorts, and boxing shoes. They had on T-shirts that had a logo for the Camp Rapture Boxing Club. There was a solid-looking older man in the middle serving as a referee. He looked like he had gone a few rounds in his life.

Across the way, standing behind the fence, were four sets of boxers, all dressed the same way. All of the young men were stout-looking and fresh-faced and nervous.

"Camp Rapture Boxing Club," Coldpoint said.

Coldpoint seemed relaxed, not menacing at all. "That's what we do here. They haven't got enough money to train at the actual club all the time. Place shares with gymnastics and children's tae kwon do. It's not really an official club, that place. It costs to be there. Not much, but for most of these boys if they had to pay a quarter to fart, they'd have to burp. They train there, but the club is mostly T-shirts and a place to gather, so they train here too. We don't charge. Two of these boys, ones in there now, they're training for the Olympics.

Fellow in the middle, that's their coach. Maxwell Landing. He won a few titles in his time, nothing big, but he's a good coach."

"I've heard of him," Leonard said.

I watched the two boys move around, and they were pretty good, though one kid had a habit of dragging his back foot; keeping it in the bucket, we used to say. He also had a habit of going too wide when he punched. The other kid was fast and circled, and had the most potential, but the bucket-foot kid could really hit.

"So, you brought us at gunpoint to see the Camp Rapture Boxing Club?" Leonard said.

"I didn't think you would have come otherwise," Coldpoint said. "You got it all wrong, fellows. We're trying to do something for the community. Sometimes we got to step on a few toes to do it, bend a few laws, but we get it done."

"Does this include killing a young man for taking photos and threatening his sister with your brand of law if she didn't put out?" I said.

"There are human failings in the mix," Coldpoint said. He nodded at the boys in the ring. "We let them train here. We raise money for the club. In time, maybe we can get them someplace to train more regularly, not just a couple hours on Wednesday over at the recreation center, trying to find spots and time between the girls' gymnastics lessons and the like. Get the poorer kids free admission to the club, get money off their minds and put boxing on it full-time for a while."

"You are such fucking humanitarians," Leonard said. "And here we thought you were just assholes. Oh yeah, there was the gun thing, and threats from Bobo and the dancer. That doesn't make things seem nearly as polite as you make out."

"Again, you might not have come," Coldpoint said. "I wanted to nip this all in the bud before you got too worked up and started trying to pin that kid Jamar's death on us."

"I'm no dancer," Sheerfault said.

"Hush," Coldpoint said to him. "You see what's going on here. This place, it's not supposed to be used for anything. Supposed to be dangerous. But it's what we got for free, so it's where we come. Yeah, it's illegal and I'm a cop. Building code, safety regulations, and all that. But they need a place to train for those who can't go to the club, and for those who can, they only get two nights a week. We add to that."

"You're just some sweet fellas helping some sweet kids," Leonard said.

"Exactly," Coldpoint said, and gave me his magazine-model smile.

We stood and watched the kids finish up. When they came out, two others went in, smiling at each other, lifting their gloves to touch, the referee giving them the signal.

That fight was a good one, better than the two kids that were supposed to be up for the Olympics. Both had game and skill, both were fast and hit hard for their age and size.

"And who are all these people?" I said.

"Investors," Coldpoint said.

"In what exactly?" I said.

"These boys. Their futures. We're trying to get them to sponsor buying this old place, turn it into a boxing club. Some repairs would be needed. But in this crowd, there's some real money, and a few people who work as carpenters and the like are part of it, and they could make it better with free labor, if we get them to believe in what we're doing."

When the fights were all done, the boys filed out, and then the crowd followed. In time it was just me and Leonard and the three humanitarians. Bobo appeared to have gone to sleep on his feet, his mouth hanging open, his eyes glazed over.

"Sheerfuck," Leonard said. "We got a ring, and we got the time, how about you and me do it again? You dance the Charleston, and I'll fight."

"I already proved what I have to prove," Sheerfault said.

"In a dance contest," Leonard said.

"Shit, burr-head, you don't want me on your ass again."

"You afraid I'll show you up? I was you, and it was me you had to fight, I'd worry too. Name-calling don't break a bone, motherfucker. But fists and feet do. No pointing rules. None of the referee stuff."

"Seems like a good idea to me," I said. "Sheerfault is so certain, here's his chance for a repeat performance, but not on points."

"What do you think?" Coldpoint said, looking at Sheerfault.

Leonard had Sheerfault where he wanted him, and in front of his asshole friends.

"Sure," Sheerfault said. "We can do that. But I'll tell you, Leonard, we go in, when it's over, you wake up at all, it will be in the hospital with a tube up your nose."

"Done got me trembling all over," Leonard said.

"No eye-gouging and no throat strikes," Coldpoint said. "I'm going to insist on some rules. Gets too bad for one of you, I'm breaking it up."

"Don't think it's too bad before it is," Leonard said.

"For the record," I said, "you got nothing to prove, Leonard. I know you can whip him, and you know you can whip him."

"Yeah, but he don't know it yet," Leonard said.

Sheerfault said, "You know that's right."

"And another thing, no gloves," Leonard said.

Coldpoint glanced at Sheerfault.

"Sure," Sheerfault said.

"I get through, Hap here will punch Bobo's lights out," Leonard said. "All two watts."

"Leave me out of this," I said. "Bobo can keep his lights on."

"Lights?" Bobo said.

"It's an expression," Sheerfault said. "I'll explain it to you later."

"All right," Coldpoint said. "You called it, Pine. What do you two need to do to get ready?"

"I'm always ready," Leonard said. "They pulled me out of my mama, I was ready for lunch and a fistfight."

30

They stripped off their coats and shirts, and Sheerfault took off his ring and watch and handed it to me along with his coat and shirt because I was the closest to the edge of the fence. Leonard came over and gave me his stuff.

"Leonard, you are a dumbass."

"Yeah, but I can fight."

Leonard went to the center. I folded the ring and watch up in Sheerfault's shirt. The ring was a peculiar thing, a hefty silver skull on a thick silver band. I placed the shirts and coats on an apple box by the edge of the fence.

In the center of the wire enclosure they stood ready. Sheerfault was a little heavy, but not fat. Just a guy with a light winter coating of meat. Leonard was not at his peak, but when he's out of shape he's in better shape than most.

Leonard and Sheerfault began to move, circling at first, looking for a hole, meaning a spot where they could slip a punch through. Leonard held his hands a little low. It was a ploy of his, get you to think you could come in and find a spot to hit, and then up came the hands and he hit you. Also, higher you held your hands, more tired you got. Sheerfault had a more classic style, hands high. They both held their chins up; didn't put them to their chests like boxers of old.

Sheerfault faked high with his right hand and brought a round kick around to Leonard's thigh, but Leonard turned his leg and slid off most of the attack. They circled some more, and then Sheerfault tried a similar trick on the other side, and that's when Leonard closed.

He hit Sheerfault two quick ones in the head with a motion so swift the blows sounded almost like one. Sheerfault ducked enough to take them on his forehead. That can be hard on bare knuckles. It can be hard on your head, for that matter. Neither seemed fazed.

Sheerfault was swift and his hands came quickly, like flesh missiles. Leonard dodged a few, but the others hit, and that worried me at first, but then I realized what Leonard knew. Those hits, though fast, were arm hits, meaning Sheerfault didn't put his body behind them, didn't turn his hips in a way that generated power. This was what Leonard meant about Sheerfault winning on points. The touches would count in a ring fight, a controlled fight, but in a real fight, not so much.

Sheerfault flicked again, and this time Leonard slipped inside and body-punched Sheerfault twice with the same hand, once in the solar plexus, once in the kidney. Sheerfault let out some air and tried to disengage, but Leonard wouldn't let him, kept on coming, throwing his punches hard, hitting Sheerfault with most of them. Sheerfault couldn't seem to get it together. Leonard had stolen his balance and every time Sheerfault tried to regain it, Leonard was there to steal it again.

Sheerfault finally disengaged by managing to hit Leonard with a jab in the face that was a pretty good punch. It stunned Leonard a little, and that gave Sheerfault some room.

Sheerfault dove in for a tackle, but as he grabbed Leonard's front leg, Leonard threw his reverse leg back and dropped down on his belly, driving Sheerfault to the ground as he went. Then he hit Sheerfault in the nape of the neck with an elbow. Sheerfault lost his grip on Leonard's front positioned leg, and Leonard swiveled like a trick rider and was on Sheerfault's back.

Sheerfault tried to roll out of it, but he wasn't rolling anywhere. Leonard had his weight distributed just right, and then he had his arm around Sheerfault's neck, positioning it in such a way that he didn't have his forearm in Sheerfault's throat, just his bent elbow. He was going for the constriction choke, what my dad used to call the Japanese stranglehold.

Sheerfault thought he was finally managing to rise a bit, pushing up with his arms, but that was Leonard's ploy. He was making himself lighter by lifting up on the balls of his feet, giving Sheerfault a false feeling of accomplishment. As Sheerfault rose, Leonard clamped his legs around Sheerfault's body and rolled on his back with a movement so quick it took us all by surprise. Now Sheerfault was facing the ceiling, his body in Leonard's clamps. Leonard lay comfortably on his back, choking Sheerfault by squeezing his arms together and expanding his chest.

Leonard didn't cross his ankles around Sheerfault's abdomen. He did that, Sheerfault could push down on Leonard's ankles with his hands, even throw his own leg over them, and cause excruciating pain. Leonard dug his heels into Sheerfault's thighs.

Sheerfault tried to twist loose. He managed to slide Leonard a short pace across the sawdust flooring, but he couldn't pull Leonard's hands off. Sheerfault tugged to dislodge Leonard's arms, without results. It was as if he were making a polite suggestion to a hungry python to loosen its coils, but pythons and Leonard didn't play that way.

I saw Sheerfault's eyes roll up, and his feet wiggled desperately, as if pedaling a bicycle, and then Sheerfault's arms dropped to his sides, as useless as a dead man's dick. Leonard didn't quit squeezing.

"Let him go," Coldpoint said.

But Leonard didn't let him go.

"Bobo," Coldpoint said.

Bobo started for the gate. I put a hand on his shoulder, said, "Hey, look, she's naked," and pointed.

Bobo looked where I was pointing, and I hit him in the jaw. I really brought that one by express train, but it merely made Bobo's head nod.

I stuck my heel into his thigh, way you would use it to push a shovel into the dirt. His leg went out from under him. I got my knee in his face a couple of times, jammed an elbow into the back of his neck. He went facedown in a scattering of dirt and sawdust.

I walked around Bobo, through the gate, and into the ring. I bent close to Leonard.

"You showed him," I said. "Let him go."

"I don't like him," Leonard said, and squeezed harder, pushing in with his chest, his chin in the top of Sheerfault's head.

"I know," I said. "But you want it so he remembers it."

"I want that?"

"Sure you do."

"Silly me," Leonard said. "I thought I wanted to kill the son of a bitch."

"If you get everything you want for Christmas, there's nothing to look forward to."

"That's true," Leonard said, let go and pushed Sheerfault off him.

Sheerfault lay still in the sawdust. Coldpoint came through the gate and inside the fence.

"You better not have killed him," Coldpoint said.

"He'll come around," Leonard said.

Bobo was up now, staggering a little, starting through the gate toward me.

"That's enough, Bobo," Coldpoint said. "Get out of there."

Bobo let that command move around inside his head like a blindfolded man in a new house. Finally he stopped and stood by the fence. He looked at Sheerfault, said, "Is he dead?"

Sheerfault certainly didn't look as if he were merely taking a nap. Maybe Leonard was wrong about him coming around.

I sighed, grabbed Sheerfault under his arms, and pulled him up a little. I stuck my knee in his back, rubbed at the sides of his throat, rubbed down on his chest with my palms, bent him forward, hammered him a few times in the small of the back. He coughed and spat up a wad of blood and fell over onto his side in the sawdust, breathing heavily. His eyes came open, fluttered, closed again.

Leonard stood over Sheerfault.

"I was wrong," Leonard said. "You don't even dance that well, Sheerfuck."

I took Leonard by the elbow and we started toward the gate.

"You took me by surprise," Bobo said as me and Leonard went past him.

"That was the idea," I said. "Me and Leonard call it the elephant of surprise."

31

They dropped us off by our car at the high school and drove away. Leonard had his coat under his arm. He was still heated up from having fought Sheerfault.

"I don't know about you," he said, "but I don't believe any of that shit about helping the poor kids have a place to train."

"They're doing that, all right," I said, "but that's not all they're doing. The idea that Jamar was murdered and Charm was sexually harassed just bounces off of him. He's one of those guys think their misery in life makes them special. Allows them to justify anything they do and say it's the best for the people. Jesus."

"Really think they believe we'll buy that line of shit?"

"No. I think Coldpoint thinks we just can't see the bigger picture, but I doubt he honestly thinks we'll toe the line. But if we push it, and someone says, hey, what did you see out there, and we tell them, there isn't much that nails anyone to the wall for a crime. And they are cops. It's something's being done progressive for the neighborhood, and it's only a little bit illegal. No one is going to give them too much shit for that. They're showing us how unconnected we are in Camp Rapture, showing us that we have our ass hanging out over here, and if we keep showing it, someone is going to drive a spike up it. They were trying to scare us."

"That didn't work."

"Did for me," I said. "It scared me plenty. I was envisioning us being in that sawmill pond by night's end, if not sooner."

"But you weren't scared enough to quit, I figure."

"Of course not. I was scared, but I'm also stupid."

"There you go. That's the Hap I know and love."

I unlocked the car. Leonard tossed his coat in, picked his fedora off the seat, and put it on as he slid inside the car.

"I want to drive by Barker's office," Leonard said.

"Suits me," I said. "I find myself a little put out with that bastard. Hey, know what?"

"What?" Leonard said.

"You tenderized Sheerfault like a hamburger steak."

"Choked him out and threw him away," Leonard said. "And you, my brother. You knocked Boo-Boo on his ass."

"Bobo," I said.

"Whatever."

32

I parked us behind Barker's office. Leonard checked himself in the mirror on the sun visor, adjusted his hat.

"Yeah, I be looking good," he said.

We got out and Leonard put on his coat and adjusted his fedora again, and we tried the outside door. It was locked. Leonard took the key from me and went to the car and got a tire tool out of the trunk, came back and stuck it into the edge of the door and heaved.

There was a cracking sound and the door came loose and swung open.

"They call that breaking and entering," I said.

"They do indeed," Leonard said.

We went down the hallway like before and came to Barker's office. The door was locked. Leonard, without hesitation, knocked the pebbled glass out with the tire tool, reached in, and flicked the lock. A moment later we were inside.

Barker, wearing only a T-shirt and boxer shorts, opened his inner office door with something in his hand, but it was too late. We were already standing there. Leonard whacked his hand lightly with the tire tool, and Barker dropped what he was holding. A little silver automatic.

I picked it up and put it in my coat pocket. Leonard pushed him into the office and turned on the light. Barker said, "Okay. You got me. Cut the light, though. Cut it. We can talk in the dark."

"I don't like what you might have in the dark," I said. "In more ways than one."

"I got nothing. What I had, you got. I got nothing."

"All right," I said, "but don't try to get cute. As you might expect, we are not in the best of moods."

I turned off the light. It might have been a paranoid move, but no use advertising we were all upstairs, not after what had gone on tonight. For all we knew, Coldpoint and his band of merry assholes might decide they wanted to take us out.

"They let you go," he said, rubbing the hand Leonard had hit with the tire iron.

"They did at that."

"Why?"

"Personality," Leonard said.

There was light coming in through the window behind the desk. It was from a streetlight. It wasn't much, but it was enough to see around the room after my eyes adjusted.

Barker sat on the couch and dipped his head.

"I had to do it, boys. I had to."

"Did you now?" Leonard said.

"I tell you I had to, had to."

"Tell us why? And then tell us why you're surprised to see us."

"Make it good," Leonard said, "'cause I'm thinking of hitting you with this tire tool so many times they'll have to build a wing on the hospital just to take care of your ass."

"I didn't know what they were going to do, but they threatened me, and my family. They can have my wife, the coldhearted bitch. But my daughter, that's different."

"They said they'd hurt her?" I said.

"Indicated it. Sheerfault and Bobo, they're the muscle, and Coldpoint, he calls the shots, though I get the impression Sheerfault is getting tired of him. Coldpoint's kind of a politician, crooked as a dog's leg, but clever. He knows piling up bodies isn't the best thing to do. He's piled up a few, I feel certain, but he's got cautious over time. He gets the police chief job, connections he's got, he's got a license to steal. Doesn't see any reason to rock the boat when they're giving him the ocean. Those other two would just as soon wear your ass for a hat. I admit I'm surprised to see you here, surprised. But you got to understand, what I did, it wasn't personal, wasn't personal."

"You said that before," Leonard said. "Don't say it again. I don't like it. And for the record, the muscle got their asses handed to them."

Barker smiled a little. "I'm glad that's how it worked out. I'm glad. Really. I didn't want you hurt, but I didn't know what else to do, didn't know what else."

"What you're going to do now is you're going to straighten some things out, answer some questions," I said.

"Yeah," Leonard said patting the tire tool against his open palm. "That's what you're going to do, and you're going to be clear about it and it's going to sound pretty to us. Everything is going to fall right in place."

"I know what I know," Barker said, "but I don't know it's all you need to know."

"Start with this," I said. "Timpson Weed. Did he or did he not ask you to tell the police he saw Jamar beat to death by cops?"

"Not exactly."

"And what, pray tell, did he have you say?" Leonard said.

"Timpson... Well, you need some background. He spent a lot of time in jail, and it got so when they wanted him at the jail, they picked him up on some charge or another, real or otherwise. They took him in when they had someone they wanted to put him with."

"What does that mean?" I said.

"They run fights with the prisoners. Pick some guy up for dope or some misdemeanor, whatever they like to call it, and they set him up to fight. Provided they got someone in there can fight back. Weed, he could fight, could fight good. He made a lot of money and made the gamblers more money until he got so good no one would bet on him losing, not bet on him at all. When he was younger, I think he boxed professionally. Way I heard it anyway, way I heard it."

"That's not quite in focus," I said.

"First time he goes in, he gets in a fight with a cell mate, and he cleans his clock, and Bobo, who's a jailer, sees it and tells Sheerfault."

"So that little bastard has gainful employment," Leonard said.

"Instead of giving Timpson more time for fighting, they ask him to do it again, say they can drop any charges he's in on, make it go away like it never happened, never happened at all. Thing is, he's got to fight, and so does the other guy."

"And all this happens at the mill," I said.

"That's right, the mill, at the mill."

"But not on Sunday nights," Leonard said.

Barker nodded. "That's the boys' fight club night. That's kind of the way they beard themselves. Weed, he was whipping all comers, and there was a lot of money made until no one would bet against him. It's not just some of the people on the force come there to bet, it's people around town. The fighter's black, that's even more a part of it. They have a thing about black people, a thing, want to see them hurt."

"Just like the good old days," Leonard said.

"How long has this been going on?" I asked.

"Some time now. You see, Jamar, he was a boxer who was fighting at the club, and they seen him, and he was good. He was smoking the Olympic kids, but he didn't have any interest in that, wouldn't go to the sawmill for fight training. They pushed at him to do it, but he wouldn't. That's why they stopped his sister. They were messing with him. Showing him they could do what they wanted when they wanted to. See, they wanted him to win a few amateur fights, push him into being a pro. They wanted the money he could make them. Even if it was just at the sawmill."

"Typical white-man shit," Leonard said. "No offense, Hap."

"None taken."

"Only Jamar didn't play along," Leonard said. "Started filming them. Didn't like them bothering sis."

"Right. That's right. Filmed them, had a scanner, followed them around, followed them when he could and made it hard for them to do anything he wasn't putting on film. They got mad and one night they decided they'd had enough, grabbed him, put him in the ring up there, made him fight. It wasn't a public fight. They had him fight until he couldn't, and they beat him to death. See, it was Timpson, it was him. He was brought in to fight because they wanted to teach the kid a lesson, a permanent one. No betting on that fight, they just paid Timpson good, brought him in, and since no one bet on him anymore, he wasn't making that good fight money. I don't know Timpson meant to beat him bad as he did, but he did, and then when the kid went down and couldn't get up, the rest of them, Sheerfault, Bobo, and Coldpoint—though I doubt he got his hands dirty—finished the kid off, finished him off."

"And you know all this through Timpson?" I said.

Barker nodded. "You see, it kind of got to him, doing what he did. But what got to him more was the idea he could have me go in and tell the cops he was going to go to other authorities, they didn't pay him off not to tell what happened up there. He thought he could work a regular payday out of it."

"Blackmail," Leonard said.

"That's right, that's right."

"And you would take a cut," I said.

"Yep, you're right there, right as rain. They didn't care though, didn't care. They own the town, everyone in it, or at least they know the people own the town and work for them, that's more it, more it. That's when Timpson got mad and started telling his story, putting it out in the projects. He didn't use common sense, not at all. He got vengeful, way they used him, used him up. And he wanted to make it hard on them, force them to give him some money, and then he'd recant his story if it ever got so he was actually brought in for it, but if they didn't pay him he'd rant and rave."

"So they killed him," Leonard said.

"They sort of asked me to have him meet with me, say I had some money for him from the cops, some money."

"You set him up like you set us up," I said.

"And told them Timpson might have a loose lip?" Leonard said.

"I needed the money, needed it, real bad."

"You sleazy little shit-greased weasel. You gave up Timpson for a buck, and he was your client, and you gave us up. You knew they'd kill him and figured they'd kill us too."

"I didn't really think about it," Barker said.

"Oh," Leonard said, "well, that makes it all right."

Leonard moved toward Barker. I put my hand against his chest.

"Easy," I said.

"Come on, let me hit fat boy once?" Leonard said.

"Maybe come Christmas," I said.

"How much was Timpson's life worth, dick cheese? How much?"

"Three hundred dollars," Barker said.

"Goddamn it," Leonard said. "Timpson was a bastard, but you're ten times worse, you money-grubbing asshole. Come on, Hap, just a couple punches to his head. That ain't nothing compared to what he done."

"No," I said. "We are the good guys."

"I don't know why they didn't kill you two," Barker said. "I'm glad they didn't, I am, glad, really."

"I think you'd have spent your money, jacked off, and slept just fine," Leonard said. "Did I mention I might break your neck?"

"It came up," Barker said. "Or something in that range."

Leonard took a step toward him. I pressed my hand against his chest again. I could feel him vibrate.

"And why the fuck do you repeat yourself?" Leonard asked.

"Childhood habit," Barker said. "Habit. Insecurity, insecure, that's it, insecure."

"My guess is Jamar and Timpson ain't the only ones died at the sawmill," I said.

"I have heard rumors there are others, others," Barker said.

"Rumors," Leonard said. "I got a little rumor for you. You know too much now, so I was you—and if I was, I'd have someone saw my head off—but I was you, I'd be special careful."

"Will you protect me, will you?" Barker said. He seemed small then, and as sad as anyone I had ever seen.

"Nope," Leonard said. "You made your bed of nails, now lie down on it. Hap, hold this tire tool while I hit him some."

"No, Leonard. That won't change things."

"But it would brighten my night," Leonard said.

"Oh, all right. Give me the tire tool."

I took it.

"Stand up," Leonard said to Barker.

Barker looked at me. I shrugged.

"You're going to let him bully me," he said.

"Considering you nearly got us killed," I said, "just this once. One shot, Leonard."

Barker stood up slowly. Leonard stepped close and gave him an uppercut in the stomach. He didn't really put a lot into it. Barker's knees bent and he fell back on the couch in a sitting position, dropped his head, gasped for air.

"That's to let you know we got a sour streak," Leonard said. "That's to let you know you tell them any more shit on us, have anything to do with them making a run at us again, that's just a sample of what I'm going to do to you. Wasn't messing with you about them having to build that wing on the hospital, and next time Hap may not be with me, may not be here to hold me back and talk me down. You listening?"

Barker lifted his head a little and nodded but didn't say anything. He couldn't. Didn't have the breath for it.

"We're going to go now," Leonard said. "Think of something we ought to know, get back to us. Think of something you think they ought to know, keep your mouth shut. Here's another thing. As soon as you get your breath, arrange for your daughter to leave town. Do not pass go. Do not stop to jerk off or take a piss, do it now. Oh, and you might want to take your own self out of here too. But that's up to you. Your well-being is not a big thing with me. Good night, and fuck you very much."

33

Sitting in the car, Leonard said, "They came after Timpson, and then us. Who's next?"

"Mrs. Elton and Charm."

"Could be that way, or fat ass in there, but he's not my concern."

"Ought to be," I said. "He has the word from Timpson on how things went down."

It was late when we arrived at Mrs. Elton's house. I knocked on the door and pushed the doorbell. To the right of the door a curtain slid back at a window. The curtain closed; a moment later the door opened.

It was Mrs. Elton.

"You got news?"

"We got to move you."

"I don't understand," she said.

"We'll tell you about it," I said.

"Come in," she said.

She was wearing a heavy robe and house shoes; her hair was under a scarf. She sat on the couch, said, "It's bad news, isn't it?"

"Bad information. You already know the news. We just have more details, but the bottom line is this: We may have stirred the pot a little too much, and they may be more dangerous than we thought. It's a simple thing, but it's a bad thing, and it has deep roots."

"Tell me," she said.

Leonard broke it down for her. When he finished she was trembling and crying.

"Thing is," I said, "you got to get some stuff together, wake Charm, have her get her stuff together. We'll take you someplace safe until we can sort this all out, get those bastards behind bars."

"Or somewhere in a ditch," Leonard said.

Always a ditch, I thought. Always a ditch.

"Charm isn't here," she said. "She's out. She went to a party. Said she'd be in late."

"How late?" Leonard asked.

"Late. That's all."

"All right, no big deal. If they don't know she went to a party, it's all good. Here's what we're going to do, just to be sure you're safe. Get some things together for you and Charm, go with Leonard. I'll stay here and wait for her. She have a cell phone?"

"Of course she does," Mrs. Elton said.

"Let's start there," I said.

She went away, came back with her own cell. She called.

"She's not answering," she said.

"Send her a text," I said. "Young people answer texts better than phone calls."

"I don't know how," she said.

"May I see it," I said.

She handed me the phone. I wrote as if I was Mrs. Elton, typed in: *Really need for you to come home right now, please. Not an emergency,*

but important. I won't be here. Hap Collins, the private investigator, will be
here to pick you up. Call me if you have questions.

I gave her back the phone, said, "Take a phone charger with you.
Keep it charged, and keep calling or texting or both. Leonard will
help you text. Want to make sure she gets the message."

"They call me Mr. Technology," Leonard said.

"I know of no one who calls him that," I said.

"But why do I have to move from here?"

"We can explain the why later," Leonard said. "Get some possibles
together."

She hustled off to do that. When she was gone, Leonard said, "So,
what's the plan?"

"Across the street to our office. That way we're close together,
but you're also up high with a good view. The office is a pretty good
Alamo."

"Folks at the Alamo lost," Leonard said.

"I'll take that under advisement. They may not show up anyway,
but it's as safe a place as one can expect until we can do some serious
thinking. Shit. What if they decide to take a run at Brett and Chance?
I hadn't considered that."

"Brett will shoot them," Leonard said.

"She will, won't she?"

"Goddamn right. Should I call Marvin?"

"Yeah. I'll call Brett and give her a heads-up, see if she wants to
move her and Chance to a safer place."

Mrs. Elton came back with two small bags. Leonard took them and
they went out to the car. Leonard drove it across the street and behind our office. I watched him do it through the front window, the one
where Mrs. Elton had seen Leonard and Marvin come and go.

The car wasn't exactly hidden, but it seemed good enough for the
moment.

I called Brett. The phone rang, went to voice mail. I had an uncomfortable five minutes thinking about how knocked out she might be due to the flu medicine she was taking. I could call Chance, but I didn't want to frighten her. She wasn't entirely indoctrinated into our way of life, not yet, and I wasn't sure I wanted her to be.

I called again. This time, on the third ring Brett answered.

"Brett, sorry, baby, but you and Chance and Buffy have to leave the house."

"Oh, shit, what now?" she said.

"The usual mayhem, and I should add this is just a precaution. Take a gun with you. Might as well be straight with Chance, though you can boil it down to the bone if you want. Bottom line is our investigation may have stirred up some bad men who might want to take things out on me and Leonard and anyone around us."

"I feel like shit still, and so does Chance," she said.

"All the more reason to get out of the house."

"I can handle myself."

"I know, but it's not necessary."

"Give me the scoop, Hap."

I told her more details but boiled it pretty much to the bone.

"I wasn't sick, I wouldn't go," Brett said. "I'd send Chance away, but I wouldn't go. But since we are both sick, I'm going."

"All I'm asking, go because you're sick and take Chance with you."

"Duh," Brett said. "Of course she goes with me."

"Don't forget your flu medicine. And remember, text me when you find someplace safe."

After that I called Manny.

She answered on the first ring.

"This better be good, whoever you are," she said.

"Define good," I said.

"Who is this?"

I told her.

"Oh. I hope you didn't call me in the middle of the night because you decided I would be a swell date. Though tomorrow might work. I need a nice dinner and a movie. If you're calling about those contacts I said I'd make, I tried, but they didn't call back."

"Nothing like that," I said. I gave her the stripped-down version, finished with "I need you to watch yourself. I got a feeling they may be planning to clean house."

"You think this why?"

"Gut reaction."

"What do you need from me?"

"Just warning you."

"I'm a big and capable girl. Let me state it again, so you hear me: What do you need from me?"

She sounded like Brett. But she wasn't sick.

"Backup."

"Where are you?"

I told her, said, "You might bring something to eat as well."

"Would you like some little initialed dinner napkins?"

"That would be swell."

"I'll wear a nice little maid outfit and bring them to you on a silver tray and later we can make whoopee."

"That really would be nice, but alas, my girlfriend doesn't let me date."

"Ah, then I'm bringing a friend, my nine-mil," she said.

34

I was sitting there thinking what do I do if they show up, call them bad names and declare king's X? I didn't have a gun. I didn't like guns, but I was in a business where guns mattered. What I had was some pocket lint and a headful of empty dreams.

Maybe if they showed up, I could just keep the door locked and tell them no one was home. Or like the bandit who hid in the henhouse, I could say when the bad guys came, "Nobody in here but us chickens."

Then I remembered the gun I had taken from Barker and put in my coat pocket with the lint. I reached in my pocket and pulled it out. It was shiny and it was small. A .22. That will kill you good as any firearm, but it might not be the best gun in a shoot-out, considering the kinds of weapons the other team might have.

Then again, there was no reason for them to know I was here. None. However, they might come for Mrs. Elton and Charm, and if they found me, I'd do just as well. Way I figured it, me and Leonard were on their list.

Lights flashed through the curtains. Holding the .22 automatic in my hand, I eased to the hallway where there were a row of windows, gently slipped a curtain aside, and looked out.

Someone got out of a car. It wasn't Sheerfault or Bobo, unless they had taken to wearing a short dress and high heels.

The door unlocked; a voice said, "Mr. Collins?"

"Charm," I said. "Step inside and close the door."

She did.

"You are supposed to go across the street to our office," I said.

"Got a text saying to come home. Nothing after that. My phone went dead."

"That was an error on my part," I said. "Your mother is there with Leonard. He'll watch after you. Safer there than here. Leave your car, and I'll walk you over. Your mom gathered you up some things. Give me your house key."

We locked up and walked across the street. I escorted her upstairs, called out gently to Leonard. He opened the door and let her in. He had a shotgun from the closet. It was the only one there at the moment, so nothing extra for me. But at least both of us were armed now.

Leaving Charm in Leonard's care, I started back down the stairs.

"Maybe you should stay here," he said, standing in the doorway, looking down at me. "Not divide our forces."

"I think it's better I'm over there. Should they show up, I'll call you."

"That's a good idea because?"

"We got them on both sides."

"So the two of us have them surrounded?"

"Manny is coming."

"We don't know Manny. Not really."

"Beggars can't be choosers, buddy. I figure she hates the department enough, she'll do all right. Marvin? You call him?"

"Didn't want anyone else to know what was going on at the station, because it's pretty complicated and not easy to digest unless you're a part of it, so I left a message for him to call me. Called his home too. Went to voice mail."

"Stay observant."

"The fucking Invisible Man couldn't get past me."

"Nice to know," I said, and went down the stairs.

Back at Mrs. Elton's house, I wandered around and found some sodas in the refrigerator. I took one and made a mental note: Owe one diet soda. I went back to the window and looked out. Nope. Nothing. I sat in a chair and tapped my fingers. That didn't make anything happen. Good. My magic was working.

Some dogs barked down the way. I strained to listen, but the barking stopped. I finished the soda, went back to the kitchen, and put the can in the trash, as I didn't see any recycling business like at our house. I got another soda out of the fridge. I owed two now.

I sat down in my chair, soda in my left hand, .22 on my knee, tapping my fingers on the arm of the chair. So far that had brought me good luck, so why stop now?

Time limped by on a walker.

Lights shone through the curtains as cars drove by on the street. None of the cars stopped. I put the empty soda can beside the chair. I was feeling a little sleepy.

No naps, I told myself. That would be bad. Ever vigilant. Ever alert. Frosty as hell and ready to go.

Actually, I nodded a little.

That's when I sensed someone was behind me. Sensed may be too strong a word. Maybe I heard something, felt a faint change in the temperature of the room due to another presence. I quit tapping my fingers and put my hand on the .22 on my knee. I was about to hit the floor and roll from a possible shot when a voice said, "You are not a ninja."

It was Manny.

"Damn, girl," I said.

"Came through the back. Picked the lock. Had I been a bad guy, they'd find your head in the yard with a turd in your mouth."

Manny was dressed in black and was wearing a holster with her sidearm in it, had her hair tied back. "I parked down the street, three blocks, walked over. No one saw me but some dogs."

I had heard them bark and hadn't suspected a thing. Hap Collins, ever ready.

"So you'll feel better about it, I'm a really good sneak. What is that you have in your hand? A cap gun?"

I let it rest in my palm and held it out to her.

She picked it up and looked at it. The streetlight outside gave us enough light to see by.

"You might as well throw this at them and hope it hits a vital spot."

"Not the way I shoot," I said.

"Let's hope you're a better shot than you are a sentinel."

"Thankfully, I am."

"If they should come here," Manny said, "my guess is they'll do what I did. One of them, anyway, and when the one out front thinks the sneak has had enough time to pick the lock and slip in the back door, the other one will come through the front door, guns blazing. You know, of course, this can all go south even if we put them down. It's police you're dealing with. They can make up any story they like."

"If they don't act like police, they're not police."

"If you can prove they aren't acting like police, then you will be in good shape."

"I'm very optimistic."

"I suspect that's a great comfort. Got any more sodas?"

"Aren't mine, but yes. In the fridge."

She went to get one. I told myself, Okay, now I owe three sodas.

When she came back she was carrying a chair from the kitchen table. She placed it against the wall to the left of my chair, sat down, pulled the tab on the soda.

"Any more information I need to know?" she said.

"I sometimes stay up past my bedtime. I try not to snack after six, but right now I could eat the ass out of a dead pig."

"I'm a little snacky myself," she said. "Speaking of a dead pig's ass, I like pork skins. You like those?"

"I do."

"Good. We like pork skins. I think this is like a bonding moment."

"Could be. We always called them pork rinds, though."

"Did you now?"

"We did."

"Hap, you are one hell of a conversationalist."

We sat silent after that. I considered another soda but figured I'd have to pee at the wrong time if things started to go down. Actually, I needed to pee then and I went to do it.

When I came back, Manny met me in the hallway. She had her pistol in her hand. She was moving and speaking softly.

"There's someone fucking with the back door," she said.

35

Manny went to one side of the door and I went to the other. A voice said, "Hap. It's me. You got a gun, don't shoot."

"Who is me?" Manny said.

"Marvin Hanson," I said, and opened the door.

Marvin came in and closed the door.

"Hey, Manny," he said.

"Hey," she said.

I forgot they knew one another.

"What the hell, man?" I said. "Shaking a door could get you shot."

"I wanted to stir things a little, just in case someone had already got to you. Figured someone other than you was here, they weren't going to say anything if I called out your name. If you answered, well, I been hearing your voice a lot longer than I've wanted to, so I'd recognize it."

"It's a nice voice," Manny said. "Kind of baritone."

"He just uses that to impress the girls," Marvin said.

"Or when I have sinus," I said.

"Didn't know you were here, Manny. Wasn't in the message. Hope hanging with this guy doesn't become a habit."

"We both like pork skins."

"That's something. I think a friendship could be formed around that," Marvin said.

"What I said. Hap and I consider it a bonding moment. He calls skins pork rinds, though."

"He's out of touch," Marvin said. He looked at me. "Got Leonard's message."

"Well, that part's easy to figure," I said.

"You are such a detective."

"Cops coming too?"

"I am the cops."

"The rest of them?"

"Not exactly. You know, one town, one ranger."

"You're not a Texas Ranger."

"Don't remind me. I wanted to be. Thing is, I got your message right after I got another one about some guy named Barker, ambulance chaser. Well, he caught one. Though, to be more accurate, he caught a hearse."

"What?"

"Dead. Beat to death."

"Son of a bitch," I said.

"Yeah, son of a bitch," he said. "Thing was, he had Brett's agency card in his coat pocket."

"Leonard gave it to him."

"And then I got Leonard's message, this address. He said the Camp Rapture police department might want you and him dead. I can absolutely understand that."

"We have trouble making friends. I blame Leonard."

"I got Leonard's call, and I'm starting out, and I get a phone call from a dispatcher I know in Camp Rapture. He knows I know you guys. Who doesn't? A blessing and mostly a curse. He says there's a dead guy that's been found behind the old high school, and the unknown someone called it in got your license number, saw your car over there, Hap."

"Uh-oh," I said.

"Yeah," Marvin said. "Uh-oh. And that's not all. This dead body, he's got Brett's agency's card in his pocket."

"And the dead guy is a sleazy lawyer named Barker," I said.

"Bingo," Marvin said.

"Shit."

"Yeah," Marvin said. "Shit."

"We got set up. The boys who gave the license plates to the cops were the cops. They got it when they met us there tonight. We went by and saw Barker on account of he set us up."

"And how's that?" Marvin asked.

I explained, left out the part about Leonard punching Barker in his office, then said, "We gave him a card so he could call us. We told him his life was probably in danger and he ought to get the hell out of town. Maybe he was on his way when they got him. Maybe he was still sitting there thinking things over. I think the Camp Rapture cops, at least two of them, and a jailer named Bobo, decided he might talk too much. He may have, before he bit the big one, squealed on how he talked to me and Leonard, gave us the scoop."

"Leonard gave me a little of it on the phone," Marvin said.

"Here's the rest of it," I said, and told him what Barker had told us.

"So you're sitting here thinking they might come for Mrs. Elton and Charm or you and Leonard?"

"Yep."

"And Manny, you just happened to drop by for a cup of coffee?"

"Actually, I had a soda and talked about pig skins," she said.

Marvin shook his head. "You admit to me you were at the old school, and at his office, and I believe you didn't kill him, but that story and your license plate number doesn't do you and Leonard any good."

"I know," I said.

"Look, I'm the fucking police chief. I can't show favoritism. I got this information from the dispatcher over there, in a friendly way, and I got to take you and Leonard down to the station."

"Are we going to have a movie night?" I said.

"Nope."

"Since you're taking me and Leonard in, can you have someone watch after Mrs. Elton and Charm?"

"We can arrange that."

"Can I come to the station too?" Manny asked. "I'm up. I got nothing to do. Maybe I could put an application in for a job."

"Good. Manny gets a job and me and Leonard get the shaft," I said.

"I'm not hired yet," Manny said.

"And there's the whole business about you being here with a mur-der suspect," Marvin said.

"Oh yeah. That could be an impediment," she said.

Marvin studied me carefully, said, "And there's just a little more information I got for you."

"Ah, shit," I said. "The hits keep on coming."

"An officer named Sheerfault pressed charges against Leonard for attempted assault and battery, but he said in self-defense he had to hand Leonard his ass."

"Bullshit. Sheerfault voluntarily climbed into the ring with Leonard, and Leonard beat him like a redheaded stepchild with a harelip, choked him out."

"And they say you hit Bobo with a board when he wasn't looking," Marvin said.

"I am not above that, and I did distract him, but I didn't hit him with a board, and he was actually about to hit me. I used the elephant of surprise."

"What?" Manny said.

"Ignore him," Marvin said. "Look, I got to take you and Leonard in."

"You have had a big night," Manny said, and she clapped me on the shoulder.

"What is that you're holding there, Hap?" Marvin said. "A cap gun?"

"This is going to complicate things," I said, handing him the gun. "It belongs to Barker."

36

Me and Leonard were in the main interrogation room at the newly renovated police station. The room was larger than the old room and the table had yet to be carved on with keys and pens and stout fingernails. Things got serious, you'd end up in one of the smaller rooms at closer quarters with your interviewer, your hands cuffed to a rail in the table that was fastened to a ring in the floor. So far, we were getting the luxury treatment, the guest suite, not the galley-slave quarters.

Marvin said, "Don't mention Barker's gun unless somehow they bring it up. Don't mention Manny being there with you either."

Manny was in the main office filling out an application. Mrs. Elton and Charm were somewhere under protection. I had called Brett and let her know what was happening, told her to be alert. She pretty much said fuck it, bad guys or no bad guys, she was going to sleep. She had Buffy to protect her and was too tired and sick to come down to the station.

I was not that confident in Buffy's protective abilities.

"And another thing," Marvin said. "Going to say you guys turned yourselves in."

"How did we know we were supposed to turn ourselves in?" I said. "Figure that one, smart guy?"

"Right now we don't have to explain it. I can look cool and enigmatic. Later on, we got to tell them something, we will. Things don't add up right, I got to throw you under the bus, and I'll probably be sliding under there with you. I might quit being police chief, and you two might go over to Huntsville for a little stay and a cocktail party that involves a very sharp needle and a long nap."

"That's not nice," Leonard said.

"Judging by our arrangements, I get the impression we'll be having visitors soon," I said.

"Yep," Marvin said. "Coldpoint, Sheerfault, and Bobo are coming over. They want to play pin the tail on the donkeys."

"I presume we are the donkeys," Leonard said.

"Bingo," Marvin said, and he went out.

We sat and waited.

Leonard said, "Right now, that cocktail and a nap sounds pretty good."

Finally, Marvin came back. He had Coldpoint, Sheerfault, and Bobo with him. Sheerfault looked like he had been in a car wreck. Black eyes and cuts on his cheeks and forehead, one ear mashed and swollen. Bobo wasn't bruised or injured in any way. Damn. I hit him pretty hard.

Marvin said to us, "Although you aren't under arrest, I want to warn you that you have the right not to say shit and all that, and you can have a shyster if you want one."

"We don't need a goddamn lawyer," Leonard said. "We ain't done shit."

"After tonight," Coldpoint said, "you're going to need a magician to get you out of this."

"Everyone shut up," Marvin said. "I'll ask the questions. This is being recorded, by the way."

"Recorded?" I said.

"Upscale shit is going on here," Marvin said. "This room records sound and sight, and we got a doohickey that freshens the air."

"Good," Leonard said. "Let me go on record saying these three motherfuckers are liars and assholes. I beat Sheerfault's ass like a dead goat, and Hap knocked Bobo's dick in the dirt."

"Noted," Marvin said.

"We're fellow cops," Coldpoint said. "You can't let him talk to us like that."

"He was going on record," Marvin said.

"What the hell?" Sheerfault said.

"You're in my jurisdiction now," Marvin said, "so put away the high hat."

"This is our case," Coldpoint said. "Happened in Camp Rapture. Our jurisdiction."

"And they were picked up in my jurisdiction," Marvin said, "and right now, there's no real evidence of them committing a crime."

"Sure there is," said Coldpoint. "There's an eyewitness says Hap's car was at the old school."

"Anonymous witness," Marvin said.

"Still, we got to take them back on account of them attacking an officer," Coldpoint said.

"And a monkey," Leonard said. "Don't forget the monkey took a beating too."

Bobo swelled his chest, looked as if he might leap at Leonard.

"Hope you took your vitamins," Leonard said to Bobo.

"Everyone, calm down," Marvin said. "You fuckers are in my station now."

"We go with them, let me tell you how it works out," Leonard said. "They'll say we tried to escape and they had to fire a few warning shots into the back of our heads. That would be a treat for you, wouldn't it, Coldpoint? One dead nigger and a white-trash motherfucker stacked at the curb."

"Thank you for including me," I said.

"What I'm going to need for these two to go anywhere with anyone is some real facts," Marvin said.

"Just told you some real facts," Coldpoint said.

"No," Marvin said. "You gave me some opinions and some stories I don't believe. Leonard got in a fight with Sheerfault, but he didn't get his ass whipped, for one." Marvin nodded at Sheerfault. "Look at you, boy. Looks like someone climbed your ass with cleats, set you on fire, then shit on you until the flames went out. You won that fight, you must have taken a little extra time afterward to beat yourself up."

"Whose side are you on?" Coldpoint said, glaring at Marvin.

"I haven't picked a side yet," Marvin said.

"We know you guys are friends," Coldpoint said to Marvin. "You may find your time as police chief brief, you keep this friendship up. And you two. I've heard about you. You're the kind that ends up in prison bending over a toilet bowl with a dick in your ass."

"Been there," Leonard said. "But not a prison, and the bending was by consent."

"Shut up, all of you," Marvin said. "I'm not kidding. Hap. Leonard. You want to spend the night in the jail on general principle, keep it up."

Leonard drew a zipper motion over his mouth.

Marvin looked at me. I did the same.

Marvin turned to Sheerfault, said, "Have Barker's death photos sent over to me."

"We can get them for you tomorrow," Coldpoint said.

"You can get them for me now," Marvin said. "Give me your body cutter's number, and I'll call him. We got all kinds of technology these days, and those photos, which I'm sure were taken at the crime scene, can be here within seconds, faster than you can get a delivery pizza."

"You have always been an asshole," Coldpoint said.

"Yeah," Marvin said. "I have. And I remember when you worked here, both of us cops together, and you have always been a scum-sucking bottom-feeder trying to look sharp and cool and well dressed. In final evaluation, you're just a cheap hood with a badge. Maybe once you did something right and lawful, but I can't prove it."

"This is all recorded, remember?" Coldpoint said.

"For posterity, I hope," Marvin said.

37

Marvin sent everyone out of the room but us. We were brought some coffee by Officer Carroll, a cop we had recently met. He was new to the force. A stout, nice-looking guy with a shaved head.

"Where have you guys shit this time?" he said.

"You might say we missed the toilet," Leonard said.

"Never mind, I'll read the reports," he said.

"Good," Leonard said. "I've told it about as much as I want to."

"Just have your coffee," Officer Carroll said.

The station had been renovated, but the coffee was still the same crap as before. Acid with a touch of colored water and caffeine and the slight aroma of mouse droppings.

"All right," the officer said. "I got to ask this. Bobo, what's up with him?"

"Got hit by a train," Leonard said. "Did you know it raised his IQ?"

"Damn," Carroll said, and went out. Leonard carefully watched him go.

"I kind of like the way he looks," Leonard said.

"He looks like a large-caliber bullet," I said.

"I know."

A short time later Officer Carroll came back.

"Hey, guys. Chief wants to see you. You can bring your coffee with you."

Leonard looked into his cup, said, "Do we have to?"

38

Marvin was behind his office desk, leaning back in his chair. He had his heels on the desk. He had a cup of coffee from Starbucks.

"Hey," I said, "we have to drink the cop-shop shit and you had Starbucks brought in for you."

"Yep."

We sat down and Officer Carroll leaned against the wall.

I said, "What happened to Manny?"

"Filled out an application and I sent a patrol to drop her off at her vehicle."

"She got off easy," I said.

"Yes, she did," Marvin said. "Got the photos of Barker's body."

"Already?" Leonard said.

"Told you, faster than a pizza. Take a look. See anything interesting?"

Leonard took them from where they lay in front of Marvin and spread them on the desk in front of us. They were nude shots of Barker stretched out on a table. It made me long for him to be wearing his cheap suit.

"Very small dick, for one," Leonard said. "Ugly feet."

"The wounds," Marvin said. "The beating."

There were standard shots, and there were close-up shots. Marvin opened his desk drawer and took out a magnifying glass.

"Look at you," Leonard said to Marvin. "Sherlock Homey."

Marvin handed me the glass.

"Why him?" Leonard said.

"More responsible," Marvin said.

I put the magnifying glass against the photo, roamed it over the close-up off Barker's head. At the back of his ear I saw something. A bloody imprint.

I put my finger on what I saw, looked up at Marvin.

Marvin swung his feet off the desk, pulled the photo away from me, held it up to us with his thumb next to the spot I had indicated.

"That wound right there, it's an odd mark," Marvin said.

He put that photo down and snatched up another.

"Visible in most of the shots, but this one is really good. I don't think Coldpoint had any idea what was there, wasn't looking for it. Had his folks send it over because he felt he didn't have to worry. They weren't investigating anything because they had you two framed for it."

Marvin tapped the photo with a finger. "Look close."

Leonard leaned forward. "A little skull?"

"Yep," Marvin said. "It is not a mark that naturally appears in nature. Barker did not have a case of the skulls, nor do fist and feet have skulls on them."

"But rings can have skulls on them," I said. "I noticed that ring when Sheerfault took it off to fight with Leonard."

"Damn, look at you," Leonard said. "You're like Ellery Queen."

"Who?" Carroll said.

"My opinion of you just went slightly downhill," Leonard said, and he and Carroll grinned at one another.

I hadn't gotten it until right then. He and Leonard were flirting.

"And I saw that ring on his finger tonight in the interrogation room," Marvin said.

"I didn't notice," Leonard said. "I was thinking about how bad the coffee was."

"That is why you will never be the keen detectives that Marvin and I are," I said.

"Way I figure it," Marvin said, "Bobo probably helped Sheerfault beat Barker to death. Maybe Coldpoint too, but I doubt it."

"Manny said he didn't do his own dirty work," I said.

"And she'd be right," Marvin said. "I've known him for a long time, and I've disliked him just as long."

"I assume this helps our situation?" Leonard said.

"It does. Another thing will help is there was no gun taken from Barker. Right?"

"None at all," I said.

"And I'm going to give the gun that was not taken back to you to get rid of so that it is not in my possession. You get caught with it before you get rid of it, then the gun will exist, and your balls will be in a vise. A gun I didn't know about will have turned up, and it will complicate matters."

"I didn't shoot him with it," I said.

"Yes, but it is probably registered to him, and if you were to have beat him to death, you might have taken it off his body. Dig? No use giving them any kind of ammunition for a defense."

"Dig, daddy-o," I said.

"Get rid of this nonexistent gun and go home."

"Are you going to arrest Sheerfault?" Leonard said.

"That's the plan, but I'm going to lay this case out really good. We're checking for someone else's DNA on Barker's body. Beat a guy to death wearing a ring like that, it might have cut into you, might have caused you to bleed and leave some DNA. Maybe Sheerfault or Bobo slobbered on the body while it was being kicked and punched. We get that, well, they can't say that anyone could have had a skull ring. We find DNA and we got the ring too, we got those motherfuckers by the short hairs."

"Charm and Mrs. Elton?" I asked.

"We'll take care of them," he said. "Might want to watch yourselves as well as keep a close eye on Brett and Chance."

"So we can go?" I said.

"You can go. And remember, the gun that doesn't exist needs to not exist at all. Least not on your person or in any location near you, and keep your fingerprints off of it."

"Gotcha," I said.

Marvin reached in the drawer again and took out Barker's cheap pistol. It was wrapped in a handkerchief. He handed it and the handkerchief to me.

"Get rid of it," he said. "I've wiped it clean."

39

Officer Carroll drove us over to our office.

"You look like you work out regularly," Leonard said to Carroll when we stopped. "Maybe you could use a partner? We could work out together."

"I might could do that," Carroll said. "I'll consider it, sure will."

"Good," Leonard said, and he got out of the car and closed the door and watched Carroll drive away.

"Okay, you're both gay, right?"

"Wow," Leonard said. "You are so tuned in."

"And you are interested in him?"

"And him in me."

"How do you know?"

"We have hidden gay impulses that tell us things that you heteros don't know about. We had an entire conversation telepathically."

"What was the subject?"

"Quantum physics, of course," Leonard said.

We went upstairs and locked the door. I said, "This isn't exactly a safe house. I mean, hell, we work here. Even Buffy could track us here, and she is the worst dog ever when it comes to dog stuff."

"Let's have a Dr Pepper and then figure it out," Leonard said.

"I still need to get rid of the gun."

"I want a Dr Pepper first."

"Will you kick and scream if you don't have one?"

"Probably."

"All right, Dr Pepper, then we get rid of the gun, and then I'm going to check on Brett and Chance and the ever-vigilant Buffy."

Leonard pulled a Dr Pepper from the fridge and I got a bottled water. We sat at the desk with our chairs turned so we could look out the window through the gauzy curtains. We had the lights off. We could see out, but as long as the light was off, no one could see in.

"You know what would be nice?" Leonard said.

"Winning the lottery?" I said.

"That's good too. But I was thinking of cookies."

"People in hell want ice water."

"I don't know about that, but I could sure use a cookie."

"Sounds like a personal problem," I said.

I pulled out my cell and called Brett.

She answered on the first ring, sounding less sick.

"So," I said, "you're healing?"

"Both of us are doing pretty good," Brett said. "And just so you know, we're not home anymore. I decided to take your advice. We were too sick to wrestle a paper bag and win. Anyone had come for us, most likely we would have been asleep."

"What about the ferocious Buffy?"

"Most likely she too would have been asleep."

"So where are you?"

"Safe house where you and Leonard stayed," she said. "I called

Marvin and told him I didn't want to worry you two, but way I was feeling, I ought to go somewhere safe and take Chance and our hound with us. He set it up."

"He didn't mention it to me," I said.

"Probably thought I told you."

"Whatever," I said. "Glad you and Chance and Buffy are there."

"There's a pretty big yard, and Buffy likes that."

"And there's a barn across the road from the house?"

"There is," she said.

"Yep," I said, "that's the one where we stayed a while back, along with Jim Bob, Vanilla, and the cosmopolitan Booger."

"One other thing."

"Shoot," I said.

"Chance lost her job at the paper. Since she was part-time, she doesn't have sick leave, and with her out as long as she's been with the flu, they let her go."

"Ah, shit."

"She says she wants to work for us," Brett said.

"Hell," I said. "I don't want to work for us."

"She thinks it might be exciting."

"It might be," I said, "which is why I don't want her to do it."

"What say we kind of go at it on a trial basis? I can give her donkey work to do, and if she holds up to that, she can maybe move into other areas. She could make a bit of money that way."

"We barely make a bit of money," I said. "But sure. I don't want her not to have a job. She'll most likely bore of it anyway."

"So it's a go?"

"Yep. But for right now, you two just get well."

I heard Chance squeal in the background.

"She's been listening, hasn't she?"

"Maybe," Brett said. "Good-bye."

While Leonard slowly sucked on his Dr Pepper and enjoyed his cookies, which he had replaced at some point without telling me, I told him about the safe house, about Chance wanting to come on board.

"I like it," Leonard said. "She's a lot smarter than you, and that would certainly help. You know what would make a great sign? 'Brett Sawyer Investigations, along with Leonard Pine, Hap Collins, and Baby Daughter.'"

"Hurry up," I said. "Let's dump this gun."

40

We went downstairs and out to the car.

The light that was supposed to be shining in the parking light was not shining. It had been shining moments ago. I looked at the post. The light had been knocked out, maybe with a rock.

"Shit," Leonard said.

He caught on to the sudden absence of light about when I did.

Two black men were waiting in the dark near a line of shrubs that connected to a house on the side of our business and the bicycle shop. They came out into the open and joined us where we stood next to our car. One of them had a limp, the other wore a base-ball cap with DAIRY BOB on it, an East Texas hamburger and hot-dog chain ran by a guy named, you guessed it, Bob. His father before him and his grandfather before that were named Bob. I just thought you might want to know.

The guy with the baseball cap moved as if itchy.

They were very large men with very ugly faces and they had some huge black pistols that were equally unattractive. One was holding a flat, black automatic on us; the other held his similar weapon to the side of his leg. I thought they looked familiar.

"There they are, Mr. and Mrs. Fucked-Up America," said the one with a limp. "King White Trash and King Black-Ass Nigger."

"Which is which?" Leonard said. "And do we get both awards?"

"We got the guns, and you're running your mouth," said the limping man.

"It's not like I figure we cooperate, things are going to turn out well," Leonard said. "Might as well go for it. And what the fuck is your beef? We don't know you."

"But we know you," said Limp. "We know you just fine. We also know a lot about you."

"Nice stuff, I hope," Leonard said.

"Not a word of it," said Itchy, and he scratched at his chest with his free hand. He kept moving and scratching like his skin was full of fleas. "Couple of smart-mouths that need taking care of, and we can do that."

"Lice?" I said, as Itchy scratched again.

"Scabies," he said.

"What we're gonna need you to do," said Limp, "is get in your car. One of you drive. We sit in the back with guns and you do what we say."

"Why would we do that?" I said.

"We have guns."

"I've had enough of that shit," Leonard said. "I'm at the point where you got to shoot me right here. I'm not going anywhere."

"Me too," I said. "This would be our second abduction tonight."

Limp and Itchy looked at each other.

Limp said, "We want you to get in the car."

"Nope," Leonard said. "Shoot us right here."

"We ain't supposed to do that," said Itchy.

"Life is just full of little disappointments," I said. "We're not going anywhere with you two. You can make noise and a mess here in the neighborhood, but we're not getting in a car with you."

You could almost see and hear the machinery working in their heads. This wasn't how it was supposed to go. They weren't supposed to make a mess here, not where they could be heard firing guns and be seen.

I put my hand in my coat pocket. Barker's little pistol was there. I casually took hold of it, still wrapped in the handkerchief, and shifted it a little and pointed it at Limp, who was closest, and pulled the trigger.

The little gun made a snapping sound, not too loud, not the way their guns would have, and Limp made a face. Neither he nor Itchy seemed to understand what was happening.

Limp's gun sagged in his hand. "That's some shit," he said, and went to his knees.

Limp was so surprised he dropped his gun. I kicked it away, and by that time Leonard had moved, surprising a distracted Itchy. He had hold of Itchy's hand. He pushed Itchy's gun aside and hit him on the jaw with his free hand. Itchy went back against my car. Leonard hit him again. Blood ran out of his nose and over his mouth.

Itchy moved as if to fight back, and Leonard hit him again.

Itchy sat on the ground and Leonard took the pistol from him about the same time I picked the other one up. Leonard looked at the pistol.

"The safety was on," Leonard said.

41

My shot had hit Limp in his gimp leg, in the upper thigh, and he was bleeding, but not as much as I had feared. The bullet had gone into him and stopped. It was a bad load, and I was glad for that. I wasn't going to have another man's death on my head. Leonard wanted to shoot both of them and call it in as a random shooting in our parking lot.

I doubted anyone would believe that. I pulled Limp over so his back was against my car, his butt against the rear tire. He was about four feet from Itchy, who hadn't tried to get up. Itchy sat where he was, shaking a little, scratching.

"All right," I said. "You are going to have to spill it."

Limp said nothing. Itchy said, "We gave our word not to rat."

Leonard put the gun he had taken from Itchy against Itchy's head.

"I got the safety off," Leonard said. "I don't like you."

"We don't even know you," said Itchy.

"What I was thinking," Leonard said. "So why kill us?"

"Money," said Limp.

"How much?" Leonard said.

"Five hundred," Limp said.

"That's it?" said Leonard. "That hurts, man. That hurts."

"Who was it hired you?" I said. "Best talk. Leonard there, he's got a short fuse and you two have lit it."

"Roscoe."

I looked at Leonard, and Leonard looked at me.

"Roscoe?" Leonard said.

"Who's Roscoe?" I asked.

"Roscoe Washington," Limp said.

"All right," I said. "Let's go at this a different way. Who's Roscoe Washington?"

"Bartender at the Joint," Itchy said.

"No shit?" I said.

Itchy nodded at Leonard. "He didn't like this one peed on his floor."

"In my defense," Leonard said, "I did ask where the restroom was."

"That's right," I said. "He did.

"Ah, hell," I said. "I remember you two in a back booth."

"He found out who you guys were, and he sent us," Itchy said.

"Roscoe might as well have hired a couple of squirrels and given them guns," I said.

"We had our own guns," Itchy said.

"How nice," Leonard said.

Leonard held the gun on them and I pulled out my cell phone and called Marvin. I didn't call 911. I called Marvin's private cell.

He actually answered.

"We got a little something for you," I said.

"Shit," Marvin said. "I hate it when you have that tone. It's never anything good."

"This one is kind of fifty-fifty," I said, "but I done a bad thing."

"Of course you did," Marvin said. It sounded on the other end as if his life force had left him. "Okay, Hap. Tell Daddy what you done."

"I shot a guy with a limp with Barker's .22 pistol. He limps worse now."

"No, you didn't?"

"Yep. I did."

"I want to express my complete hatred for you," he said. "I told you to get rid of that goddamn gun."

"Was on my way to do it, and, well, these two guys came up and they had guns and they wanted to make us get in my car and were going to drive us off somewhere and shoot us."

"If only," Marvin said.

"Hey," I said.

Leonard said, "Tell him how much we were worth."

"They were going to shoot us for five hundred dollars," I said. "Wait." I turned my attention to Limp. "Was that apiece?"

"To split," Limp said.

"Really?" I said.

Limp nodded.

"We got some raccoons out of an attic for the same price," Itchy said.

"They were going to kill us and then split five hundred dollars, the same they got for getting raccoons out of an attic."

"Raccoons are underrated," Marvin said. "They are tough little buggers. You know, they can pick locks, and once they do it, they can remember how to do it easily for up to three years, case they need to come back."

"That's some fascinating shit, Marvin."

"Where are you?"

I told him, and he said, "I'm coming. You are going to really love seeing me."

"Not as much as you might think," I said.

42

E verybody hates us," I said.

We were back at the cop shop, but this time in the smaller inter-rogation room.

Officer Carroll came in. He looked at Leonard, said, "We may have to put those workouts off for a while."

"I hear that," Leonard said.

Marvin opened the door and came into the room.

"You make it so hard," he said. "If I let you go up for a few things sometimes, that would make my life easier. Actually, you might do better in prison."

"Been there," I said. "Didn't love the food."

"It was self-defense," Leonard said. "We didn't start it."

Marvin collapsed into a chair like a discarded ventriloquist's dummy. "I know, but I still hate both of you."

"We are on a lot of people's lists," I said.

"Sometimes at the very top of them," Leonard said.

"Those two idiots said what they did," Marvin said, "and why, and even said you shot in self-defense."

"That's nice of them," Leonard said.

"They are dumb as two bricks in a sack of shit," Marvin said. "Problem here is you shot that gun. You know the one. One I told you to get rid of. Small. Twenty-two-caliber that didn't used to exist but might exist now. Was in your coat pocket wrapped in a handkerchief. Ring any bells?"

"I know just the one," I said. "But here's one thing. The handkerchief was wrapped around it, so my fingerprints aren't on it."

"True," Marvin said, "but it was in your coat pocket, and there's a hole in your coat pocket that the bullet from the gun came out of, and the bullet, when ballistics gets through, will be from the same gun that belonged to Barker."

"But he wasn't shot with a twenty-two," I said.

"No, but since that's his twenty-two, even Laurel and Hardy in there could figure out that with you having it in your pocket, you might have taken it from Barker."

"That is a problem," I said.

"So are your fingerprints on Laurel and Hardy's weapons?"

"We disarmed them," Leonard said. "Course our prints are on their guns."

"What we got here is what we call a detective's dilemma," Marvin said.

"They call it that?" I said.

"Of course not, donkey dick," Marvin said.

He sighed and sat still for a long time. Finally he said, "Give me your coat."

I stood up and pulled it off and gave it to him.

Marvin took it and went out of the room and a moment later Officer Carroll came in.

"He said for me to drive you two home," Officer Carroll said. "And he said too that you two shouldn't think you're going to slide out of this one. But between you and me, I think you will. We want the bad guys, not you guys. We'll get around the twenty-two slug somehow."

43

Officer Carroll drove me back to my car in the office lot and let me out, said, "I'll drive Leonard home. I'm supposed to make sure he gets there. Chief thinks you two do better when you're not together."

"What about me?" I said. "I am a known desperado."

"You'll be all right," he said.

He drove away with Leonard sitting on the front passenger side.

He hadn't even said good-bye.

I drove home then, and it wasn't until I was in the house that I realized Brett and Chance were in the safe house still nursing the flu. I felt weak and tired and lonely and disappointed and small and worthless right then. I got a blanket out of the hall closet, and a pillow, and put them on the couch. I went upstairs and got my revolver from the nightstand and brought it down and laid it on the floor beside the couch. I went into the kitchen and poured a glass of milk and made myself a cheese sandwich, but after three or four bites, I put it in the garbage.

I checked to make sure all the doors were locked and no windows were open, and then I turned out the lights and stretched out on the couch, nestled my head into the pillow, and pulled the blanket over me.

I lay there and the ceiling got close, and then the walls got close. I had experienced something like this before, and right then I knew I had been too cocky about my recovery.

Reality was coming down on me now that I had had time to relax and let it all soak into me. I'd been abducted twice in one night and held at gunpoint, and the feelings I had missed out on after coming back from the dead had been jump-started. I trembled for a while. I had faced worse than those two goons a number of times, but right then it all came down on me, them and everything else I had ever done that I shouldn't have.

I wondered about Leonard. But I knew the answer to that. He was fine. And if he wasn't fine, I might never know, even as close as we were. There were some bridges he didn't cross even with me, at least not yet. I lay there and trembled for a long time, and then I told myself, *It's over. I'm fine.* No use feeling this kind of fear when there was nothing to fear.

Then why do you have a revolver lying by the couch if you're doing so good, tough guy? Why's that?

Just because, I told myself, but then, as fast as it had come over me, the trembling stopped and I found my center and started to relax. I thought of Brett. I thought of Chance, and of course I thought of my brother, Leonard.

He was probably in his apartment with Officer Carroll doing what a client of ours had once called the dirty dog.

You're all right, I told myself. *You're good. Don't worry now. You didn't die and you're fine and you'll be okay. Everything will work out. You know what happened to Jamar now, and all that remains is to tell his mother, sad and horrible as that will be.* Figuring out who killed him was solved too, though not proved. That was the next step, and we had given the information we had to Marvin, so it was in his court now.

Eventually, I slept.

44

The next day I woke up and made coffee and had a granola bar for breakfast. I called Brett to make sure everything was okay, and it was. She and Chance were almost well and planned to come home later that day.

When we finished talking I poured myself another cup of coffee and called Leonard.

"And how are you this morning?" I asked.

"Better than I been in a long time."

"I got the impression that you and Officer Carroll may have gone home together."

"His name is Curt. I call him Pookie."

"To me he will always be Officer Carroll."

"Well, he is very official. I had to work hard not to let him take charge in bed. You know I don't like that."

"Actually, I didn't know that, and now that I do, I wish I didn't. How is he?"

"Very firm."

"Generally."

"Very firm."

"Leonard, come on, man."

"I like him. Quite a bit."

"I thought way it worked is you wanted someone softer than you, more feminine. Two tough gays, I don't know. That might throw the universe out of whack."

"Since I know you're trying to be funny, I'll let that pass," Leonard said.

"He still there?"

"Nope. Had to go to work. By the way, I now have an inside track, and when I was listening to Pookie talking to Marvin this morning, I learned they arrested Roscoe. He admitted it all. He says he was only going to have us beat up good, take us out in the woods and have those two knuckleheads pound on us awhile, tell us why he did it, and leave us out there to make our way home. Not only was the one gun on safety, it and the other one were unloaded."

"Maybe they were just stupid."

"They were that, okay, but I'm not sure I believe Roscoe. I think he picked a couple of turnips. He may have given them the guns and they were too stupid to check the safety and the loads."

"They said those were their guns."

"Turned out they lied. Changed their story. Said Roscoe gave them the guns."

"That Roscoe," I said. "What a kidder."

"Thing is, they got him," Leonard said. "I'm going to take a shower and have a big cup of coffee, some ham and eggs and a side of grits, all cooked by me."

"So, a nasty meal, way you cook."

"You offering to take me to breakfast?"

"I had a granola bar and coffee," I said. "I'm done."

"Cheap man."

"You ate my salad. I have not forgotten."

"Yeah, well, I'll check up on you later."

"Officer Carroll, huh?"

"Good-bye, Hap."

45

Brett and Chance and Buffy came home about lunchtime. The flu had finally faded and they were feeling spry, even if they looked a little watery-eyed and tired.

"Don't kiss me," Brett said. "I'm over it, but who knows, I might still be contagious."

"Yeah, we better not hug either," Chance said.

Buffy sniffed my pants cuff. Her I could pat and hug, and I did.

We decided to go out for lunch, as none of us were in a cooking mood, and we ended up at a Mexican restaurant. We all had tortilla soup. I might add that Buffy did not have tortilla soup. She stayed home, most likely asleep on the couch. She always climbed up there when we left. When we touched the doorknob she dropped to the floor with a thud and lay on the rug in front of the couch. She thought she was sneaky.

On the way back to the house, my phone rang. It was Marvin. He said, "You know a black girl kid with all the personality of a water moccasin?"

"The four-hundred-year-old vampire?"

"What?"

"What Leonard calls her. It's a long story."

"And I'd love to hear it, but do you know her real name?"

"Reba. Don't know her last."

"We picked her up under an overpass, or rather near it, in some bushes."

I was pulling into the driveway then, and both Brett and Chance were silent, letting me finish the call.

"She okay?"

"In the larger scheme of things she's all right, just beat to hell. A cruiser come across her coming out of the woods, right on the edge of LaBorde, out where the woods get thick on the east side. She tried to run from the cops, but her leg was broke and she was using a stick to get around. She fought like a tiger, but she was in bad shape by then. Good thing. Officer Thompson, a nice lady who once beat up two male thugs using her fists, said it was a hell of a fight. Said she got hit with the stick a couple of times, but finally got Reba in the car. Had to handcuff her. Drove her to the hospital. Girl tried to leave twice since she's been there, and she can't actually walk. Caught her opening a window to get out, and she's on the second floor. I got Officer Carroll outside her room. She won't tell us what happened; not all of it, anyway. She won't talk to anyone but you or Leonard, preferably both. Come to the hospital. I'll call Leonard."

When I clicked off, Brett said, "Everything okay?"

"Not sure yet. I have to go to the hospital."

"Should I go with you?" Brett asked.

"I don't know," I said.

I explained about Reba and how she was fastened to the case we were looking into, and when I finished, Brett said, "Sounds to me you boys just need to do it. Me and Chance don't know her, and you appear to have a special relationship."

"Yeah, she blackmailed us into buying her a giant un–Happy Meal at McDonald's and she talks mean to both of us and Leonard hates her. Special relationship? I don't think so."

"She wants to talk to you two for a reason, and I think that reason is she trusts you," Brett said.

"The relationship may be more special than you think," Chance said.

"And maybe she just wants a lunch from McDonald's," I said.

46

I have never liked hospitals, and as of recent I have liked them less, it only being a few months ago when I was in this very one. Leonard was already there when I arrived, waiting at the front of the emergency room. He had a large sack in his hand.

"I kind of understand the impulse to beat up the four-hundred-year-old vampire," Leonard said as I walked up, "but I don't like that it got done."

"I hear you," I said.

Inside we asked about Reba. We got the information and rode the elevator up and started down the hall. I hadn't mentioned to Leonard that Officer Carroll, aka Curt, aka Pookie, was the cop on duty.

When Leonard saw Curt, his face lit up, and so did Curt's. As we neared the room, Curt opened the door and I went through. I glanced back and saw Curt and Leonard bump fists. That must have been some night.

In the room, Leonard closed the door and we went over to the bed. The bed seemed huge, like a white cloud, and there was a black dot at the top of it, Reba's head. She looked so small there on that cloud. Her face was swollen and one eye was closed and the lid was a mound of inflammation and her lips were cracked and bloody. One arm was in a cast and lay outside the sheets like a large piece of plumbing pipe.

Leonard took one side of the bed, I took the other.

Reba had her eyes closed. We stood there, not knowing exactly what to do, but in a few moments she felt our presence and opened her eyes, looked first at Leonard.

"Damn, that there a thing to open my eyes to," she said.

"Yeah, well, you ain't looking so good neither," Leonard said. "You try to bite an oncoming train?"

"Two niggers beat me up," she said.

"Black men," I said.

"Whatever," she said.

"It's best not to call people that," I said.

"He does," she said.

"Him, I can do nothing about, and you, most likely nothing as well, but I got to try."

"Quit trying," she said.

"But you haven't told the cops about these two men?" Leonard said.

"I don't like cops."

"Marvin, the police chief, he's a good man," I said.

"I don't like cops. You got stopped-up ears."

"Okay," I said. "You asked to see us."

"I guess."

"Did you or didn't you?" Leonard said, and placed the sack on the sliding table beside the bed.

"What's that?" Reba said.

"You know what it is," Leonard said. "It says 'McDonald's' on the side of the sack. There's two hamburgers in there, giant batch of fries, and two fried pies. I didn't get you a drink. I can go down the hall and get one. Better yet, Hap can do it. I ain't your slave."

"Ain't nobody do much for me," she said.

"We're here for you," I said.

"He is, anyway," Leonard said. "Me, I'm just here on account of I ain't got nothing else to do today."

"Tell us about the men who beat you up," I said.

"They come looking for me," she said. "I was out in my tree, and they knew right where to look for me, and one of them picked up a rock and threw and hit me. I tried to move fast then, and I fell. That's how I broke my arm. My leg done broke too. They did that when I fell. One of them kicked me there. Then they dragged me off and put me in their car and drove me out to the river bottoms, pulled me down in them woods. They done stuff to me then. You know."

"Yeah," I said. "I'm sorry."

"Ain't the first time. You live up there in them projects, things happen."

"I'm really sorry," I said.

"Not as much as me," she said, and this time she shed a tear. I thought for a moment she was going to break out crying, but she got a hold of herself. She was too tough for that, and she was so tough it made me tear up.

"I bit one of them niggers good," she said. "I stomped one of them's foot good, and then he got real mad and they started beating me. They beat me bad."

"We can see that," Leonard said.

"Yeah, my modeling career done out the window. They dragged me off deeper in them woods and started whaling on me. I had me some beatings before, from some of Mama's boyfriends, but none like that. They done knocked me out a bit, but I come to. They thought I couldn't get away, 'cause my leg was broke. I fooled them and started crawling, going like a crippled dog. I fell down a hill, onto the edge of the river, and they couldn't get down to me on account of it was steep and there was lots of briars and such. I got a bunch of stickers in my ass. I lay there like I was dead, and they figured I was, or close enough to it, 'cause they went on. I crawled awhile, got me a stick for a crutch, and work on up to the highway. That's where I see a cop car. I tried to get away from it, go back in the woods, but I couldn't move fast enough, and this white lady cop got me and brought me to the hospital, then other cops come in. That big nigger, the chief, he interviewed me and here I am."

"Why didn't you tell Chief Hanson what happened?" I said.

"Yeah, your ears done stopped up for sure," she said. "I told you. I don't like cops."

"Bet you don't like those two thugs either," I said. "Want to get them, you need to tell the cops."

"I want you two to get them," she said.

"Why would we do that?" Leonard said.

"'Cause we done worked together."

"Have we?" Leonard said. "In some quarters, how you and us worked together is called extortion."

"Is that like working together?" she said.

"Not exactly," Leonard said.

"Listen, I think I got a little Easter egg for you," I said.

"Easter egg?" she said.

"A surprise. Describe those two grabbed you."

She did.

I said, "One of them still has the limp you gave him, and the two of them are in custody."

"You sure?" she said.

"Pretty sure," I said. "They fit the description."

"You got to be sure," she said.

"Why did they want to hurt you, Reba?"

"Hurt? They was trying to kill my ass."

"Why?"

"I don't know exactly. I seen them around before, though. They come to see Chicken Fucker a few times. He used to thug a little, beat on anyone didn't pay for their drugs, and they was the same."

"Timpson sold drugs?" Leonard said.

"No. He was one of them collector types."

"Who did Timpson thug for?" Leonard said.

"He work for the same one them two big niggers worked for, Roscoe Washington."

I looked at Leonard. He said, "Click."

47

What upset me more than what had happened to Reba was how she took it. She had been raped and beaten, and there was a part of her that seemed to accept it, as if she had been there before and expected nothing better. By the time we went out of the room I was sick to my stomach.

I told Leonard I needed a bathroom trip. He paused to talk with Curt while I found the men's room. I splashed water on my face and used a paper towel to dry off with. My eyes were full of tears. I washed my face again and got it together and went out to the car with Leonard.

"You're upset, ain't you?" Leonard said.

"Yeah."

"Me too, but the way we do good for that girl is to put this right."

"How can we? They're already in custody and Reba says she won't talk to the cops."

"She'll come around. But before she does, we need to go on over to the projects."

We left Leonard's pickup in the lot, and I drove us over to the projects. When we got out of the car, the thug gang, about five this time, including Tuboy and Laron, were standing out by the drive leaning on a car, trying to look cool. Way they really looked was scared. They hadn't forgotten Leonard.

Leonard stopped near Tuboy, and when he did, Tuboy unconsciously licked his lips in a snakelike fashion. I figured they had suddenly gone dry.

"You ain't gonna hit us again, are you?" Tuboy asked.

"That depends," Leonard said, standing close to Tuboy.

"On what?" Tuboy said. He was trying to sound like a tough guy, but his voice had gone up an octave.

"Watch our car for us," Leonard said, "'cause I know you wouldn't let anything happen to it."

"Your car ain't our problem," Tuboy said.

"Is now," Leonard said. "I'm assigning it to you."

"I don't want nothing to do with it," Tuboy said.

"Me neither," Laron said.

The others grumbled in agreement.

"You don't get to choose," Leonard said. "All you got to do is make sure it ain't touched. A bird shits on it, I hold you responsible."

"Man, that's cold," said Laron.

"Is indeed. Let me ask all of you something. You know about Reba getting beat up?"

"Shit, she gets beat up a lot. She's got an uncle, Uncle Chuck, who beats her up when he gets drunk and can catch her. I think he gets an arm workout like that. Soon as he's drunk, he's looking for something to hit, and she's it, he can catch her. She's gotten faster."

"Last night, smartass," Leonard said. "Any of you know anything about that shit happening last night? Good information is worth a twenty."

"A twenty," Tuboy said. "You can't get a hand job for less than fifty."

"Oh, I bet you'd give me one for a lot less, I insisted," Leonard said.

Tuboy stepped back without really thinking about it. He studied Leonard. The others looked first at Leonard, then at Tuboy, as if at any moment Leonard might hang his wang out and have Tuboy go to work on it.

"They say she was knocked out of a tree, put in a car, and hauled off," Tuboy said.

"They say?" Leonard said. "What kind of shit is that?"

"I guess I might have seen it."

"Did you call the cops?"

"Not my business."

"What if it had been you," I said.

"Then it would have been my business," Tuboy said.

One of the group laughed.

"You know how I've made that car your business?" Leonard said. "Now I'm making information about Reba your business, 'cause I find out you knew something and didn't tell me, after I get through sticking your head in a hole in the ground so I can kick your ass for entertainment, I'm going to call the cops and have them come down on you so hard you'll think the sky done fell on you."

"We ain't doing nothing," Tuboy said.

"That's right," Leonard said. "You ain't, with your life, anyway. But I know your kind."

"Can't judge a book by its cover," Laron said.

"Yeah, but you ain't no book, and you smell like lying shit, and if you're giving me shit, handing me a pile of lies, I'm going to rub your noses in it. Don't think I won't. Now, that little girl may not mean anything to you, but she means something to Hap here, and

Hap means something to me, and none of you mean a goddamn thing to me. You starting to get where I'm coming from?"

"You don't like us," Tuboy said.

"I don't like what you want to be," Leonard said. "I don't like what you are now, and what you are now is pretty much what you want to be, and I call that fucking stupid. Now, why would anyone want to hurt Reba, besides her uncle, and by the way, we get through with this other question, I got one more question for you. But let's take these quizzes one at a time."

Tuboy and Laron looked at one another, and then all the gang looked at one another and back to Leonard. Tuboy cleared his throat.

"You got to understand, we could end up way Reba did, or worse," Tuboy said.

"And worse could start in less than a minute," Leonard said.

"I seen them two that was here," Tuboy said. "They hang out at the Joint. I done been up in there a couple of times, but the bartender, he don't like me."

"I don't like you either," Leonard said, "but I like the bartender less. Let me give you a jump start. We know those two thugs grabbed Reba, and we know the bartender, Roscoe, put them up to it. But I'm thinking there's a bigger picture here. You give us something, hear?"

One of the boys who had not spoken before, a thin fellow with a wool knit hat on, stepped up to the front of the group.

"I get the twenty?" said the boy.

"Maybe," Leonard said. "What's your name?"

"David."

"Tell us something worth twenty," Leonard said.

"Everyone knows the cops run the game. Take drugs from buyers and dealers, but you don't hear about no drug busts. They just run it back through the community."

"Timpson helped them sell drugs?" I said.

"He helped, but he don't sell," David said. "Just collects. It's his old lady runs the show for the cops. She gets paid for making sure things go smooth, and if they ain't smooth, she makes sure things get smoothed out."

"You mean Tamara?" I said. "She runs things?"

"That's the one," Tuboy said.

"Hey, this is my twenty I'm trying to get," David said.

"Yeah, and when you do, you gonna buy us all something with it," Tuboy said.

"No," I said. "He gets to keep it, but if we get the real stuff, there's a twenty for each of you."

"I ain't having shit to do with this," said one of the boys, and then walked off.

"Anyone else walking?" Leonard said.

"Tamara be the one," David said. "Everyone knows that. She tell Timpson what to do when he was around to do it. He say something, it come from her, you can bet on that."

"Do you know her contacts?" Leonard said.

"Just like I done said," David said, "the police."

"Cops here, they run things like they see them, like they want them," Tuboy said. "They ain't no more cops than we are, 'cept they got rides and shooters. Well, I got a pistol."

"Look in Tamara's apartment, you'll find enough meth and other shit to fill up a dump truck," David said. "I know, I buy me a little taste of this and that from time to time."

"Good to see your life's right on track," Leonard said.

"I ain't gonna stay up in here forever," David said. He had gotten a lot braver now, taking the head-dog position away from Tuboy, at least for a few moments.

"Naw," Leonard said. "You ain't never coming out of the projects, except carried out. You're too stupid."

"Does this mean I don't get the twenty?"

"It means you get the twenty," Leonard said.

"You said we all get twenties," said Tuboy.

"Hap, give them twenties," Leonard said.

"What?" I said.

"Give them twenties."

"I don't have that kind of money."

"What you got?"

I opened up my wallet. "Forty dollars."

"Give it to me."

I gave it to Leonard. "All right, he's got forty and I got thirty-five," Leonard said.

"That ain't twenty apiece," said Tuboy.

"At least you can count. First grade wasn't a waste after all. But we're going to give you what we got and put the rest of it on the installment plan."

"The fuck?" Tuboy said.

"And you're going to like it," Leonard said. "Now I got that second question. Where's that uncle of Reba's?"

48

Leonard got the apartment number from one of the boys, went and knocked on the door. When a big man with more muscles than Charles Atlas opened it, Leonard asked if he was Reba's uncle. The man eyed Leonard, said he was and that if he was wanting to buy him a piece of her ass, that was all right, but it cost extra for white guys. He meant me, of course.

"Naw, we ain't here for that kind of thing. What we're here for is because of that kind of thing."

"There's a difference?" the uncle said.

"Oh yeah," Leonard said. "Mighty big difference."

"You're starting to rub me the wrong way," the uncle said.

"You have no idea," Leonard said, then turned to me and said, "Hold my hat."

I took it from him, and that's when Leonard wheeled and hit Chuck the first time. It was like a missile landing on an aircraft carrier. The uncle dropped hard on his ass. Leonard dragged him out of the doorway by his ankles and let him get up, and then he hit him a couple of sharp blows that made the man bleed. I knew the ass-whup boogie had really begun. He hated Sheerfault, but this was beyond hatred. Leonard knocked the uncle against the building where he couldn't get away, and then he went to work; a surgeon couldn't have been more precise. The man tried to hit back, but he might as well been trying to fight a tiger with a toothpick.

A couple of people came out of doors, saw what was going on, and went back inside. I kept watch in case the uncle had any defenders, and by doing that, I didn't always have my eyes on Leonard, but I could sure hear him at work. Rhythmic, without hesitation between blows. Leonard certainly seemed to have his wind that day. When the uncle was on the ground unconscious, Leonard started kicking him in the head. I let him do that a few times, then I went over and got Leonard by the shoulder, and then by the waist, and pulled him back.

"Murder doesn't help any of us," I said.

"That motherfucker dies, that helps the universe," Leonard said.

"Come on, I don't want to visit you in Huntsville."

"You stay away from that little girl," Leonard said as I dragged him off. "You hear me, asshole?"

"He's not hearing anything at the moment," I said.

"Then he better get him some telepathy," Leonard said.

I eventually got Leonard away from there, got him walking toward the car. As we went, the gang of boys stood there with their mouths open.

"Damn, Chuck was someone Timpson was afraid of, and he bad," Tuboy said.

"Think I was bad today, you ought to see me on a Wednesday after breakfast," Leonard said.

In the car Leonard took a deep breath as I backed out.

"And I don't even like the four-hundred-year-old vampire," Leonard said.

"Of course you don't," I said.

49

We didn't talk to Tamara, and we didn't call Marvin. We had other ideas and they weren't necessarily good ones, but they were what we had.

First, though, we drove back to my house to give some attention to Leonard's shoulder. He had pulled the rotator cuff a little from hitting Uncle Chuck so often, nothing that wouldn't be okay, and not so bad he was out of commission. He was just pained.

Back at my place, Brett had him take off his shirt. She got a bag of peas out of the freezer and laid those on his shoulder and had him hold it there.

"That's cold," Leonard said.

"No shit," Brett said. "Hold it, and don't be such a big baby."

Chance came out of the back room then, looked at Leonard. "What happened to you?"

"Tennis injury," Leonard said.

"Yeah, I bet," Chance said.

Brett gave some ibuprofen to Leonard, and then we ended up in the living room. Chance made us coffee, and we sat there sipping, Leonard balancing a bag of frozen peas on his naked shoulder.

When we were relaxed, I said, "Coldpoint and his minions, Sheerfault and Bobo the Clown, have been using the projects to run drugs. They are feeding that stuff right back to the kids there, as well as branching out. They hide behind being cops and being respectful, helping kids make it to the Olympics in boxing."

"They got a little girl beat up and raped and tried to kill her on account of she talked to us," Leonard said. "Someone told that she did, and I figure that someone is one of the assholes we talked to today, and there will be hell to pay. Shit, I'm not through with her uncle."

"It could have been anybody in the projects," I said. "That place has a thousand eyes and ears. Thing is, we got connections to Coldpoint and his crew all over the place," I said, "but we don't have the hard stuff on them. Timpson was their bitch, but he was also his girlfriend's bitch. He helped kill Jamar, and then he tried to make money off of it with the cops, and they gave him a permanent attitude adjustment. Figure Roscoe was in on all this too, and he wasn't going to have us beat up or killed because his feelings got hurt and Leonard peed on his barroom floor."

I had to stop and explain about that part, catch Chance and Brett up some more.

"I got my suspicions," I said. "And it's if you're going to sell product, you got to have someplace to do it, and the projects and the bar are part of it. Timpson had us meet him there, and my guess is it was a way for Roscoe to tag us, which is why Timpson made a point of introducing us. Roscoe tagged us, and so did the two dumbasses at the back of the bar. Lucky for us, him using them was like trying to get a couple of Chihuahuas to take down a grizzly. Me and Leonard, collectively, are the grizzly bear."

"You know that's right," Leonard said.

"So Timpson set you up, had you identified by meeting you at the bar," Brett said.

"He thought he'd get rid of us, keep us out of his and Tamara's hair, out of the way of their drug business, not to mention his plan to blackmail the cops. Stupid plan."

"That all makes sense," Leonard said. "I hate to say it, but I think you got it figured."

"What about Charm and Jamar?" Chance said.

"Charm was merely taking pictures for a class, and the cops thought she was taking pictures of their illegal fights, had some clue what was going on up there. They gave her shit, tried to throw a scare into her, and her brother tried to protect her. He had a bit of a rep as a boxer, and they thought, Well, he's going to give us shit, we won't kill him outright, we'll get some sport out of it. That's when Timpson killed him, or beat him bad enough the others finished him off. That part may be hard to know."

"But we know Reba heard what she shouldn't have heard," Leonard said, "and then she told us stuff that Tamara didn't want told, and somehow it got back to Tamara what Reba did. Maybe Reba ran her mouth. She strikes me as someone might do that. I don't know, but it got found out, and that's when Tamara and Timpson got Roscoe and the goons involved. Had I known they'd done to her what they did, I'd have killed them right then and there. Wouldn't have been no jail for them."

"Did you tell the cops all this?" Chance said.

"No," I said.

"I thought cops were good," Chance said.

"They are people," I said, "and therein lies the problem. Some are good, some aren't. Marvin certainly is. But the cops in Camp Rapture, not so much. They're like thugs with a license to steal and murder and pretty much do what they want. It goes all through the city officials. You get rotten apples at the top, it spoils the apples all the way down, or, rather, a head rotten apple attracts others of its kind by design."

"Those are some crafty apples," Brett said.

"What are you going to do about it?" Chance asked.

"Me and Leonard came up with something of a plan on the way over here."

"How about you give us the working parts," Brett said, "and I bet me and Chance can make it less stupid."

50

It was a cold night and it was colder for us because we weren't at home or in the car. Brett and Chance were parked near the police station in Camp Rapture. Before they'd dropped us off, we described Coldpoint, Bobo, and Sheerfault for them and determined Coldpoint was at the station. We had spotted his car in the lot. The four of us even saw him come outside once, smoke a cigarette, and go back in.

"He's kind of good-looking," Chance had said.

"Yes, and he is kind of a devil as well," I said.

"Easy, tiger," Brett said.

After that, Brett and Chance let us out on the hill near the sawmill and drove back into position, which took about twenty minutes, the hill being on the edge of town. Chance called and said Coldpoint's car was still there. As far as they could tell, so was he.

The lot where Brett and Chance parked was for a country-music nightclub. It was partially filled with cars. It was across the street from the police station. They found a position near the front facing the street, behind one car.

Through their windshield and the back and front windshields of the car in front of them, they had a good view of the cop shop and the parking lot with Coldpoint's car in it. They were calling themselves the Sneaky Bitches, and even signed off together on the phone with "Sneaky Bitches rule."

"They may have to be sedated at some point," Leonard said.

We were hiding among the trees above the sawmill, wearing heavy coats and wrapped in blankets. We had a couple large thermoses of coffee, sandwiches, and a bag of vanilla wafers. Since I knew Leonard was not big on sharing those, and so did Chance, she had bought me a box of animal crackers and packed them for me. We had brought raincoats. It looked like wet weather might be coming. We had backpacks to store everything in. Leonard had a pistol. I had decided not to bring one; they had their place, but I hated the damn things. I had a golf club I had found buried in the grass of our side lawn, must've been left there about the time Arnold Palmer took his first swing on a golf course. Some kid probably dragged out his father's club one day, then lost interest, dropped it, and forgot about it. I had racked a mower blade on it last summer, but I'd kept the club, leaned it against the side of the carport, meaning to throw it away. It was rusted but surprisingly sturdy. I was glad to have it.

Where we sat was on a rise above the sawmill. We weren't that high above it, but it was a pretty good-size hill, and from where we crouched we could see the mill, the worn-out drive, and the pond. The pond was dark, as the moon was mostly behind a cloud. It looked like a tar pit. We had cell phones with us, on vibrate, and the plan was simple and slightly refined by Brett to include cell-phone contact.

We reasoned tonight might be when things happened, if any of our information was correct, and then again, it might merely be a cold night and we'd go home with frozen asses and nothing solved.

But I doubted that. There was money to be made on betting. For the better-positioned folks in the community, dogfights, chicken fights, or human fights, it was all the same; it wasn't their pain or their blood that was in those matches, only their dollars. With everyone from city officials and law enforcement in cahoots, they felt protected.

About midnight, I began to think my speculation wasn't good enough. I was starting to miss Brett and my warm bed. We had drank about half our coffee and had eaten our sandwiches. I had also consumed an entire box of animal crackers, and Leonard was well into his bag of wafers. Why he didn't weigh three hundred pounds, I couldn't figure.

It had grown colder, and now there was a light rain, more of a mist, really. We put on our raincoats and pulled up the hoods and sat there in misery.

"It comes two in the morning, we're taking our asses home," Leonard said. "I'm cold as a sled dog's nut sack."

"Agreed," I said.

About thirty minutes later we saw several sets of car lights hazing through the rain, coming up the hillside road. A second later my phone buzzed.

"Coldpoint has left," Brett said.

"Someone is already here," I said.

"Can't be Coldpoint. He just this minute left."

"We'll see who pretty soon," I said.

"You going to be okay?"

"Have I ever not been okay?"

"Lots of times," Brett said.

"I'm going to text you when to call Marvin. He doesn't know you're calling, so you don't get him, get Officer Carroll, and be sure and call him Pookie."

"Fuck you very much," Leonard said.

I gave her Curt Carroll's number, said, "If what we think is going on is in fact going on, we're going to need a Texas Ranger, some Highway Patrol, someone not bound by jurisdiction. Marvin has friends everywhere, so he'll know who to send. The Camp Rapture sheriff's department might be in on it, so not them. If Batman is available, send him."

"Got you."

"If I don't text in thirty minutes, get someone starting this way. Make that twenty."

"Be careful," Brett said, and we ended our call. The crowd below wasn't near enough to hear me on the phone, but in a few more minutes they would be walking under us. I could hear car doors slamming and people talking as they came.

Glancing downhill, I saw Sheerfault and Bobo get out of a car, which Sheerfault had parked up close to the mill. Others had left their cars, which were parked in the line farther away, and were making their way toward the mill. There were about twelve people, not counting Sheerfault and Bobo. Everyone was wearing a raincoat or carrying an umbrella.

Bobo pulled back the plywood barrier and slid inside the mill with Sheerfault. A moment later you could see a crack of golden light through the slit in the wall and a beam of the same rising up under the pine tree that poked through the roof. Confident as they were, they weren't exactly in sneaky mode; who was going to punish them? Well, I had an idea.

Everyone outside filed in.

Headlights bounced up the drive. They belonged to a white jailhouse bus, the sort they use for transporting prisoners. The bus slipped to the side of the parked cars, and the hydraulic door hissed open. A brief moment later a man came out. It was someone I had never seen before. I could tell from the back glow of the headlights that he was wearing a sheriff's deputy shirt, jeans, tennis shoes, and a jailer's jacket and a ball cap. He had a holstered gun on his hip. A moment passed and out of the bus came four men in handcuffs, followed by a fat man with a shotgun slung over his shoulder. They were followed by some of the men I had seen there before, some of the town's bigwigs. They came off the bus and walked behind the criminals like Roman soldiers lazily making their way to a crucifixion. They went inside the mill.

More car lights cruised up the drive, and then cars began to spread out and park in a row behind the bus. Car lights were turned off and six men came out of the cars and so did one dark-haired woman, opening an umbrella as she did. I knew her from newspapers. She was a judge. Jill something or another. I think she was running for mayor next election. Her politics had been described as being to the right of Attila the Hun's. Tonight, that would most likely be confirmed.

"I don't think them convicts are having a field trip to see how the old sawmill worked," Leonard said.

"Nope," I said.

We sat and waited for some time to pass. No more cars came along. We could hear voices rising inside the mill, and then there were shouts, and even from where we sat, we could hear the sound of fists smacking.

"No gloves," Leonard said.

"Nope," I said.

We left our goods, except for our phones, Leonard's gun, and my golf club, and slipped from the hill. At the bottom of it, we crouched behind Sheerfault's car.

"I'm going to see I can get a phone video and sound recording of what's going on," Leonard said. "I'll send it to Brett as insurance."

"Video and sound recording," I said. "You sound so cute trying to be technological."

"Fuck you."

"Watch your ass."

"You'll be watching it. Try not to get a boner."

With that Leonard slipped away and began a soft trot toward the mill.

51

The voices in the sawmill rose up and fell down, yelled out, moaned and hissed, and then became a conversational hum. A moment later, the voices were loud again.

I kept an eye on Leonard. He was the near the slit in the mill, lifting his phone to film through the opening. After a few seconds, he stopped filming, looked back at me, and began to text.

TOO MANY PEOPLE. CAN'T GIT CLEAR VIEW. THEY ARE BUSY. WALKIN UP BEHIND EM TO FILM.

I sent a text quickly: THAT'S NUTS.

His return text popped up. YEP.

Leonard grinned at me, then turned back to the mill. I watched him pull the rain hood tighter around his head and slip through the crack in the door.

What a dumbass, I thought.

I should have sent Brett a text, but I didn't take time for it. I was already easing out from behind the car. I ran as softly as I could across the worn drive and to the gap that led into the mill. I leaned the golf club against the wall, peeled off my rain slicker, and tossed it aside. I picked up the club and took a peek in the mill.

Leonard was walking casually toward the back of the crowd. No one noticed him. They had their minds on what was going on inside the wire enclosure. There were some beer coolers on the ground, and a man I recognized as a councilman had a beer in his hand and was walking away from the crowd gathered at the fencing. Had he turned his head slightly, he would have seen Leonard.

Leonard stood at the back of the crowd near where they had piled their rain gear and umbrellas, raised his phone, and began to film between a split in the spectators. Through that split I glimpsed Coldpoint, Sheerfault, and Bobo close to the fence. Beyond them I caught a sight of two ragged-looking men swinging wildly at each other. There was no skill or plan to it. It was wild arm hurling. Both of them looked as if they might keel over at any moment from exhaustion. If something bad happened and one keeled over for good, there was the sawmill pool waiting.

"I think maybe we ought to bring you inside." I turned, and there was Coldpoint behind me with his handgun drawn. Our impulsiveness had caused us to lose focus, not wait until the man we knew was coming arrived.

Now he had arrived.

He was standing about five feet from me and he had the gun in one hand and an umbrella in the other hand, cocked against his shoulder. Rain ran off the umbrella and off my rain hood.

"Know you're pretty good with your hands and feet, you get up close, so let's keep the distance the way it is. And the golf club, drop it. Go inside, and don't give me shit. I want to shoot you anyway."

"The boys you hired failed you," I said. "You ought to let it go at that."

"Maybe we can get some good out of you yet."

"I don't do anal," I said.

"Go inside. I'm out of patience and I don't have a sense of humor."

I went inside and there was Leonard, behind the crowd, filming with his cell phone. You couldn't see the boxers, just the backs of people.

Leonard glanced at me and Coldpoint.

"Motherfucker," he said.

The crowd was so loud and involved they had yet to notice us.

"Hey," Coldpoint called out. "Back here."

What that led to was part of the crowd turning toward us, and coming out of it was Sheerfault. When he saw that Coldpoint had me at gunpoint, he smiled and showed his teeth wide as a piano row.

Coldpoint pushed me until I was near Leonard. Now the crowd had moved toward us. They gathered about us and forgot the two fighters in the ring of wire, and the fighters were still at it, not having noticed they'd lost their audience.

The crowd was tight around us now.

Leonard touched his phone and then dropped his arm and held the phone against his leg. Sheerfault came over and took it without a struggle. Bobo shouldered his way through the onlookers and came to stand by Sheerfault.

I glanced through a gap in the gathering, saw the two fighters had sat down in the ring, arms around one another to keep from toppling over.

"What we have here," Coldpoint said, "is a predicament."

"What you have here," I said to the crowd, "is a crime in progress. You folks don't want to be part of it, you ought to hike out, get away from this asshole and his ass hairs."

No one moved.

Sheerfault said, "That little speech wasn't very persuasive, was it." He turned toward Leonard. "What's with you, nigger, all out of smartass remarks?"

"Reached my monthly quota," Leonard said. "Next month I'll start up again."

"Always a clown, even to the last," Sheerfault said.

"You got clown-ass-whipped, is what you got," Leonard said. "I made you my bitch."

Sheerfault stepped toward Leonard. Coldpoint said, "Stop right there. Enough of this shit."

Sheerfault paused.

"Naw, let him come on," Leonard said. "He does best when there's a gun involved. He needs an edge."

"You shut up too or I'll drill Hap's spine," Coldpoint said. He sounded amazingly like a child on the playground who had just responded to being called a stupid-head.

Leonard went quiet. I could tell from the look on his face it was painful to do so.

"Just so you know," Coldpoint said, "the cop outside that little girl's room, I think he's going to come out poorly."

He let that comment hang in the air.

"What the hell does that mean?" Leonard said.

"It means I got some folks going to pay him and the girl a visit. It means he probably won't be around when morning comes, and neither will the girl. Anyone gets in the way, I've sent two of the best to surprise them. The two Roscoe sent were not so good."

"All niggers," Sheerfault said.

"Shut up," Coldpoint said.

"Don't get all sophisticated now," Leonard said. "Stick to what you really are. And let me tell you, that cop and that girl, anything happens to them, I'll skin you, starting with your dick. If you have one."

"But I haven't given my pair the word yet," Coldpoint said. "I'm waiting until a little later. I can move things forward, I have to. Make it happen sooner. My men, they are very good at what they do. These two"—he nodded at Sheerfault and Bobo—"not so much."

"Hey," Sheerfault said.

The man with the shotgun snickered.

"You best get hold of yourself," Sheerfault said to him. "I know where your big ass lives."

Shotgun man went silent, turned red-faced.

The lady judge, well dressed and out of place, said, "Wait a minute. Are we talking about killing someone?"

"Like it hasn't happened before," Coldpoint said. "Don't get self-righteous now, Jill. None of you. You all are part of this, and we got enough stuff on all of you, you say a word, we all go down. Way down."

The judge maybe wasn't as far to the right of Attila as some suggested, but she was far enough to know when to go along to get along. She swallowed heavily, dipped her head so that her brown teased hair caught the light and bounced off her hairspray. Then she sort of faded like the Invisible Woman. It was as if her personality had been pulled out of the top of her head and cast to the wind.

"Might go easier on you if you did speak up," I said. But that judge wasn't hearing me. Her mind was drifting along somewhere on the River Styx.

"Better wake up," I said to her.

Coldpoint hit me in the back of the head with the gun barrel. It dropped me to my knees and made me see double for a moment.

"Here's what we're going to do," Coldpoint said. "All you people.

All of you. You have gotten your hands dirty, and you're going to get them dirty tonight, and for some of you it'll be dirtier than before. But you think I don't have your asses in my pocket, just try and rat on us. And here's another thing, we may get some fine entertainment out of it."

"Will there be a pony?" Leonard said.

He was ignored.

"I like ponies."

I struggled to my feet.

"You like ponies, Hap?"

"Fuck the pony," I said.

"You two, get in that ring and fight," Coldpoint said.

"Not likely," I said.

"I think it'll make for a good match," Coldpoint said, "and here's the thing: you don't, the two at the hospital get dead."

"We do, they'll get dead," Leonard said.

"I can let them live," Coldpoint said. "I can work things out, I make that choice. It's easier they die, but I can spare them. But not if you two don't get in that ring."

"Bullshit," Leonard said. "I'm not fighting Hap."

"Sure you are," Coldpoint said.

"Like we can trust your word," Leonard said.

"We ought to do," I said.

"What the fuck, Hap. He ain't gonna spare nobody."

"I might," Coldpoint said. "I will."

"I tell you this, I come out of here with arms and legs and my nuts swing, and either one of them people are dead, I'm coming after you," Leonard said.

"You said that already."

"I didn't say I'm coming after all of you, though."

"Now you've said it. Get in the ring."

Leonard looked at me. I said, "It's okay. Got to do what we got to do."

I could tell he got it then. No one else would have noted the subtle shift in his features, but I had. Brett had reinforcements coming. All we had to do was fight and stall.

52

They pulled the two fighters sitting on the ground out of there, and the big guy with the shotgun who had helped get them off the bus took them away. After a few moments he came back.

"They're on the bus," he said to Coldpoint.

Coldpoint nodded.

Sheerfault had opened the wire gate and was grinning at us. I really hated him. Bobo stood nearby, his mouth hanging open. I don't know why, but in that moment, I felt sorry for the poor chucklehead. He was like a dog that belonged to bad people.

Once we were inside the fencing, Sheerfault closed the gate. Coldpoint held up his hand. His phone was in it.

"I get the sense you're slacking, I call," he said. "I only have to call. I don't have to wait for anyone to answer. I call, and they go. You got that."

"We got it," I said.

"I better see some serious movement in there, and some hard hits," Coldpoint said. "You can do anything you want to do, but you got to do it for real."

"Shit, Hap," Leonard said.

"I know," I said.

Leonard took off my slicker and hung it on the fence. I remembered he had a gun in the pocket of the slicker, but right then didn't call for trying to shoot it out. Coldpoint and Sheerfault also had guns. And then there were the ones who got off the bus, brought the fighters in. What we had to do was steal some time.

I took off my shirt, and Leonard took off his.

"You boys been working out," Coldpoint said.

"Why, thank you," I said. "Personally, I feel a little fat."

"Do it," Coldpoint said. "Do it now. And be all in about it."

I let out my breath and took a deep one in. I said, "Watch for the low ones, Leonard. I cheat."

"Me too."

"Same alike," I said.

And now the world outside of the ring went away. We had to fight, and we had to keep at it until Brett hooked up Marvin and the others. As far as Coldpoint knew, there weren't any cops about to be involved. Marvin had bearded them in his own den, made them feel foolish, but I was pretty sure that the way it looked to Coldpoint was two lone rogues had slipped up here to get proof of what was going on, and had fucked up and were going to pay for it.

He was right about that last part, of course.

Leonard and I sparred frequently, and we opened up a bit now and then, but not since many years ago, when we'd fought in a kick-boxing tournament, but we had never truly gone for broke.

So now we began to circle, and then I began to dance, skipping a little. Leonard grinned at me. He knew I was best when the other guy started, that I was a counterfighter in the ring, though less so on the street. We skipped around each other.

Coldpoint said, "Get to it."

"Don't cramp our styles," Leonard said.

And now Leonard moved, came fast, punched for my head. I nodded to the side and slipped the punch; another came, and I slipped that. He kicked out to my thigh with his right leg, the lead leg, and I lifted my leg and sloughed it off and came at him with a push off my back leg. He was ready for that, knowing I can get off the line faster than him, and knowing my hands were faster, and me knowing he was deceptive and could hit like a mule kicks if a mule was turbo-powered. We clashed a bit, and I grabbed him around the neck and we came in close, him hitting me in the stomach a couple of light shots. I leaned my head in, said, "Make it look real. Lives are on the line."

He butted me. My nose sprayed blood. I tried to move back. He gave me a front kick to the midsection and then dove at me to grapple, but I rolled out of the way. He hit the ground and tumbled and came up and turned and I hooked him to the ribs and skipped back, more hurt than I was letting on. My head rocked and I couldn't breathe. I could hardly hold my body upright, that midsection kick having taken my wind and polished the inside of my backbone.

He gave me a concerned look. He knew that had been pretty damn real, but I gave a gentle nod, not only to let him know I was okay but that what he did was fine. We had to keep it moving, had to keep it real, had to buy Brett and Marvin time.

Now we came together again and Leonard darted a jab, but I double-palmed his arm, kind of climbed it on the outside, and hit him with a ridge hand in the jaw. It was a damn good shot and sent him flying backward. He hit on his back, and damn if he didn't do a back roll and come up on his feet. He looked at me, grinned, and spat a wad of blood in the dirt.

The crowd was going now, cheering, and I was thinking how weird that was. They were loving what we were doing, and when we were done we'd take shots to the head and be slipped into the sawdust pool, and the ones we were trying to protect at the hospital would be dead, but for now they loved us, two pit bulls in the ring, fighting.

I bobbed and weaved, mostly just to give some show, and me and Leonard eased together. He faked a right and caught me with that goddamn cannon-hot hook in the ribs again. I felt something move inside of me that wasn't my last meal. I grabbed at Leonard, trying to pin his arms, and then in that moment, years of training, years of having been in sport battles and real battles linked together, and I just became a man in a ring with another man, not my brother but a fighter. Punches and low kicks were thrown, and one of those low kicks caught me inside the thigh, and without even knowing it was about to happen, I collapsed to one knee. Leonard leaped on me like a giant angry toad, knocking me onto my back. He straddled me and I bumped him. It rolled him on his side. I tried to slip away, but he was on top of me again, straddling me, raining blows on my head. I deflected them with my hands, caught one of his arms, pulled it to me, and tried to throw a leg up and around his neck, going for a triangle hold, but this wasn't Leonard's first rodeo either. He leaned into me and that gave him room to bend his arm a little, and I couldn't hold him. He grabbed my neck with one hand and used his other hand to shove a thumb into the notch in my throat and pressed down.

I lost my grip on his arm, and he grabbed my arm in turn. He swung his body and threw himself back into a lying arm bar, and if he was holding back any I couldn't tell it. Like me he was caught up in the moment. But his grasp wasn't firm. I wiggled free, got to my feet, and so did he.

We threw fist and hammer fist, and close in I palmed him under the chin, and I was sick when it hit, because it was a solid strike, and

I could see I had him staggered, and now I knew he was mine, and if I stopped, the phone call would be made, so I started in, threw some solid punches, but not too solid. Had to make it last. But then I realized Leonard was playing possum. He dropped suddenly and spun around close to the ground with an extended leg and swept my feet out from under me.

I came up immediately, but let me tell you, the lights seemed fuzzy and my heart seemed weak, and every move I made was no less trouble than trying to climb a greased pole.

Leonard kicked again; I slid past the kick and grabbed him around the waist, shifted my body, and threw him over my hip. He hit the ground hard. I heard the air go out of him. But as was his manner, he came back from it quickly. He probably couldn't breathe, but he could still move. He rolled and came up and then we exchanged kicks. I couldn't tell you if I hit him or if he hit me because I was out of it. I was beyond pain. I felt myself going numb all over, and then I heard something I thought was familiar, but in my state I couldn't identify it.

"The law," Leonard said.

And then I knew. It was sirens.

There was a mad rush toward the door. The crowd had panicked.

I put my hands on my knees and bent over. I felt faint. Leonard stepped in and got hold of me and straightened me up. All of a sudden, things switched and it was me holding him up.

He said, "I take it back, what I said once about you being fast but not able to hit hard. You hit hard."

"And you're faster than you look."

"We aren't going to do that again under any circumstances," Leonard said.

"I hear that," I said.

Coldpoint, Sheerfault, and Bobo were trotting toward the front of the building, the last ones out, but then Coldpoint turned and came back toward us with his gun held forward. I guess he figured he was going to go ahead and take us out.

Leonard had gotten hold of his jacket now, and he brought out his gun. Coldpoint stared a moment, made a sour face, turned and ran out of the door and into the rain, stood in the opening holding his phone. He pressed it, gave us a shit-eating grin, and ran out of sight.

"Chickenshit," Leonard yelled after him.

53

Me and Leonard got our shit together enough to head out of the fencing, across the mill, and out of the door. The crowd broke and was running in every which direction. Some of them were trying to climb the hill Leonard and I had come down.

I picked up the golf club I had been forced to drop, and soon after one of the guards came running by, heading for the back of the mill, hoping for a way out. He was the one with the shotgun, and he still had it, but he tossed it into the weeds as he passed. Or almost passed. I swung the club as he came near, caught him alongside the jaw and sent teeth flying.

"Fore," I said as the big man hit the dirt.

The rain had grown more fierce and was cold on my head and neck and was soaking through my clothes. I don't know how Aquaman takes it. I saw Coldpoint running toward his car. What was his plan now? Drive to Mexico? Go home and shoot himself?

No plan he could come up with would be any good.

"I'm going to see I can find Sheerfault," Leonard said.

"Good. I got Coldpoint."

I splashed along through puddles after him. He was running toward the line of parked cars, but there was no help there. Cruiser lights strobed through the wet night. At the bottom of the road, cruisers were blocking the way out. Highway Patrol and all manner of law were out of their cars and coming up the drive in a herd of law enforcement cloaked in black slickers, their pistols drawn. I could see them nabbing runners left and right, throwing them on the ground and yelling for them to stay put.

I was twenty feet away from Coldpoint when he realized he had no way to go forward, turned and came back in my direction, saw me. He decided in that instant he was going to at least shoot me before all was said and done. His lifted the pistol. I swung the club hard and let it go. It sailed across the distance between us, almost invisible in the rain and the night, caught Coldpoint somewhere in the face. I heard him grunt like a constipated man trying to pass a football, and the pistol went up in the air, and he fell onto the ground and rolled up against one of the parked cars.

By the time I reached him, he was trying to use his butt to push away from the car, but that hit had been a good one. His jaw was hanging down on one side.

He tried to say something but couldn't, just held up his hands in an *I quit* position.

"Reba or Officer Carroll are hurt, I'll kill you, Coldpoint."

He smiled, closed his eyes, and leaned against the car. I could see cops coming toward us; within moments they'd have Coldpoint and, if I stood around, me as well.

I turned and looked toward the mill. The crowd had gathered again and were flowing toward me. They had charged to the rear of the property only to discover there was a sharp drop-off with the highway thirty feet below. They had the drop-off on one end, the law on the other, a hill on one side, and a pond full of toxic water and sawdust on the other.

The crowd started running back in my direction. I could see Leonard at the rear of it all, on slightly higher ground, which made him easily visible for a moment. I saw Sheerfault too, running with all his might. Bobo was to the side, mixed into the crowd of runners. Leonard was trying to get to Sheerfault, but the crowd's motion was not working in his favor. I tried rushing to cut Sheerfault off, but he had too much of a lead.

Sheerfault reached the edge of the mill, dashed toward his car. Bobo yelled out to him, "Sheer," and held his hand up, as if he were trying to get the teacher's attention.

Sheerfault ignored him, jumped in his car, hit the wrong gear, backed into the jail bus, whipped it into the correct gear, and whirled the car around with ease. A stuntman couldn't have done it any better. He raced his car down the drive, the lights off, almost hitting me, causing officers to leap aside. But then he hit the brakes as he realized the exit was blocked by cop cars. He jerked it into reverse, hit the gas, went backward up the drive, came to a wide spot, wheeled the car around with another incredible brake stomp and spin, came racing onward. He turned on his lights like he was really going to need them, but there was nowhere he could go that way either, no farther than the end of the drive, anyway. The mill was in front of him, the side of the hill on his right, and the dark sawdust pond to his left. Maybe he thought if he drove fast enough, the car would levitate.

A couple of men from the crowd had gotten into his path as they scrambled for their cars. He didn't slow for them, hit them and knocked them winding. He wheeled left and tried to brake, maybe planning to jump out and make a run for it. There was a way he might go on foot down there, around the pond and down the hill below it and on out to the highway. But the car didn't stop. It began to skid at the edge of the pond in the wet earth. The headlights punched at the water. Sheerfault got the door open, had one leg out. His foot hit the ground and I heard a faint snapping sound as the crowd ran past me and right into the waiting arms of a lot of law.

I wasn't watching the crowd closely, however. I had my eyes on that car and Sheerfault. He couldn't get out and his foot was dragging and the car was sliding. It went over the lip of the dark pond and down into it. I heard Sheerfault scream, then I saw Bobo running that way, yelling, "Sheer, Sheer."

Bobo dove into the pond after the car, only the taillights visible now, like two red primordial reptile eyes.

I ran down there. I hated both those guys, but not so much I wanted to see them drown in that mess. By the time I got to the bank of the pond, the car was gone, gobbled up by the goo.

Bobo was trying to swim in that muck. He was strong. He dove down twice and came up twice, spitting that horrid yuck out of his mouth, but the sawdust water was heavy. It grabbed at him and held him and washed over him. He yelled out for Sheerfault once more, dove down again, and didn't come back up.

There was nothing I could do.

I turned and looked toward the driveway, saw Highway Patrol officers with guns drawn. They were loading the whole gang of them into the jail bus. I saw the two guys who had been the original entertainment looking out of the windows of the bus.

It was all happening fast and smooth by then. I saw a tall black man in a white shirt, white hat, and cowboy boots standing in the middle of it all, lighting a cigar. Texas Ranger, no doubt.

Leonard had slipped down by me by then.

"I didn't get to shoot nobody," he said.

"I'm sorry."

He looked out at the water.

"I seen Bobo go in," he said.

"He won't be coming up. Shitty way to end up, even for those two. Turned into Rusty Puppies."

"Deserved way to go," he said, and casually flipped the pistol he was holding into the muck.

"Had it been me, would you have tried to pull my ass out of that mess?" I said.

"Of course not. I'd hire a backhoe to get your body later."

We turned with our hands raised and walked toward the Texas Ranger.

54

When we were standing by the Ranger, we saw Marvin walking past the bus. "I got these two," he said. "They were our inside men."

The Ranger said, "You're out of your jurisdiction."

"Yep," Marvin said. "But without me and these two knuckleheads, you'd still be at home watching *Gunsmoke* reruns."

The Ranger grinned. "I like *Gunsmoke*."

"What's not to like," Marvin said.

The Ranger went down the hill.

"Reba and Curt?" Leonard said.

"Two men tried to kill them," Marvin said. "Officer Carroll killed both of them. One shot apiece."

"Is Curt all right?" Leonard said.

"Actually, he said he sprained a finger reaching for his pistol fast as he did."

"You know this for sure how?" I asked.

"We have a thing called radios, and we talk on them," Marvin said.

"We're thinking about getting phones we can carry in our pockets so we talk on those too. Oh, wait. I got one."

He pulled his cell out of his coat pocket and held it up.

"Of course," I said. "I knew that. And they can make moving pictures with sound now too, can't they?"

55

The Ranger used LaBorde as his command center. We told our story to him with Marvin present. We were in the very nice interrogation room. Now that some time had passed, I was really hurting from mine and Leonard's bout. We had found out Coldpoint was in custody but not talking. Wise move, since his two main coconspirators were dead. But then there was the judge and the other bozos who had been at the mill. One of them would talk, that was for sure.

"You two look terrible," the Ranger said. "Like you got hit by a truck and dragged a few miles."

"You think it looks bad, ought to be on this end looking out," I said.

"Yeah," Leonard said. "I think I shit one of my lungs out in the jailhouse toilet."

"You're friends, but you beat on each other like that?" the Ranger said.

"Had to make it look real and kill some time while y'all were fucking around at the doughnut shop."

"I saw you throw a pistol in the pond," the Ranger said to Leonard.

"Did you now?" Leonard said.

"Yep," said the Ranger.

Leonard nodded. "Picked it up inside the sawmill where someone dropped it. I panicked and tossed it in the pond."

"Why would you panic?"

"They call it panic for a reason," Leonard said. "It isn't supposed to make sense."

"Was the gun registered to you?" the Ranger asked.

"Nope. I got it in the sawmill."

It was in fact a cold piece, part of Leonard's stash, and he had brought it with him, but he didn't want to admit that. If he did, some shit might follow.

"We could drag the pond for it," the Ranger said.

"You could," Leonard said. "And you'd find it, but it isn't registered to me."

"And you didn't bring it with you."

"An unregistered gun? Not hardly. That would be unlawful. I just wouldn't do that."

The Ranger looked at me.

"That would be wrong," I said. "Leonard, like myself, is an upstanding citizen."

The Ranger didn't seem to be a man that enjoyed bullshit, but unfortunately for him that night, we were full of it. We had been helpful at the sawmill, but he had an accurate suspicion maybe we had been too helpful, out of line for citizens.

Marvin said to the Ranger, "Could you and me talk outside a moment?"

The Ranger nodded and they went out. They were out there for a long time. Leonard and I sat politely, waiting.

"I think a different coat of paint would be nice in here," Leonard said.

"Looks all right," I said.

"Don't you think it's too dark? I mean, you come in, you're already being interrogated, which is a drag. So something more festive could make life a little better, at least for a few moments."

"Maybe a mobile hanging over the table."

"What I'm talking about. Something shiny."

Finally they came back. The Ranger looked at us.

"You're upstanding fucking citizens that were just there to record bad things on your phone, and the bad things got out of hand, and you got in the middle of them. They made you fight, the cops that you had alerted earlier showed up later than you expected, and there you were. Though for some reason, why you were there still doesn't set right with me."

"We want to be newspaper stringers," Leonard said. "We thought that would be a good place to start."

"Don't push it," the Ranger said. "You can go. I advise you to go. But don't go far away, we might need to talk again, and thanks for the video."

"Thank you, Mr. Ranger," Leonard said.

As I went by Marvin, I whispered, "Thanks."

"Eat shit," he said, and didn't whisper.

56

My car was in the parking lot where Brett and Chance had dropped it. She and Brett had gone home from there, optimistic that we wouldn't be spending our lives in jail.

We had also been optimistic, but not as much. Now, we felt pretty good. We climbed in the car, me behind the wheel. I had the spare key in my pocket, and since it was a Prius, I didn't even have to take the key out of my pocket. That always made me feel like a big dog. Magic.

"You know," Leonard said, "I wouldn't want to fight you again, you being a brother and all, but I think had we not been stalling for time, and if a few other factors had not been in play, I could have licked you."

"Nope."

"Could too."

"Nope, nope, nope."

"Yep, yep, yep."

"Nope," I said, "and don't say anything else, or you walk home."

"My ribs hurt."

"You can say that. I don't feel so good either."

I eased the car out of the lot.

"Can I stay at your place, Hap?"

"The couch."

"Sure, since Chance has my room."

"It *was* your room."

"Couch is fine. Buffy can keep me company."

"She sleeps with Chance."

"Oh."

I drove along the streets slowly, as if my car felt as bad as I did. As the moments moved by I felt worse and worse from that beating I had taken from Leonard. Good thing he loved me or I'd have been dead.

"We are seriously a couple of badasses," Leonard said.

"Look up *badass* in the dictionary, and our fucking picture is right under the word."

"Got that right," Leonard said. "But I'm a badass might need to rest for a few days, shit some blood, and get my ribs looked after. Maybe get some bionic parts."

"I got my own health problems."

"Man, you getting out of my lying arm bar," Leonard said. "That was some shit."

"Wasn't it?" I said.

"You're supposed to compliment me on something now," Leonard said.

"You fall down good," I said.

57

A few days later when Marvin decided he didn't hate us so much after all, he told us they'd picked up Tamara at the projects and she squealed like a pig. She wasn't so tough. She confirmed what we knew and added a few things, mostly that Timpson had helped beat Jamar to death and that his having me meet him at the Joint was merely so Roscoe could put an eyeball on us and the two dumbasses in the back could see us too. I really hated those bastards, hurting Reba like that, trying to kill her. Marvin promised to make sure when they went away word got spread at the prison that they raped and beat a kid. Even the worst of the worst in prison generally hated anyone who did that kind of stuff, and it often led to a shiv party in the shower.

Couldn't happen to two nicer guys.

They dragged Sheerfault's car out of the muck. He was still in it. Bobo had beat the glass out of the driver's-side window with his fist, which is no easy feat on land and would have been even harder under dark, mucky water. Fact was, I would have thought it impossible.

Bobo had an arm cocked inside the window and had died that

way, clutching at the door frame, trying to pull Sheerfault out. I kind of admired him for that.

On a Sunday afternoon, Leonard and Officer Carroll, as I preferred to call him, picked up Reba at the projects and brought her to the house where we were having an indoor cookout. It was raining that day and had been raining all week. Reba still had her arm and leg in a cast and was precariously on crutches.

As they came through the door, Leonard said, "Found the four-hundred-year-old vampire. She's forgoing blood today and having a grilled burger."

"You ain't got no French fries?" she said, crutching her way toward the table.

"We do," Brett said, "they're frying."

Brett and Chance introduced themselves to her.

"Before we picked her up, we got her some fried pies at McDonald's," Officer Carroll said. "Leonard said she'd want them."

"Course I do," Reba said. "You got something against pie?"

"Not a thing," Officer Carroll said. He was wearing off-duty clothes. I thought he looked odd out of uniform. He had a finger taped up, the one he had sprung, and he looked as happy and alert as always. I wondered how he was dealing with having shot two people. I had a larger number of dead folks on my head, and there were times at night when it was as if all their bodies were stacked on my chest.

"You and Leonard sure do look like hell," Officer Carroll said.

"Gives me character," Leonard said.

"No, it makes you move kind of slow," Officer Carroll said, and they passed a smile between them.

Leonard, moving stiffly, got Reba positioned in a chair, her broken leg and cast stuck out under the table.

"You done blown up the projects," Reba said, "and you fucked over them bad po-pos, but they gonna be someone else selling that sugar pop sometime soon. Some other cops gonna run things."

"I'm a cop," Officer Carroll said.

"I got my eye on you," she said. "Even if you did keep me from getting killed."

"Well, we're hoping for the best," Officer Carroll said.

"Hope ain't nothing but shit misspelled," Reba said.

"My, you have a mouth on you," Brett said.

"Shit, you ought to have heard my mama. And on them hamburgers. Like mine well done, and don't put no goddamn sweet pickles on it, but you got a little mustard, I could take that, you spread it thin."

ABOUT THE AUTHOR

JOE R. LANSDALE is the author of nearly four dozen novels, including *Honky Tonk Samurai,* the Edgar Award–winning *The Bottoms, Edge of Dark Water,* and the Spur Award–winning *Paradise Sky.* He has also received eleven Bram Stoker Awards, the American Mystery Award, the British Fantasy Award, and the Grinzane Cavour Prize. He lives with his family in Nacogdoches, Texas.

. . . AND *JACKRABBIT SMILE*

Hap is celebrating his wedding to Brett, his longtime girlfriend— and his and Leonard's PI boss when their backyard barbecue is interrupted by a couple of Pentecostal white supremacists. They're not too happy to see Leonard, and no one is happy to see them, but they have a problem and only Hap and Leonard will take the case.

It isn't long before our heroes find themselves mixed up with a revivalist cult that believes Jesus will return flanked by an army of lizard men. And if that weren't enough, in the process Hap and Leonard solve a murder to boot.

Following is an excerpt from the novel's opening pages.

1

Even when I'm doing something enjoyable, it seems death and destruction lurk nearby. I might not recognize those dual demons right away, but they're out there.

They might arrive in a pickup truck, and those in it may seem at first like a lot of people I might see. Just folks going about their business.

But they may be carriers of a repulsive kind of disease, and there are many symptoms. Hate and prejudice, ignorance and a profound pride in what they don't know. They are those who go with their gut, which is about as accurate as throwing chicken bones or reading signs in frog entrails.

I don't know they're coming until they're there, and even then, I might not understand exactly what has walked into my life. I may think, considering my experience, that I'll know right away if something is going to go dark and wet, but I still get fooled, and their kind of disease can have a ripple effect; it's not just their viewpoint, it's how their viewpoint affects others—they spread their germs without even being aware of it.

• • •

I was in the side yard with Brett, enjoying our Saturday, and a fine April afternoon, cooking up burgers, bratwurst, and weenies on the grill. Their aroma in the air was thick enough, if you smacked your lips you could taste them.

We were celebrating. Three hours before, me and Brett had gotten married by the LaBorde justice of the peace. No Bible, no preacher, just the law. Me and her had talked about pulling that trigger for some years, and finally we had gone and done it. I couldn't have been happier.

When we got married we had a small crowd there at the JP's office, close friends and a few strays we had taken in, and they were coming over in a little while to enjoy our wedding picnic. We had a long folding-leg table laid out with paper plates and cups, and an ice chest with a bag of ice in it. We had folding chairs stacked on the ground, ready for use.

I was scraping a burger off the grill, flipping it.

"I thought we might go to Paris for a honeymoon," Brett said, "but then I got to thinking about a cookout in the yard and nixed it."

"Yeah. French cooking can kiss my ass, baby. I'm doing burgers and dogs."

"Don't burn them this time," Brett said.

"Nope. I'm on it. And you know what, everything goes well, we can play horseshoes after lunch, and later tonight you can play with my ass."

"Oh, you charmer."

"That's right, baby. Stick with me and you'll be farting through silk."

A white pickup coasted to the curb in front of our house and parked next to the oak tree that grew near the street. It wasn't a truck that belonged to one of our guests. It wasn't a truck that belonged to anybody I knew.

The tires on the truck were so high that when the door opened, the driver, a thin, thirtyish man with wiry muscles and sandy-blond hair, practically had to dangle himself down to the curb. On the other side a woman worked her way out of the passenger seat and came around the front of the truck. She had lowered some kind of step stool to make her exit. I caught a glimpse of it from under the truck. Both of them probably had nosebleeds from sitting so high.

They started across the yard. It made me a little nervous, especially when I saw the T-shirt the man was wearing. It was white with blue lettering on the front that read WHITE IS RIGHT. Not one of my sentiments, even though my skin is as pale as milk when it isn't tanned or sunburned.

The young man had on black jeans and lace-up boots and so many tattoos visible on his arms and neck that, from a distance, I thought he was wearing long sleeves. Close up I could see more tattoos through the thin fabric of his T-shirt. I assumed he might have others in places less interesting to see, and a box of stick-on tattoos at home along with a pointed white hood for those special evenings out with the Klan. That may sound judgmental, but hey, that T-shirt told me a lot.

The woman was probably in her late fifties, garbed up in what I think of as traditional Pentecostal style, meaning her brown hair was in a bun so tall and wide she could have hidden an electric mixer under it, and she was wearing a blue-jean dress that fell almost to her ankles and was capped off by clunky black boots that looked one grade up from orthopedic shoes. She didn't have on any makeup, not even lipstick or eyeliner. From certain religious points of view, God and Jesus get all worked up about hairdos and makeup but couldn't seem to end a war anywhere or kill a disease. I thought maybe God had his priorities out of whack.

Those two looked so much like stereotypes it wouldn't have surprised me to discover they had venomous snakes in their pockets and could speak in tongues.

The man slowed and let the woman take the lead. She came right to me, stuck out her hand, and I shook it. She didn't offer it to Brett. The man didn't offer his hand to either of us. He stood there with his hands in his pockets. One eyelid spasmed from time to time, as if being periodically electrocuted. I could have sworn I saw one of his neck tattoos crawl under his shirt, but I suppose it was a shifting of the light.

Up close I could see some of the tattoos were professional and some were the sort you do yourself or get in prison, or perhaps a three-year-old with a carving knife and a bottle of ink had been hired to mark him up.

"You're the one's got that private detective agency, aren't you?" the woman said.

"She does," I said, nodding at Brett. "I work for her."

"Oh, I thought you owned it and had her and that . . . colored fellow working for you. What's he do there?"

"Eats cookies and drinks coffee, from what I can tell," I said.

"He works there, same as this man, who, by the way, is my husband."

I liked the way Brett said that. I felt like a big dog. I was so happy I wanted to wag my tail.

"You work for your wife?" the man said. It was like his mind had just snapped to attention.

"It's either that or she doesn't let me eat."

"Sometimes, when he's sassy or acting a little hysterical, I make him stand in the yard and hold a heavy rock over his head," Brett said.

The woman grinned a little, but the young man looked at me as if he were concerned I not only didn't wear the pants in the family but might have accidentally cooked my dick on the grill in place of a sausage.

"We looked you up in the phone book. Drove by your office a few times," the woman said. "We asked around about y'all, trying to decide."

"Decide what?" Brett said.

"We got this problem, and truth is, everyone else turned us down."

"Who's everyone else?" I said.

"The other private detective in town."

"There's another one?" I said.

"And all them over in Tyler and Longview too. Ain't none over in Marvel Creek, which is where we've got the problem, so there wasn't no one to ask there. Cops here can't do nothing. It's out of their jurisdiction."

"Thing is, we heard you had that nig . . . colored man working there," the young man said, "and that put us off some. At first we thought he just cleaned up the office."

I thought: Bless your little ignorant heart.

"Here's something might put you off even more," I said, and pointed.

Marvin Hanson's car pulled up at the curb, and he and Officer Carroll, as we always called Curt, got out.

Hanson was carrying a twelve-pack of diet sodas under his arm, and Officer Carroll had a twelve-pack of beer under his. The sodas were mostly for me, the beers were for some of the others.

From the backseat came the niece of Leonard's ex-boyfriend John. Her name was Felicity, and she was just out of her teens and had her hair in pigtails today, tied up on both sides with bright blue ribbons.

Finally, there was Reba, the little girl Leonard called the Four-Hundred-Year-Old Vampire Midget. Truth was, twelve years old or not, Reba could be a bitch. She had a mouth like a sailor's and a mind as sharp as a butcher's knife. I had to make sure she didn't get in the beer when no one was watching.

All of them except Officer Carroll were black as black could be, and you could see the man and the woman taking that in, the way soldiers might count their enemies' artillery mounted on a hill. Officer Carroll was Leonard's boyfriend. I kind of figured same-sex relationships were probably on the pair's no-no list as well.

"What's all them colored people showing up for?" the young man said. The way he said that, you could tell he didn't go out and about among those who held different beliefs than his own.

"We're filming a Tarzan movie after lunch," Brett said. "Need a lot of them colored folks for that. Cannibal scenes, you know."

"Yeah, I get to play Tarzan," I said.

"No. You get to be Tarzan's monkey," Brett said.

I made a soft chattering sound. I thought it sounded like a monkey, and a damn sexy monkey.

"By the way," I said, motioning to Marvin and Officer Carroll, "this gentleman is the police chief, and this white fellow works for him."

No hands were shook. Everyone merely looked at one another for a moment as if all fingers had been dipped in shit.

Marvin said, "We'll put these in the ice chest," and he and Officer Carroll went to do just that.

I heard the screen door slam and looked up to see Chance step out on the porch with a large bag of potato chips in either hand. She wasn't going to please them either. Physically, she was not only made up of whatever I was made up of, but she had her mother's coloring, her dark skin, fine American Indian and Hispanic features, black hair tied back in a ponytail long enough to use for a lariat. She was beautiful.

Right behind her came Leonard, in charge of a box of vanilla cookies, his black face split with a bright white smile.

I watched the young man fold his arms across his chest, obscuring the writing on his shirt.

Everyone came over and wished us congratulations again— everyone except our surprise guests, of course.

It was then a second wave of guests arrived. Our friend Manuela Martinez got out of her car carrying a large paper bag. She was looking fine and petite in tight jeans and an equally tight orange top, her black hair cut to the shoulders; the white scar that ran from below her left ear to the tip of her chin gave her near-model features a kind of rugged class. I watched her walk toward us. I watched very carefully.

Brett elbowed me. "Watch it, mister."

"Hey, what was that for?" I said.

"You know," she said.

On the other side of the car, Cason Statler got out. He too had a paper bag with something in it. We were going to have enough food to feed the proverbial army. I had introduced him to Manny, as we called Manuela, and since that time they had become as tight as superglue in a gnat's ass.

Cason was one of those guys that got better looking as he got older. White guy with thick, dark hair and a cock-of-the-walk stride, always in shape.

Brett said, "Now I got something to look at."

"Then we're even," I said.

"Not exactly," she said.

The woman and the man from the two-story pickup truck stood stiff, like trees growing in the yard. We had sidelined them. And realizing we were being dicks, even though I thought they deserved it, I said, "Look, you want to talk, we can. On the porch."

They pulled roots and went to the porch and sat down on the glider and waited for us.

Leonard walked up to me, said, "Who are those crackers?"

"Why, those are racists who are a little worried we might have a colored boy working for us."

"Ah, now, Massa Hap, you know I'm one of the good ones."

"Yes, but don't forget your place."

"You mean with my foot up your ass?" he said.

Chance listened to us and smiled. She carried the chips to the table. Me and Brett greeted everybody while Leonard went on over to the porch to make the honkies nervous. He smelled blood in the water.

I gave the spatula to Manny, said, "Don't let the food burn."

"I warn you," Manny said, "what I cook best are kitchens. I've burned down two of them."

"No worries," Brett said. "We're outdoors. If the meat starts to smoke, use the spatula and take them off the grill. If they catch fire, use the spatula to beat out the flames."

"Gotcha," Manny said.

2

Me and Brett went over to the porch. As we were walking up, I heard Leonard say, "And I had me four of them fat white women in that barn. Lined 'em up against the wall, said, 'Strip off and bend over and call me Daddy.' Whole thing only cost me three dollars, and they let me brand them with a hot tire iron for free."

"Ignore him," I said.

The woman and the young man looked as if they had just survived a home invasion. The man especially appeared confused, and maybe a little angry, and yet at the same time there was a hesitation. I think he was afraid to say anything directly to Leonard, fearing his mouth might be writing a check his ass couldn't cash.

All of us were on the porch now, our guests in the glider, me and Brett sitting on the steps, and Leonard leaning against the front door.

"Them two, the colored and the white man, they really law?" the white guy asked.

"Naw," Leonard said. "We just let Marvin wear a badge and the other one got a cop suit for Christmas. Only reason he isn't wearing it now is for fear of mustard stains."

That got a blank look, an expression those two did especially well.

I said, "Yes. They are the real deal. First things first. I sense a disturbance in the color barrier. If you have trouble with black people, brown people, highly attractive redheads like my wife, or exceptional people like myself, then there's no use in us talking."

"All except that part about Hap being exceptional is real," Leonard said.

The man looked at his mother. His eye was twitching a little more frequently now.

His mother said, "I guess we're okay."

"I don't know," the man said. "I'm not sure a colored is up to the job. So we need to know how much he'll be involved."

"As much as any of us will," Brett said.

"Though during the middle of the day, I might have to have me a nap," Leonard said.

The man and woman looked at each other, didn't speak, but when they turned back to us, the woman said, "All right, then. Beggars can't be choosers."

"That's the spirit," Leonard said. He was talking cool, but the anger was coming off him like a high fever.

Brett reached out and gently touched Leonard's arm. He calmed beneath her hand.

"Okay, tell us who you are, what you want," Brett said.

"My name is Judith Mulhaney. This is my son, Thomas. What we want is to hire you to find my missing daughter. His sister, Jackie."

"We called her Jackrabbit," Thomas said. "She has these big

front teeth. Looked good on her, though. That's how we got to calling her a jackrabbit, saying she had a jackrabbit smile."

"She's been gone from home five years," Judith said. "Be honest, I don't think she's alive. Not to say she's been dead for five years. She was alive during most of that time, we know that. People saw her, but we didn't, just heard how she was doing here and there. Thought eventually, things would work out, that she'd come back to see us, but in the past few months, no one has seen her that we're aware of. Got to say we don't know many people over there well enough to be sure if we're getting the correct news. We kind of keep to ourselves. But I got a bad feeling. A mother knows."

"If anything was done to her," Thomas said, "I got an idea who might have done it."

"We want her back," Judith said, "be it flesh, or be it bones."

"All right," Brett said. "Before we know if we can be of any help, we need to hear the whole story. Need to know if you got money. Investigations don't come cheap."

"You get right to it, don't you?" Judith said.

"I do," Brett said. "You want us to do this, put us to work, you got to understand I don't like you or your son. You've insulted Leonard here several times and are too dense to know it or too insensitive to care. You've done everything but call him the N-word."

"I can say 'nigger,'" Leonard said. "It's okay I do. 'Nigger, nigger, nigger.'"

"Goddamn it, Leonard," Brett said.

"Just saying," Leonard said.

"That's what I don't get," Thomas said. "You can say it, but I can't."

"Oh, you can say it," Leonard said, "but say it with me standing here, next time you say it, it might be through a gap in your teeth. I say 'nigger,' we call it ironic, don't we, Hap?"

"Ironic," I said.

"You say it, and we knock your teeth out."

"It don't seem fair," Thomas said.

"It's on account of things having been so damn fair for us dark-skinned folks all these years. That too is irony, if you're wondering. And that doesn't mean something you do with starch and an ironing board."

"I know what 'irony' means," Thomas said. I didn't think he sounded all that convincing.

"Look here," I said. "Me and Brett, we're celebrating, and I don't want to deal with this. I'm sorry, but Jackie's been gone five years, she can wait a day. This is our day. Meet us at our office tomorrow at ten a.m., if you're serious. You know where the office is, I take it?"

Judith and Thomas both nodded in concert.

"And by the way. How did you find our house?" I said.

"Address is in the phone book," Thomas said.

"We looked up Brett Sawyer, like on the agency listing, and there's a house address for Brett Sawyer," Judith said. "We just drove over."

"Oh," I said.

So much for our Fortress of Solitude.

3

Me and Brett lay in bed breathing hard, our bodies covered in sweat. I was holding her in my arms and the air was beginning to cool. She reached over and grabbed the sheet and pulled it over us.

"Ah," I said, "you're blocking my view."

"You've seen enough for one night. My ass hurts."

"That was our first sex as a happily married couple," I said.

"Not to look a gift horse in the mouth, but it was a whole lot like the sex we had before we were married."

"This is true," I said. "But good, nonetheless."

"Absolutely. I'm glad we finally did it, Hap. Married, not had sex. Well, that came out wrong. I'm glad we did both. I don't know why being married matters, but it does. I didn't think it would. I knew you wanted to, and then I wanted to because you did, and now that we're married, I do feel different. I like it. Of course, I had a couple beers at lunch."

"It's a solid commitment, and I think it helps on our taxes."

"Married people break up all the time," she said.

"Not this time."

"Right answer," she said. "Do you think we were kind of mean to those people today?"

"I do. And they had it coming."

"Maybe we just fulfilled their idea of what liberal-minded folks are supposed to be like. Well, you're the most liberal-minded, and Leonard, he's not liberal, so maybe I don't know shit."

"Leonard was a real asshole," I said. "Talking about lining women up against the wall. He should have said men if he really wanted to get to them. Women aren't his attraction."

"I understand the sentiment," Brett said, and rubbed my thigh under the sheet.

"I don't know if I want to help those two," I said. "I really don't like them."

"It's not about their beliefs, Hap, it's about the missing girl."

"Jackrabbit."

"I bet she hated that name."

"Probably didn't use it with the general public," I said.

"Thinking it over," Brett said, "I think Leonard showed tremendous restraint."

"Yeah, couple years back he would have set their truck on fire with them in it."

"Think they'll show up at the office in the morning?"

"I don't know. But if you keep rubbing my thigh, I can tell you what will show up."

"That's kind of the idea," she said. "Question? You mind I'm keeping my last name, not taking yours?"

"Of course not. I'm keeping mine. I don't want to be Hap Sawyer any more than you want to be Brett Collins. I have thought about changing my name to Swinging Dick, though. Think that suits me better."

"Oh, baby. Name like that, wouldn't you need enough to swing, to give it meaning?"

"Oh, that hurt."

Brett laughed that throaty laugh she has and took hold of my head and pulled me to her and kissed me.

MULHOLLAND BOOKS

You won't be able to put down these Mulholland books.